THE
LIFE
WE
BURY

THE LIFE WE BURY

A Novel

ALLEN ESKENS

SEVENTH STREET BOOKS®

AN IMPRINT OF PROMETHEUS BOOKS

59 JOHN GLENN DRIVE • AMHERST, NY 14228
www.seventhstreetbooks.com

Published 2014 by Seventh Street Books®, an imprint of Prometheus Books

The Life We Bury. Copyright © 2014 by Allen Eskens. All rights reserved.

Cover design by Jacqueline Nasso Cooke
Cover photograph by Jarek Wyganowski

Inquiries should be addressed to
Seventh Street Books
59 John Glenn Drive
Amherst, New York 14228
VOICE: 716–691–0133
FAX: 716–691–0137
WWW.SEVENTHSTREETBOOKS.COM

19 18 17 16   13 12 11

Library of Congress Cataloging-in-Publication Data

Eskens, Allen, 1963–
    The life we bury / by Allen Eskens.
        pages cm
    ISBN 978-1-61614-998-7 (paperback)—ISBN 978-1-61614-999-4 (ebook)
    I. Title.

PS3605.S49L54 2014
813'.6—dc23

2014016018

Printed in the United States of America

I dedicate this novel to my wife, Joely,
my most trusted advisor and best friend.
I also dedicate this novel to my daughter, Mikayla,
for her constant inspiration
and to my parents, Pat and Bill Eskens,
for their many lessons in life.

CHAPTER 1

I remember being pestered by a sense of dread as I walked to my car that day, pressed down by a wave of foreboding that swirled around my head and broke against the evening in small ripples. There are people in this world who would call that kind of feeling a premonition, a warning from some internal third eye that can see around the curve of time. I've never been one to buy into such things. But I will confess that there have been times when I think back to that day and wonder: if the fates had truly whispered in my ear—if I had known how that drive would change so many things—would I have taken a safer path? Would I turn left where before I had turned right? Or would I still travel the path that led me to Carl Iverson?

My Minnesota Twins were scheduled to play the Cleveland Indians that cool September evening in a game to crown the central-division champion. Soon the lights of Target Field would flood the western horizon of Minneapolis, shooting up into the night like rays of glory, but I would not be there to see it. Just one more thing I couldn't afford on my college-student budget. Instead, I would be working the door at Molly's Pub, stealing glances at the game on the television above the bar as I inspected driver's licenses and tamped down drunken arguments—not my career of choice, but it paid the rent.

Oddly enough, my high-school guidance counselor never mentioned the word "college" in any of our meetings. Maybe she could smell the funk of hopelessness that clung to my second-hand clothing. Maybe she had heard that I started working at a dive bar called the Piedmont Club the day after I turned eighteen. Or—and this is where I'd place my bet—maybe she knew who my mother was and figured that no one can change the sound of an echo. Regardless, I didn't blame her for not seeing me as college material. Truth is, I felt more comfortable in the dinge of a bar than I did in the marbled halls of academia, where I stumbled along as though I wore my shoes on the wrong feet.

I jumped into my car that day—a twenty-year-old, rusted Honda Accord—dropped it into gear and headed south from campus, merging with a stream of rush-hour traffic on I-35 and listening to Alicia Keys on blown Japanese speakers. As I hit the Crosstown, I reached over to the passenger seat and fumbled through my backpack, eventually finding the piece of paper with the address of the old folks' home. "Don't call it an old folks' home," I mumbled to myself. "It's a retirement village or senior center or something like that."

I navigated the confusing streets of suburban Richfield, eventually finding the sign at the entrance to Hillview Manor, my destination. The name ceded to that place had to be some kind of a prank. It viewed no hills and lacked the slightest hint of grandeur suggested by the word "manor." The view from the front was of a busy four-lane boulevard, and the back of the building faced the butt end of a rickety, old apartment complex. The bad name, however, may have been the cheeriest thing about Hillview Manor, with its gray brick walls streaked green with moss, its raggedy shrubs run amok, and its mold, the color of oxidized copper, encasing the soft wood of every window sash. The place squatted on its foundation like a football tackle and seemed equally formidable.

As I stepped into the lobby, a wave of stale air, laden with the pungent aroma of antiseptic cream and urine, flicked at my nose, causing my eyes to water. An old woman wearing a crooked wig sat in a wheelchair, staring past me as if expecting some long-ago suitor to emerge from the parking lot and sweep her away. She smiled as I passed, but not at me. I didn't exist in her world, no more than the ghosts of her memory existed in mine.

I paused before approaching the reception desk, listening one last time to those second thoughts that had been whispering in my ear, petulant thoughts that told me to drop that English class before it was too late and replace it with something more sensible like geology or history.

A month earlier, I'd left my home in Austin, Minnesota, sneaking off like a boy running away to join a circus. No arguments with my mother, no chance for her to try and change my mind. I just packed a bag, told my younger brother that I was leaving, and left a note for my mom. By the time I made it to the registrar's office at the university, all the decent English classes had been filled, so I signed up for a biography class, one that would force me to interview a complete stranger. Deep down I knew that the clammy sweat that pimpled my temples as I loitered in the lobby came from that homework assignment, an assignment I had avoided starting for far too long. I just knew the assignment was going to suck.

The receptionist at Hillview, a square-faced woman with strong cheeks, tight hair, and deep set eyes that gave her the appearance of a gulag matron, leaned over the countertop and asked, "Can I help you?"

"Yes," I said. "I mean, I hope so. Is your manager here?"

"We don't allow solicitations," she said, her face becoming brittle as she narrowed her focus on me.

"Solicitations?" I gave her a forced chuckle and held out my hands in an imploring gesture. "Ma'am," I said. "I couldn't sell fire to a caveman."

"Well, you're not a resident here, and you're no visitor, and you sure don't work here. So, what's left?"

"My name's Joe Talbert. I'm a student at the University of Minnesota."

"And?"

I glanced at her name tag. "And . . . Janet . . . I'd like to talk to your manager about a project I have to do."

"We don't have a manager," Janet said through her squint. "We have a director, Mrs. Lorngren."

"I'm sorry," I said, trying to maintain my pleasant façade. "Can I talk to your director?"

"Mrs. Lorngren's a very busy lady, and it's suppertime—"

"It'll only take a minute."

"Why don't you run your project by me, and I'll decide if it's worth disturbing Mrs. Lorngren."

"It's an assignment I'm doing for school," I said, "for my English class. I have to interview an old person—I mean an elderly person and write a biography about them. You know, tell about the struggles and forks in the road that made them who they are."

"You're a writer?" Janet looked me up and down as if my appearance might answer that question. I straightened up to the full extent of my five-foot, ten-inch height. I was twenty-one years old and had accepted that I was as tall as I was ever going to be—thank you Joe Talbert Senior, wherever the hell you are. And while it was true that I worked as a bouncer, I wasn't the big meat you normally see at the door of a bar; in fact, as bouncers go, I was on the puny side.

"No," I said. "Not a writer, just a student."

"And they're making you write a whole book for school?"

"No. It's a mix of writing and outline." I said with a smile. "Some of the chapters have to be written out, like the beginning and the ending and any important turning points. But mostly, it'll be a summary. It's a pretty big project."

Janet wrinkled her pug nose and shook her head. Then, apparently persuaded that I had nothing to sell, she picked up the phone and spoke in a lowered voice. Soon a woman in a green suit approached from a hallway beyond the reception desk and took up a position next to Janet.

"I'm Director Lorngren," the woman announced, her head held erect and steady as if she were balancing a tea cup on it. "Can I help you?"

"I hope so." I took a deep breath and ran through it all again.

Mrs. Lorngren chewed over my explanation with a puzzled look on her face and then said, "Why did you come here? Don't you have a parent or grandparent you can interview?"

"I don't have any relatives nearby," I said.

That was a lie. My mother and my brother lived two hours south of the Twin Cities, but even a brief visit to my mom's place could be like a walk through a thistle patch. I never met my father and had no idea if he still stained the Earth. I knew his name though. My mom came up with the brilliant idea of naming me after him in the hope that it might guilt Joe Talbert Senior into staying around awhile, maybe marrying her and supporting her and little Joey Jr. It didn't work out. Mom tried the same thing when my younger brother, Jeremy, was born—to the same end. I grew up having to explain that my mother's name was Kathy Nelson, my name was Joe Talbert, and my brother's name was Jeremy Naylor.

As for my grandparents, the only one I ever met was my mom's father, my Grandpa Bill—a man I loved. He was a quiet man who could command attention with a simple glance or nod, a man who possessed equal parts strength and gentleness and wore them, not in layers, but blended like fine leather. There were days when I sought out his memory, when I needed his wisdom to deal with the tidal swells in my life. There were nights, however, when the sound of rain splashing against a windowpane would seep into my subconscious, and he would visit me in my dreams—dreams that would end with me bolting upright in my bed, my body covered in a cold sweat and my hands trembling from the memory of watching him die.

"You do understand that this is a nursing home, don't you?" Mrs. Lorngren asked.

"That's why I came here," I said. "You have people who've lived through amazing times."

"That's true," she said, leaning into the countertop that separated us. From up close, I could see the wrinkles that branched out from the corners of her eyes and creased her lips like a dry lake bed. And I could smell the faint aroma of scotch in the stream of her words as she spoke. She continued in a lowered voice. "Residents live here because they cannot take care of themselves. Most of them are suffering from Alzheimer's or dementia or some other neurological condition. They can't remember their own children, much less the details of their lives."

I hadn't thought of that. I could see my plan starting to falter. How could I write the biography of a war hero if the hero can't remember what he did? "Don't you have anybody with a memory?" I asked, sounding more pitiful than I would have liked.

"We could let him talk to Carl," Janet piped up.

Mrs. Lorngren shot Janet a glance akin to the glare you'd give a buddy who'd just screwed up your perfectly good lie.

"Carl?" I asked.

Mrs. Lorngren crossed her arms and stepped back from the counter. I pushed on. "Who's Carl?"

Janet looked to Mrs. Lorngren for approval. When Mrs. Lorngren finally nodded, Janet took her turn leaning across the countertop. "His name is Carl Iverson. He's a convicted murderer," she said, whispering like a schoolgirl telling a story out of turn. "The Department of Corrections sent him here about three months ago. They paroled him from Stillwater because he's dying of cancer."

Mrs. Lorngren huffed and said, "Apparently, pancreatic cancer is a perfectly reasonable substitute for penal rehabilitation."

"He's a murderer?" I asked.

Janet glanced around to be sure that she wouldn't be overheard. "Thirty years ago he raped and murdered this fourteen-year-old girl," she whispered. "I read all about it in his file. After he was done killing her, he tried to hide the evidence by burning her body in his tool shed."

A rapist and a murderer. I had come to Hillview looking for a hero and instead I'd found a villain. He would certainly have a story to tell, but was it a story I wanted to write? While my classmates would turn out tales of Grandma giving birth on a dirt floor, or Grandpa seeing John Dillinger in a hotel lobby, I would be writing about a man who raped and killed a girl and then burned her body in a shed. The idea of interviewing a murderer didn't sit well with me at first, but the more I thought about it, the more I warmed up to it. I had put off starting this project for too long. September was almost over and I'd have to turn in my interview notes in a few weeks. My classmates had their horses out of the starting gate and my nag was still back in the barn munching on hay. Carl Iverson would have to be my subject—if he agreed.

"I think I'd like to interview Mr. Iverson," I said.

"The man is a monster," Mrs. Lorngren said. "I wouldn't give him the satisfaction. I know this isn't a Christian thing to say, but it would be best if he just stayed in his room and passed on quietly." Mrs. Lorngren recoiled at her own words, words a person might think, but must never say out loud, especially in front of a stranger.

"Look," I said, "if I can do his story, maybe . . . I don't know . . . maybe I can get him to admit the error of his ways." I was a salesman after all, I thought to myself. "Besides, he has a right to have visitors, too, doesn't he?"

Mrs. Lorngren looked cornered. She had no choice. Carl wasn't a prisoner at Hillview; he was a resident with the same right to have visitors as anyone else. She unfolded her arms, placing her hands once more on the countertop between us. "I'll have to ask him if he wants a visitor," she said. "In the few months that he's been here, he's only had one visitor come to see him."

"Can I talk to Carl myself?" I said. "Maybe I can—"

"Mr. Iverson." Mrs. Lorngren corrected me, eager to regain her superiority.

"Of course." I shrugged an apology. "I could explain to Mr. Iverson what the assignment is about, and maybe—"

A jingling of electronic chimes from my cell phone interrupted me. "I'm sorry," I said. "I thought I shut it off." My ears turned red as I pulled my phone out of my pocket and saw my mother's number. "Excuse me," I said, turning my back to Janet and Mrs. Lorngren with the pretense of acquiring privacy.

"Mom, I can't talk now, I—"

"Joey, you gotta come get me," my mother screeched into the phone, the drunken slur in her voice melding her words together, making them hard to understand.

"Mom, I have to—"

"They fucking handcuffed me."

"What? Who—"

"They arrested me Joey . . . they . . . those pricks. I'm gonna sue 'em. I'll get the baddest fucking lawyer." She yelled her words at someone near her. "You hear me you . . . you prick! I want your badge number. I'll have your job."

"Mom, where are you?" I spoke loud and slow, trying to get my mother's attention back.

"They put me in handcuffs, Joey."

"Is there an officer there?" I asked. "Can I talk to him?"

She ignored my question and spiraled from one unintelligible thought to another. "If you loved me you'd come get me. I'm your fucking mother god dammit. They handcuffed . . . Get your ass . . . You never loved me. I did . . . I didn't . . . I should just cut my wrists. No one loves me. I was almost home . . . I'm gonna sue."

"Okay, Mom," I said. "I'll come get you, but I need to talk to the cop."

"You mean Mr. Prick?"

"Yeah, Mom. Mr. Prick. I need to talk to Mr. Prick. Just give him the phone for a second, then I'll come get you."

"Fine," she said. "Here, Prick. Joey wants to talk to you."

"Ms. Nelson," the officer said, "this is your time to contact an attorney, not your son."

"Hey, Officer Prick, Joey wants to talk to you."

The officer sighed. "You said that you wanted to talk to an attorney. You need to use this time to call an attorney."

"Officer Prick won't talk to you." Mom belched into the phone.

"Mom, tell him I said please."

"Joey you gotta—"

"Dammit, Mom," I yelled my whisper, "tell him I said please."

A moment of silence, and then, "fine!" My mom turned the phone away so that I could barely hear her. "Joey says please."

There was a long pause, but then the officer got on the phone. "Hello."

I spoke quickly and quietly. "Officer, I'm sorry about all this, but I have a brother who's autistic. He lives with my mom. I need to know if my mom's getting released today because if she's not, I gotta go take care of my brother."

"Well, here's the deal. Your mother's been arrested for DUI." I could hear my mother cursing and wailing in the background. "I have her at the Mower County Law Enforcement Center to give a breath test. She invoked her right to call an attorney before taking the test, so she's supposed to be using this time to contact an attorney, not calling you to come get her out."

"I understand," I said. "I just need to know if she's getting released tonight."

"That would be no." The officer limited his response in a way that my mother would not hear what was in store for her. I played along.

"Is she going to detox?"

"Yes."

"How many days?"

"Between two and three."

"Then she'll be released?" I asked.

"No."

I thought for a moment. "From detox to jail?"

"That is correct, until she makes her first appearance in court."

Mom heard the word "court" and began to yell again. In her inebriation and exhaustion, her words swung and lurched like a decrepit rope bridge. "Dammit Joey . . . get down here. You don't love me . . . you ungrateful . . . I'm your mother. Joey, they . . . they . . . get down here. Get me out."

"Thanks," I said to the officer. "I really appreciate the help. And good luck dealing with my mom."

"Good luck to you, too," he said.

I ended the call and turned back around to see Janet and Mrs. Lorngren looking at me like I was a toddler who had just learned that dogs can bite. "I'm sorry about that," I said. "My mother . . . she's . . . not well. I'm not going to be able to meet Carl—uh, Mr. Iverson—today. I have to take care of something."

Mrs. Lorngren's eyes softened, her stern expression dissolving into sympathy. "That's fine," she said. "I'll talk to Mr. Iverson about you. Leave your name and number with Janet and I'll let you know if he is agreeable to meet with you."

"I really appreciate that," I said. I wrote my information on a piece of paper. "I might have my phone turned off for a while, so if I don't answer, just leave a message and let me know what Mr. Iverson says."

"I will," Mrs. Lorngren said.

A block away from Hillview, I pulled into a parking lot, gripped the steering wheel with all my strength, and shook it violently. "God dammit!" I yelled. "Dammit! Dammit! Dammit! Why can't you just leave me alone!" My knuckles turned white, and I trembled as the wave of anger passed through me. I took a deep breath and waited for the throbbing in my throat to subside, for my eyes to clear. Then, once I had calmed down, I called Molly to let her know that I wouldn't be able to work the door. She wasn't happy, but she understood. After I hung up, I tossed the phone on the passenger seat and began the long drive south to get my brother.

CHAPTER 2

Most people have never heard of Austin, Minnesota, and those that have heard of it know it because of Spam, a salted pork product that never rots and feeds soldiers and refugees all over the world. It's the crown jewel of the Hormel Foods Corporation and the nickname-sake of my home town—Spam Town. They even have a museum in Austin devoted to the greatness of Spam. And if that didn't stamp Austin with the equivalent of a prison tattoo, there was the strike.

It happened four years before I was born, but kids growing up in Austin learn about the strike the way some children learn about Lewis and Clark or the Declaration of Independence. A recession in the early 1980s had taken a chunk out of the meat-packing industry, so Hormel asked the union to take a big pay cut. Of course, that went over like a kick to the nuts, and the strike began. Pushing and shoving on the picket line led to riots. The violence attracted the networks, and one television crew clocked out by crashing a helicopter into a cornfield up near Ellendale. The governor finally sent in the National Guard, but by then the violence and animosity had left a mark on the town that some would say gave it character. I just saw it as an ugly scar.

Like any town, Austin had its good points, too, although most people don't see the skin beside the pimples. It had parks, a pool, a decent hospital, a Carmelite monastery, its own municipal airport, and it was only a hop away from the famous Mayo Clinic in Rochester. It had a community college where I had been taking classes while, at the same time, working two part-time jobs. In three years, I had saved up enough money and racked up enough credits to allow me to transfer to the U of M as a junior.

Austin also had thirteen bars, not counting hotel bars and service

clubs, and with a population of twenty-three thousand—give or take—
Austin had one of the highest bar-to-citizen ratios in greater Minnesota.
I knew the bars well, having been in every one of them at one point or
another. I stepped into my first bar when I was a mere nub of a kid, probably no more than ten years old. My mother left me at home to keep an
eye on Jeremy while she went out for a drink or two. Being two years
older than my brother and him being autistic—making him such a quiet
kid and all—Mom felt that I was plenty old enough to babysit.

That night, Jeremy sat in an arm chair in the living room watching
his favorite video, *The Lion King*. I had geography homework to do, so
I locked myself in the tiny bedroom he and I shared. I don't remember
most of the rooms we shared over the years, but I remember that one:
walls as thin as crackers, painted the same bright blue that coats the
bottom of every public swimming pool in the world. You could hear
the slightest sound from one room to the next, including the songs of
The Lion King, which Jeremy played over and over and over. I sat atop
our bunk bed—a second-hand piece of crap with springs so useless that
our mattresses had to rest on sheets of plywood—covering my ears to
try and block out the noise. But it did little to muffle the incessant,
repetitive music kicking through the porous wall of my concentration.
I'm not sure if this next part is true or an embellishment of my memory
born of guilt, but I asked Jeremy to turn down the volume, and I swear
he turned it up instead. A guy can only take so much.

I stomped into the living room and pushed Jeremy out of his chair,
causing him to fall hard against the wall. The impact knocked loose a
picture above his head, a picture of me holding him when I was three
and he was a baby. The picture popped off of its nail, fell down the wall,
and crashed into the top of Jeremy's blonde head, the glass shattering
into a hundred spikes.

After Jeremy brushed the debris off of his arms and legs, he looked
at me. A wedge of glass stuck out of the top of his head like an oversized
coin jammed in an undersized piggy-bank slot. His eyes narrowed, not
in anger, but in confusion. Jeremy rarely looked me in the eye, but that
day he stared at me like he was on the verge of solving some great riddle.

Then, abruptly, as if he'd found his answer, his eyes softened and his gaze shifted to the blood drops accumulating on his arm.

I grabbed a towel from the bathroom, carefully removed the glass from his head, which hadn't penetrated as deep as I had feared, and wrapped the towel around him like a turban. I used a washcloth to wipe the blood off his arm and waited for the bleeding to stop. After ten minutes, blood still trickled from the cut, and the white towel had become blotched with large, bright-red patches. I rewrapped the towel around Jeremy's head, put his hand on the end of the towel to hold it in place, and ran out the door to find our mother.

Mom didn't need to leave a trail of bread crumbs for me to find her. Our car sat in the driveway of the duplex with two flat tires, which meant that Mom had to be within walking distance. This limited my options to a couple bars. It didn't strike me as odd at the time that my mother left me alone to look after an autistic brother and never bothered to mention where she was going, or that I automatically knew to look for her in the bars. Then again, a lot of what I considered normal in my childhood appears so completely messed up when I look back now. I found her on my first try, at the Odyssey Bar.

The emptiness of the place caught me by surprise. I'd always envisioned my mother stalking off to join an army of beautiful people who joked, laughed, and danced like they did on the TV commercials. But this place had bad country music crackling through cheap speakers, uneven floors, and reeked of feckless mediocrity. I saw my mother right away, chatting with the bartender. At first, I couldn't tell if the look on her face showed anger or concern. But she answered that question by grabbing my arm with a blood-cutting grip and dragging me out of the bar. We walked at a brisk pace back to the apartment and found Jeremy watching his movie, his hand still on the towel where I'd left it. When Mom saw the bloody towel, she lost a hinge.

"What in the hell did you do! Jesus Christ. Look at this mess!" She pulled the towel off his head and lifted Jeremy off the floor by his arm, dragging him into the bathroom and lifting him into the empty bath tub. Blood matted his fine blonde hair. She threw the bloody towel into the sink and went to the living room to scrub three tiny spots of blood from the rust-brown carpeting.

"You had to use my good towel," she yelled. "You couldn't just grab a rag. Look at this blood in the carpet. We could lose our damage deposit. Did you ever stop to think about that? No. You never think. You just make the goddamn mess, and I have to clean it up."

I went into the bathroom, half to get away from my mother and half to be with Jeremy in case he got scared. He didn't get scared though; he never got scared. Or if he did, he never showed it. He looked at me with a face that, to the rest of the world, would appear expressionless, but I could see the shadow of my betrayal behind his eyes. No matter how much I have tried to put that night behind me, to bury it someplace deep inside and let it die, the memory of Jeremy looking up at me continues to breathe.

Jeremy was eighteen now, old enough to stay alone in the apartment for a few hours, but not for a few days. As I pulled into the driveway of Mom's apartment that night, the Twins and the Indians were all tied up at one run apiece in the third inning. I let myself in with my spare key and found Jeremy watching *Pirates of the Caribbean*, his new favorite movie. He looked surprised for only a second, then he looked at the floor between us.

"Hey Buddy," I said. "How's my little bro?"

"Hello Joe," he said.

When Jeremy started middle school, the district assigned him a teaching assistant named Helen Bollinger. She knew about autism, understood Jeremy's need for patterns and routines, his preference for solitude, his aversion to touching or being touched, and his inability to understand much beyond primal needs and black-and-white instruction. While Mrs. Bollinger struggled to bring Jeremy out of his darkness, my mother encouraged him to be seen and not heard. That wrestling match went on for seven years, with Mrs. Bollinger winning more than she lost. By the time he graduated from high school, I had a brother who could carry on something akin to a conversation, even if he had to struggle to look at me when we talked.

"Maybe I thought you were at the college," Jeremy said, speaking in a strict staccato cadence, as if he were placing each word in careful order upon a conveyor belt.

"I came back to see you," I said.

"Oh, okay." Jeremy turned back to watch his movie.

"Mom called me," I said. "She's got a meeting, and she's not gonna be home for a while."

It was easy to lie to Jeremy, his trusting temperament being incapable of understanding deceit. I didn't lie to him to be mean. It was just my way of explaining things to him without the complexity or nuance that came with the truth. The first time that my mother found her way to detox, I came up with the lie that she was at a meeting. After that, I told Jeremy that Mom had a meeting every time she ran off to one of the Indian casinos or flopped at some guy's house for the night. Jeremy never asked about the meeting, never wondered why some meetings lasted a few hours and others lasted a few days, never wondered why these meetings happened so suddenly.

"This meeting is one of those long meetings," I said. "So you get to stay with me for a few days."

Jeremy stopped watching TV and began looking around the floor, a thin furrow forming above his eyebrows. I could tell that he was building up to making eye contact with me, a task that did not come naturally to him. "Maybe I will stay here and wait for Mom," he said.

"You can't stay here. I have to go to my classes tomorrow. I gotta take you with me, to my apartment."

My answer wasn't what he wanted to hear. I could tell because he stopped trying to look me in the eye, a clue that his anxiety was on the rise. "Maybe you can stay here and go to your classes in the morning."

"My classes are at the college. That's a couple hours away from here. I can't stay here, Buddy." I remained calm but firm.

"Maybe I will stay here by myself."

"You can't stay here, Jeremy. Mom told me to come get you. You can stay at my apartment at college."

Jeremy began to rub his left thumb across the knuckles of his right hand. He did this when his world made the least sense. "Maybe I can wait here."

I sat on the couch next to Jeremy. "This'll be fun," I said. "It'll just be you and me. I'll bring the DVD player, and you can watch any movie you want. You can pack a whole bag of nothing but movies."

Jeremy smiled.

"But Mom's not gonna be back for a few days, and I need you to come to my apartment. Okay?"

Jeremy thought hard for a bit then said, "Maybe I can bring *Pirates of the Caribbean*?"

"Sure," I said. "It'll be fun. We'll make it an adventure. You can be Captain Jack Sparrow, and I'll be Will Turner. What do you say?"

Jeremy looked up at me and did his favorite imitation of Captain Jack, saying, "This is the day you'll always remember as the day you almost caught Captain Jack Sparrow." Then Jeremy laughed until his cheeks turned red, and I laughed with him, the way that I always laughed when Jeremy cracked a joke. I grabbed some garbage bags and gave one of them to Jeremy to fill with DVDs and clothes, making sure that he packed enough to last a while, just in case Mom didn't make bail.

As I pulled out of the driveway, I contemplated my work and class schedules, trying to find gaps that would allow me to keep an eye on Jeremy. On top of that, distracting questions tripped through my brain. How would Jeremy get along in the unfamiliar world of my apartment? Where would I find the time or the money to bail my mother out of jail? And how the hell did I become the parent in this wreck of a family?

CHAPTER 3

On the drive back to the Twin Cities, I watched the anxiety pace back and forth behind my brother's eyes, his brow and forehead creasing and relaxing as he processed what was happening. As the miles fell behind my tires, Jeremy grew more comfortable with our adventure until finally he relaxed with a deep exhale, the way I've seen dogs sigh in that moment when vigilance surrenders to sleep. Jeremy—the boy who laid his head on the bottom level of our bunk bed and shared my room, my closet, and my dresser drawers for eighteen years—was with me again. We had never been apart for more than a night or two in all our lives until a month ago, when I moved to campus, leaving him behind with a woman who swam in chaos.

As far back as I could remember, my mom had been prone to wild mood swings—laughing and dancing across the living room one minute, throwing dishes around the kitchen the next—classic bipolar from what I understand. Of course that diagnosis was never made official because my mother refused to get professional help. Instead, she lived her life with her fingers in her ears, as though the truth would not exist if she never heard the words spoken aloud. Add to that cauldron an ever increasing measure of cheap vodka—a form of self-medication that quelled the inner scream but amplified the outer crazy—and you get a picture of the mother I left behind.

She hadn't always been that bad though. In the early years, my mother's moods used to have a ceiling and a floor that kept the neighbors, and Child Protective Services, out of our lives. We even had some good times. I can remember the three of us going to the Science Museum, the Renaissance Festival, and the Valley Fair Amusement Park. I can remember her helping me with my math homework when I struggled to multiply double digits. I could sometimes find a crack in the wall that had grown between us and remember her laughing with us and even loving us. When I tried, I could remember a mother who could be warm and soft on those days when the world stayed off her back.

That all changed the day my Grandpa Bill died. A feral restlessness descended upon our little trio that day, as though his death severed the one tether that gave my mother stability. After his death she let go of what little restraint she possessed and simply floated on the wave of her moods. She cried more, yelled more, and lashed out whenever the world overwhelmed her. She seemed determined to find the darker edges of her life and embrace them as some kind of new normal.

Hitting was her first rule change. It started gradually, but eventually she took to slapping me across the face whenever her tea-kettle brain started to boil. As I got older and less sensitive to the slaps, she adjusted her aim to hit me in the ear. I hated that. Sometimes she would use implements like wooden spoons or wire flyswatter handles to make her point. Once, in seventh grade, I had to miss a wrestling tournament because the welts on my thighs were visible around my wrestling uniform and she forced me to stay home. For years she left Jeremy out of our battles, preferring to take all of her frustrations out on me. But as time went by, she began to lose control with him, too, yelling and cursing at him.

Then, one day she went too far.

When I was eighteen and out of high school, I came home to find my mother particularly drunk and angry and hitting Jeremy in the head with a tennis shoe. I dragged her into her bedroom and threw her down on the bed. She got up and tried to hit me. I grabbed her wrists, spun her around, and tossed her back onto the bed. She tried twice more to come at me and ended each attempt face down on her mattress. After the last attempt, she paused to catch her breath and ended up passing out. The next morning, she acted like nothing had happened, like she had no memory of her craziness, like our little family unit wasn't on the brink of its inevitable collapse. I played along, but I knew—I knew that she had reached a point where she could justify hitting Jeremy. I also knew that once I left for college it would likely get worse. Those thoughts made my chest hurt. And so, just as my mother pretended nothing was wrong after her blackout, I buried my thoughts deep inside, hiding them where they would remain undusted.

But as we headed to my apartment that night, life was good. Jeremy and I listened to the Twins game as we drove—at least I listened to it. Jeremy heard the game but couldn't follow it from one minute to the next. I chatted with him, explaining things about the game as we drove, but he would rarely respond. When he did, he stepped into the conversation as if he had just come in from another room. By the time we pulled off I-35, up near campus, the Twins were laying a walloping on Cleveland, having scored four runs in the bottom of the eighth to take a six-to-four lead. I whooped as each run scored, and Jeremy whooped in imitation of me, laughing at my excitement.

When we arrived, I led Jeremy up the steps to my apartment on the second floor, his garbage bags in hand. We bounded through the door just in time to turn on the TV and watch the Twins throw the final out to win the game. I held my hand up to high-five Jeremy, but he was turning a slow circle, taking in the smallness of my apartment. The kitchen and living room were at opposite sides of a single space; the bedroom was barely bigger than the twin bed it contained; and my apartment had no bathroom, at least not within the confines of its walls. I watched as Jeremy scanned the apartment, his eyes covering the same territory over and over again, as though the next pass might expose a hidden bathroom door.

"Maybe I need to go to the bathroom," Jeremy said.

"Come on," I said, motioning to Jeremy. "I'll show you."

My bathroom was across the hall from my front door. The old house had originally been built in the 1920s to hold one of those large, turn-of-the-century families that gave birth at a pace to outrun infant mortality rates. It had been subdivided in the 1970s with a three-bedroom apartment on the main level and two single-bedroom apartments upstairs, with only one of the upstairs units big enough to have its own bathroom. So at the top of the steep, narrow stairway, the door to the right was my apartment, the door to the left was my bathroom, and the door straight ahead was the other second-floor apartment.

I dug Jeremy's toothbrush and flavored toothpaste out of one of the garbage bags and headed across the hall to the bathroom with Jeremy following at a cautious distance. "This is the bathroom," I said. "If you need to go, just lock the door." I showed him how to flip the deadbolt.

He didn't walk into the bathroom. Instead, he examined it from the relative safety of the hallway. "Maybe we should go back home," he said.

"We can't, Buddy. Mom's at her meeting. Remember?"

"Maybe she is home now."

"She's not home now. She's not gonna be home for a couple days."

"Maybe we should call her and see." Jeremy began rubbing his thumbs across his knuckles again. I could see a slight tremor growing out of his anxiety. I wanted to put my hand on his shoulder to try to settle him down, but that would only exacerbate his reaction. Jeremy's autism was like that.

Jeremy turned toward the steps, contemplating their steep pitch, pressing his thumb even harder into the back of his hand, kneading the knuckles like bread dough. I moved to block Jeremy from the steps. He was taller than me by two inches and outweighed me by a good twenty pounds. About the time he turned fourteen he surpassed me in height, weight, and looks: his golden hair curled around his head with a Nordic swirl, where my dirty blonde hair stuck out like straw if I didn't tame it with a touch of hair gel; his jaw was square, with a boyish dimple on the tip, where my chin was forgettable; his eyes sparkled ocean blue when he smiled, where my eyes were the hazel of weak coffee. Despite having every physical advantage over me, he remained my "little" brother, and therefore susceptible to my influence. I stood a step below him, my hands on his biceps, easing him back, trying to turn his attention away from the stairs and back toward my apartment.

Behind me, at the bottom of the steps, I heard the door to the foyer open and close, followed by the cadence of feminine footsteps. I recognized the sound of her footfall, having listened to her pass by my door every day now for the past month. I knew her only as L. Nash, the name on the piece of tape that crossed her letter box. She stood all of five feet two, with short, black hair that whipped around her face like water dancing off rocks. She had dark eyes, a pixie nose, and a chilly penchant for being left alone. She and I had passed each other many times in the hall or on the steps. When I tried to engage her in small talk, she smiled politely, responded appropriately, but never stopped—always doing her best to pass by my interruption without seeming rude.

She paused halfway up the stairs to watch me holding Jeremy by the arms, physically preventing him from leaving. Jeremy saw L. Nash and stopped moving, dropping his eyes to the floor. I stepped to the side to let her go by, the walls of the stairway squeezing together as she passed, the scent of her body wash and baby powder brushing my nose.

"Hi," I said.

"Hi," she returned, raising an eyebrow in our direction and walking the remaining few paces to her apartment door. I wanted to say something more, so I blurted out the first stupid thought that jumped into my head.

"It's not what it looks like," I said. "We're brothers."

"Yeah," she said, as she turned the key in her lock. "I'm sure that line worked for Jeffrey Dahmer, too." She stepped into her apartment and closed the door.

Her quip left me dumb. I wanted to shoot back my own clever retort, but my mind had seized up like a rusty bolt. Jeremy didn't watch L. Nash like I did. He stood quietly at the top of the stairs, no longer rubbing his thumb to his knuckle. His emergency had passed. The stubbornness in his eyes had been replaced by fatigue, it being well past his normal bedtime. I guided him into the bathroom to brush his teeth and then to the bedroom, where I rolled my old television in so that he could watch his movie on the DVD player. Then I grabbed a blanket and settled onto the couch.

I could hear Jeremy watching his movie, the familiar dialogue and music lulling him to sleep, distracting him from the insecurities of this new environment. Despite the drama at the top of the steps, I had to admire Jeremy for adapting as well as he did. Even small changes in his routine, like a new toothbrush or the wrong breakfast cereal, could knock him off kilter. But here he was, in an apartment he had never seen before, an apartment half the size of the one he called home, an apartment that didn't even have its own bathroom, falling asleep for the first time in a bed that didn't have a top bunk.

I'd turned off my phone earlier in the evening to avoid the barrage of calls I expected from my mother, but now I pulled it out of my pocket, turned it on, and checked my missed calls. There were twenty-one calls from a number in the 507 area code, no doubt my mother calling from the detox center. I could just hear her screaming at me for shutting off my phone and for leaving her in detox and jail—even though I had no part in that decision.

The first nine voice messages were from my mother:

"Joey, I can't believe you'd treat your own mother like this—" [Delete]

"Joey, I don't know what I did to deserve—" [Delete]

"Well, now I know that I can't count on you—" [Delete]

"I know I'm a terrible mother—" [Delete]

"Joey if you don't answer your phone I'll—" [Delete]

"You don't love me—" [Delete]

"I'm sorry, Joey. I just wish I was dead. Maybe then—" [Delete]

"You think you're some hot-shit college—" [Delete]

"Answer your fucking phone—" [Delete]

"Joe, this is Mary Lorngren from Hillview Manor. I just wanted to call and tell you that I spoke to Mr. Iverson about your project . . . and he has agreed to meet with you to discuss it. He wanted me to make it clear that he is not agreeing to do it, mind you. He wants to meet with you first. You can call Janet tomorrow to find out when is a good time to come by. We don't like to disturb the guests during their meal times. So, just call Janet. Bye-bye."

I turned off my phone, and closed my eyes, a slight smile creasing into my cheeks, absorbing the strange irony that I might soon be interviewing a savage murderer, a man who gave no thought to ending a young girl's life, a criminal who survived for more than thirty years in the worst hellhole prison in Minnesota, yet I did not dread that conversation nearly as much as I dreaded seeing my own mother again. Still, I could feel a wind at my back, one that I chose to see as favorable, one that I hoped would bring me a good grade in my English class. With my sails filled, I might be able to overcome my procrastination in starting the assignment. It never occurred to me, as I nestled on my couch, that such a wind might also be destructive. When I finally fell asleep that night, I did so wrapped comfortably in the belief that my meeting with Carl Iverson would have no down side, that our encounter would somehow make my life better—easier. In hindsight, I was at best naïve.

CHAPTER 4

C arl Iverson wasn't wearing shoes when they arrested him. I know this because I found a picture of him, barefoot, being led past the remains of a burned-down shed toward a waiting squad car. His hands were cuffed behind his back, his shoulders slumped forward, a plain-clothed detective holding one of his biceps and a uniformed officer holding the other. Iverson wore a simple white t-shirt and blue jeans. His dark, wavy hair was pressed into the side of his head as if the cops had just pulled him out of bed.

I found this picture in the bowels of the University of Minnesota's Wilson library, in a glass-walled archive where thousands of newspapers are stored on microfilm, some dating back to the days of the American Revolution. Unlike the rest of the library, where shelves were filled with stories of the heroic and the famous, the archive room held newspaper articles written by guys with pencils behind their ears and ulcers in their stomachs, articles written about everyday folk—the quiet people. They could never have dreamt that their stories would survive for decades, even centuries, to be read by a guy like me. The archive room had the feel of a tabernacle, with millions of souls packed away on microfilm like incense in tiny jars, waiting for someone to free their essence to be felt, tasted, inhaled again, if only for a moment.

I began with a search for Carl Iverson's name on the Internet. I came up with thousands of hits, but one site had an excerpt from some legal document that referred to an appellate court decision regarding his case. I didn't understand all of the legal jargon, but it gave me a date when the murder took place: October 29, 1980, and it gave me the initials of the murdered girl: C.M.H. That would be enough information to find the story in the newspaper.

I moved from task to task quickly, pressed into efficiency by my brother's unexpected presence in my life, and more than a little flustered at having one more ball to juggle. I found myself thinking about Jeremy and wondering how he was managing back at my apartment. I wondered if my mom's bail hearing would happen by Friday. I had to work at Molly's on Friday and didn't want to go to work and leave Jeremy alone. I needed to get him back to Austin before the weekend. Molly would almost surely fire me if I had to miss work again.

I'd woken Jeremy that morning before I left for school, poured him some cereal, pulled the TV back into the living room, and showed him again how to use the remote. Jeremy was eighteen years old, so it's not that he couldn't pour his own cereal. Yet the unfamiliarity of my apartment would likely have befuddled him. He would go hungry rather than open a strange cupboard door to look for food. I considered skipping my classes that day, but I had already lost too much time procrastinating. I laid out some of Jeremy's favorite DVDs and told him that I would be back in a couple hours. I hoped that he would be okay being alone for that short time, but my concern was growing with every passing minute.

I went into the microfilm stacks, found the reel for the *Minneapolis Tribune* for October 29, 1980, slid it into the reader, and scanned the front page for the story. It was not there. I moved to the following pages and still found no mention of a murder, at least not one that involved a fourteen-year-old girl or the initials C.M.H. I read the entire newspaper and came up blank. I leaned back in my chair, ran a hand through my hair. I was starting to think that the date in the court opinion was wrong. Then it dawned on me. The story would not have made the paper until the next day. I rolled the spool forward to the next day's edition. The top story for October 30, 1980, was a half-page article about a peace treaty between Honduras and El Salvador. Beneath that I found the story I was looking for, a story about a girl murdered and burned in Northeast Minneapolis. The article ran down a sidebar beside a picture of a fire. The picture showed firefighters shooting water on what appeared to be a shed about the size of a single-car garage. The flames shot skyward a good fifteen feet above the roof, suggesting the photographer had snapped the picture as firefighters were just beginning their efforts to extinguish the flames. The article read:

Human remains found in Pierce Street blaze

Minneapolis police are investigating after charred human remains were discovered yesterday in the debris of a burned tool shed in the Windom Park neighborhood of northeast Minneapolis. Firefighters responding at 4:18 p.m. to reports of a fire in the 1900 block of Pierce Street N.E., arrived to find the tool shed engulfed in flames. Police evacuated neighboring houses while firefighters battled the blaze. Fire Marshal John Vries reports that investigators combing through the debris discovered a charred body amid the rubble. The body has not yet been identified. Police have not ruled out foul play.

The article went on for a few more paragraphs with unimportant details about the estimated damage and the reaction of neighbors.

I printed a copy of the page and then spooled through the microfilm to the next day's edition. In a follow-up article the police confirmed that the body found the day before had been identified as fourteen-year-old Crystal Marie Hagen. The body had been badly burned, and authorities suspected that she had already been dead when the fire was set. The burned-out shed was located next door to the house where Crystal had lived with her mother, Danielle Hagen; her stepfather, Douglas Lockwood; and her stepbrother, Dan Lockwood. Crystal's mother, Danielle, told reporters that they had noticed that Crystal was missing shortly after word spread that a body had been discovered in the debris of the shed. Crystal was positively identified as the deceased using dental records. The article ended with the note that thirty-two-year-old Carl Iverson had been taken into custody for questioning. Iverson lived next door to Crystal Hagen and owned the shed where Hagen's body was found.

Next to this article I found the photograph of the two officers arresting a barefooted Carl Iverson. Using the knobs on the microfilm reader, I enlarged the picture. The two cops wore coats and gloves, in contrast to Iverson's t-shirt and jeans. The uniformed officer had his gaze set on something behind the photographer. From the hint of sadness in his eyes, I speculated that he might have been looking at Crystal Hagen's family, as they watched the arrest of the monster that killed and burned their daughter. The plain-clothed cop had his mouth open, his jaw slightly crooked, as if he were saying something, maybe even yelling something at Carl Iverson.

Of the three men in the photo, only Carl Iverson looked at the camera. I didn't know what I was expecting to see in his face. How do you hold yourself after committing murder? Do you strut as you walk past the charcoal-black aftermath of the shed where you burned her body? Do you wear a mask of nonchalance and pass by the ruins with no more interest than if you were walking to the corner store for some milk? Or do you flip out with fear, knowing you've been caught, knowing that you've breathed your last measure of freedom and will spend the rest of your life in a cage. When I zoomed in on Carl Iverson's face, on his eyes as he looked at the photographer, I saw no pride, no false calm, and no fear. What I saw was confusion.

CHAPTER 5

There is an odor that permeates old apartment buildings. When I was a kid, I noticed its effect on the people who came by to visit my mother's apartment, that split second of corruption as the taint of decay hits them square in the face, the twitch of the nose, the flutter of blinking, the reining in of the chin. When I was little, that mustiness was what I thought all homes smelled like. Not scented candles or fresh-baked bread, but dirty sneakers and unwashed dishes. By the time I was in junior high, I found myself looking away in embarrassment any time someone came to the door. I swore that when I grew up and got my own apartment, I would get one that smelled of old wood, not old cats.

As it turned out, that was not easy to do on my budget. The triplex apartment building I lived in had an ancient cellar that breathed dankness up through the floorboards, filling the structure with a pungency born of wet dirt mixed with the tang of rotting timber. The odor was strongest immediately inside the common front door where our letter boxes were bolted to the wall. Within that foyer, the steps to my apartment rose to the right, and to the left a door led to the main-floor apartment where a Greek family, the Kostas, lived. Sometimes the aroma of rich cooking spices seeped through that door, mixing with the cellar funk to overwhelm the senses.

I made a point of keeping my apartment clean, vacuuming weekly, washing dishes after every meal; I'd even dusted once in the short time that I had lived there. I wasn't a clean freak by any stretch. I simply refused to let my apartment succumb to its natural state of entropy. I went so far as to plug an air freshener into an electric socket that pumped out spurts of apple and cinnamon to welcome me home every day. But what caught my attention that day, as I walked through my door, wasn't the pleasantry of the artificial air freshener; it was Jeremy sitting on my couch beside the girl I knew only as L. Nash, and they were giggling.

"Now that's what you call ironic," L. Nash said.

"Now that's what you call ironic," Jeremy repeated. Then he and L. Nash broke into another laugh. I recognized the line from Jeremy's *Pirates of the Caribbean* movie. It was another one of Jeremy's favorite lines. They were watching the movie together. Jeremy was sitting, as he usually does, in the center of the couch directly in front of the TV, his feet flat on the floor, his back straight against the curve of the couch back, his hands balled up on his lap where he could fidget with them if needed.

L. Nash sat in the corner of the sofa, her legs crossed over one another, wearing jeans and a blue sweater. Her dark eyes flitted weightlessly as she laughed with Jeremy. I had never seen her smile before, at least not beyond the cursory upturn at the edges of her lips as we passed each other in the hallway. But now her smile transformed her, as if she had grown taller or changed her hair color or something. Her cheeks popped with dimples; her lips seemed redder and softer against the backdrop of her white teeth. Damn, she was cute.

Jeremy and L. Nash looked up at me as if I were a parent intruding upon a slumber party. "Hello?" I said, my tone betraying my confusion. What I wanted to say was "Jeremy, how the hell did you get L. Nash into my apartment and sitting on my couch?"

L. Nash must have seen the confusion on my face because she offered an explanation. "Jeremy was having a little problem with the TV," she said. "So I came over to help."

"Problem with the TV?" I said.

"Maybe the TV did not work right," Jeremy said, his face shifting back to his normal flat affect.

"Jeremy hit the wrong button," L. Nash said. "He pushed the input button by mistake."

"Maybe I just pushed the wrong button," Jeremy said.

"I'm sorry, Buddy," I said. I had made that mistake a few times myself, accidentally switching the internal input from DVD to VCR, causing the TV to explode with a noisy white static, which had to be a personal hell for Jeremy. "So how did he . . . I mean who . . ."

"Maybe Lila fixed it," Jeremy said.

"Lila." I said, letting the name rest on the tip of my tongue for a bit. So that's what the L stood for. "I'm Joe, and you've obviously met my brother Jeremy."

"Yeah," Lila said. "Jeremy and I are good friends already."

Jeremy had turned his attention back to his movie, paying no more mind to Lila than he did the wall behind him. Like the idiot I was—a condition often exacerbated by the presence of a female—I decided that my next move would be to rescue Lila from Jeremy, to show her a seat at the adult table, impress her with my wit and charm, and sweep her off her feet. At least, that was my plan.

"Are you surprised that I'm not a serial killer," I said.

"Serial killer?" Lila looked up at me, confused.

"Last night . . . you . . . um . . . called me Jeffrey Dahmer."

"Oh . . . I forgot." She smiled a half smile, and I scrambled to find a new topic of conversation, having missed the mark with my attempt at humor. "So what do you do when you're not fixing televisions?"

"I'm a student at the U." Her words slid slowly from her mouth to punctuate that she knew damn well that I knew she was a student. We had passed each other on the stairs many times with textbooks in our hands. Yet, as lame as my overture had been, I had to view it as progress because we were having our first real conversation. I often timed my entrances and exits from the building to coincide with hers—at least to the point where it didn't come across as creepy—and I could no more get her to talk to me than I could mix sunlight with shade. But there we were having a conversation, all because Jeremy hit the wrong button.

"Thanks for helping him out," I said. "I really appreciate it."

"Just being neighborly," she said and started to stand up.

She was going to leave; I didn't want her to leave. "Let me show you my appreciation," I said. "Maybe I could take you out to dinner or something." My words fell heavy to the ground as soon as they left my mouth.

Lila curled one of her hands into the other, shrugged her shoulders, and said, "That's okay." Her geniality faded like a toy succumbing to a dead battery, her eyes no longer weightless, her dimples gone. It was as though my words cast a pall over her. "I should get going," she said.

"You can't leave."

She started for the door.

"I mean you shouldn't leave," I said, sounding needier than I intended. "Duty requires that I return the good deed." I moved toward the door, half blocking her path. "You should at least stay for lunch."

"I have to get to class," she said, skirting past me, her shoulder brushing lightly against my arm as she went by. Then she paused at the door, or at least I think she paused. Maybe she was reconsidering my invitation. Maybe she was toying with me. Or, maybe—probably—my imagination was playing a trick on me and she didn't pause at all. I, of course, chose to err on the side of recklessness and press on.

"Let me at least walk you home," I said.

"It's eight feet away."

"More like ten feet," I said, following her into the hallway and closing my door behind me. I wasn't getting anywhere with my feeble banter, so I changed tactics and tried sincerity. "I really appreciate what you did for Jeremy," I said. "He can be a bit . . . I don't know, childlike. You see he's . . ."

"Autistic?" she said. "Yeah, I know. I have a cousin on the spectrum. He's a lot like Jeremy." Lila leaned against her door, her hand turning the knob.

"Why don't you join us both for dinner tonight," I said, shredding any semblance of subtlety. "Just my way of saying thanks. I'm making spaghetti."

She stepped inside her apartment and turned to meet my eyes, her face suddenly serious. "Listen Joe," she said. "You seem like a nice guy and all, but I'm not looking for a dinner. Not right now. I'm not looking for anything right now. I just want to—"

"No. No, I understand." I interrupted her. "I thought I'd ask. It's not for me. It's for Jeremy," I lied. "He's not good at being away from home, and he seemed to like you."

"Really?" Lila smiled. "You're gonna pimp your brother out like that just so you can cook me a meal?"

"Just being neighborly." I smiled back.

She started to close the door but hesitated as she turned the idea over in her head a couple times. "Okay," she said, "one dinner, that's all—for Jeremy."

CHAPTER 6

Janet, the receptionist at Hillview Manor, smiled at me this time when I walked through the front door. It helped that I had called ahead to get Mr. Iverson's eating and napping schedule. She told me to show up around two o'clock, which I did on the dot, anticipating the wall of Mentholatum odor that hit me as I stepped through the door. The old woman with the crooked wig still kept her vigil at the entrance, paying no attention to me as I walked by her. Before I left my apartment, I settled Jeremy on the couch, started his movie, and showed him again which buttons to push on the remote and which ones to avoid. If all went well—and Iverson agreed to be my subject—I might have just enough time to get some background for my assignment.

"Hi, Joe." Janet stood up and walked out from behind her reception desk.

"Is my timing good?" I asked.

"As good as it's going to be. Mr. Iverson had a rough night last night. Pancreatic cancer is a terrible thing."

"Is he okay to . . ."

"He's fine now. Probably a little tired. The pain in his belly flairs up sometimes and we have to sedate him just to give him a few hours rest."

"Isn't he getting radiation, or chemo, or something?"

"He could, I guess, but it won't do any good at this point. The most that chemo might do is prolong the inevitable. He said he doesn't want that. I don't blame him."

Janet walked with me to the lounge area, pointing to a man in a wheelchair sitting alone in front of one of the large windows that lined the back of the building. "He sits there every day staring out that window, looking at God knows what, since there ain't nothin' to see.

41

He just sits there. Mrs. Lorngren thinks he's mesmerized by a view with no metal bars blocking the way."

I half expected Carl Iverson to be a monster strapped to his wheelchair with leather belts for the protection of the residents around him, or to have the cold piercing eyes of a madman capable of doing great evil, or to have the demanding presence of an infamous villain; but I found none of that. Carl Iverson should have been in his mid-sixties, if I did the math right. But as I looked at this man, I thought that Janet made a mistake and brought me to the wrong person. A few thin wisps of long, gray hair dangled from the crown of his head; sharp bones poked against gaunt cheeks; thin skin, tinted yellow with jaundice, covered a neck so skinny and shriveled that I was sure I could have closed a single hand completely around it. He had a serious scar crossing the carotid artery on his neck and cadaverous forearms, their tendons prominent against the bone in the absence of any muscle or fat. I half believed that I could hold his arm up, like a child might hold a leaf up to the sunlight, and see every vein and capillary that ran through it. If I had not known better, I would have put his age closer to eighty.

"Stage four," Janet said. "It's about as bad as it gets. We'll try to make him comfortable, but there's only so much we can do. He can have morphine, but he fights it. Says he'd rather have the pain and be able to think clearly."

"How long's he got?"

"If he makes it to Christmas, I'll lose a bet," she said. "I sometimes feel sorry for him, but then I remember who he is—what he did. And I think about that girl he killed and everything she missed out on: boyfriends, love, getting married and having a family of her own. Her kids would've been about your age if he hadn't killed her. I think about those things whenever I start feeling sorry for him."

The phone rang, pulling Janet back to the reception desk. I waited for a minute or two, hoping she would come back and provide the introduction. When she didn't return, I cautiously approached what little remained of the murderer Carl Iverson.

"Mr. Iverson?" I said.

"Yes?" He turned his attention away from a nuthatch he'd been watching scamper down the trunk of a dead jack pine outside the window.

"I'm Joe Talbert," I said. "I think Mrs. Lorngren told you I was coming?"

"Ah, my visitor . . . has arrived," Carl said, speaking in a half whisper, breaking his sentence in half with a wheezing inhale. He nodded his head toward an armchair nearby. I sat. "So you're the scholar."

"Nah," I said, "not a scholar, just a student."

"Lorngren tells me . . ." He shut his eyes tightly to let a wave of pain pass. "She tells me . . . you want to write my story."

"I have to write a biography for my English class."

"So," he said, raising an eyebrow, leaning toward me, his face dead serious, "the most obvious question is . . . why me? How do I come to receive . . . such an honor?"

"I find your story compelling." I said the first thing that came to my mind, the words echoing with insincerity.

"Compelling? In what way?"

"It's not every day you meet a . . ." I stopped myself, looking for a polite way to end the sentence: a murderer, a rapist of children? That was way too harsh. ". . . a person who's been to prison," I said.

"You're pulling your punches, Joe," he said, sowing his words in a careful steady pace so as to avoid having to stop to catch his breath.

"Sir?"

"You're not interested in me because I spent time in prison. You're interested because of the Hagen murder. That's why you're talking to me. You can say it. It's gonna help with the grade, right?"

"The thought did cross my mind," I said. "That kind of thing . . . killing someone, I mean, well, you don't come across that every day."

"Probably more often than you think," he said. "There're probably ten or fifteen people in this very building who have killed."

"You think that there're ten other murderers in this building besides you?" I said.

"Are you talking about killing or murdering?"

"Is there a difference?"

Mr. Iverson looked out the window as he pondered the question, not so much looking for the answer as contemplating whether to tell it to me. I watched the tiny muscles in his jaw tighten a couple times before he answered. "Yes," he said. "There is a difference. I've done both. I've killed . . . and I've murdered."

"What's the difference?"

"It's the difference between hoping that the sun rises and hoping that it doesn't."

"I don't understand," I said. "What's that mean?"

"Of course you don't understand," he said. "How could you? You're just a kid, a college pup blowing his daddy's money on beer and girls, trying to keep a passing grade so you can avoid getting a job for another few years. You probably have no greater care in the world than whether you'll have a date by Saturday."

The vigor of this emaciated old man caught me off guard; and frankly, it pissed me off. I thought about Jeremy back at my apartment, a TV remote click away from crisis. I thought about my mother, in jail, begging for my help on the inhale and cursing my birth on the exhale. I thought about the thin edge that I walked between being able to afford college and not, and I wanted to dump that dusty, judgmental prick out of his wheelchair. I felt anger rising in my chest, but I took a deep breath, as I had learned to do whenever I became frustrated with Jeremy, and I let it pass.

"You know nothing about me," I said. "You don't know where I've been, or what I have to deal with. You don't know the shit I've had to wade through to get here. Whether or not you tell me your story is up to you. That's your prerogative. But don't presume to judge me." I fought against the urge to stand up and walk out, holding on to the arm of the chair to keep me in my seat.

Iverson glanced down at my white-knuckled grip, then at my eyes. A hint of a smile, more subtle than a single flake of snow, crossed his face, and his eyes nodded approval. "That's good," he said.

"What's good?"

"That you understand how wrong it is to judge someone before you know their whole story."

I saw the lesson he wanted me to learn, but I was far too angry to respond.

He continued. "I could have told my story to any number of people. I used to get letters in prison from people wanting to turn my life into something they could make money from. I never responded because I knew that I could give a hundred authors the same information and they would write a hundred different stories. So if I'm going to tell you my story, if I tell you the truth about everything, then I need to know who you are, that you're not just some punk in this for an easy grade, that you will be honest with me and be fair about how you tell my story."

"You understand," I said, "this is just a homework assignment. No one's gonna read it except my teacher."

"Do you know how many hours are in a month?" Carl asked, apropos of nothing.

"I'm sure I could figure it out."

"There's 720 hours in the month of November. October and December each have 744."

"Okay," I said, hoping he would explain his tangent.

"You see, Joe, I can count my life in hours. If I'm going to spend some of those hours on you, I need to know that you're worth my time."

I hadn't considered that point. Janet thought Carl would be dead by Christmas. With just a week remaining in September, that would give Carl three months to live. I did the rough math in my head and understood. If Janet was right, then Carl Iverson had less than three thousand hours of life left to live. "I guess that makes sense," I said.

"So what I'm saying is this: I'll be truthful with you. I'll answer any question you put to me. I'll be that proverbial open book, but I need to know that you are not wasting my limited time. You have to be honest with me as well. That's all that I ask. Can you do that?"

I thought about it for a moment. "You'll be absolutely honest? About everything?"

"Absolutely honest." Carl held out his hand to shake mine, to seal the agreement, and I took it. I could feel the bones of Carl's hand knocking around under his thin skin as if I were gripping a bag of marbles. "So," Carl asked, "why aren't you doing a story on your mom or dad?"

"Let's just say my mom is less than reliable."

Carl stared, waiting for me to continue. "Honesty, remember?" he said.

"Okay. Honestly? Right now my mother is in a detox center in Austin. She should be getting out tomorrow, and then she'll sit in jail until her first appearance in court on DUI charges."

"Well she sounds like she has a story to tell."

"I won't be telling it," I said.

Mr. Iverson nodded his understanding. "What about your dad?"

"Never met him."

"Grandparents?"

"My grandma on my mom's side died when Mom was a teenager; my grandpa died when I was eleven."

"How'd he die?" Carl asked the question with no more fore-thought than you give to a yawn; but he had stumbled onto my deepest wound. He had opened the door to a conversation that I refused to have, even with myself.

"This isn't about me," I said, the sharp tone in my voice cutting a swath between Mr. Iverson and me. "And this isn't about my grandpa. This is about you. I'm here to get your story. Remember?"

Carl leaned back in his chair and considered me while I tried to wash my face of all expression. I didn't want him to see the guilt in my eyes or the anger in my clenched jaw. "Okay," he said. "I didn't mean to touch a nerve."

"No nerve," I said. "You didn't touch any nerve." I tried to act as if my reaction had been nothing more than mild impatience. Then I lobbed a question at him to change the subject. "So, Mr. Iverson, let me ask you a question."

"Go ahead."

"Because you only have a few months to live, why would you agree to spend it talking to me?"

Carl adjusted himself in his chair, gazing out the window at the drying towels and the barbeque grills littering the apartment balconies across the way. I could see his index finger stroking the arm of his wheelchair. It reminded me of how Jeremy strokes his knuckles when he is anxious. "Joe," he said finally, "do you know what a dying declaration is?"

I didn't, although I gave it a shot. "It's a declaration made by someone who is dying?"

"It is a term of law," he said. "If a man whispers the name of his killer and then dies, it's considered good evidence because there's a belief—an understanding—that a person who is dying would not want to die with a lie upon his lips. No sin could be greater than a sin that cannot be rectified, the sin you never get to confess. So this . . . this conversation with you . . . this is my dying declaration. I don't care if anybody reads what you write. I don't even care if you write it down at all." Carl pursed his lips, his stare searching for something far beyond the immediate scenery, a slight quiver in his words. "I have to say the words out loud. I have to tell someone the truth about what happened all those years ago. I have to tell someone the truth about what I did."

CHAPTER 7

That evening, my head pulsed with waves of excitement. I had secured a tragic subject for my biography assignment, and, to top the evening off, I had a dinner date with Lila Nash. Okay, not a date. But I had a girl coming over to my home to share a meal with me. This had never happened before. When it came to dating, I always stuck to restaurants. I had never cooked for a girl or served a girl a meal in my home. I had come close once, but, like many of my plans back in my high-school days, it came to ruin.

Somewhere in my adolescence, I discovered that I was neither handsome nor ugly. I fell in that vast ocean of so-so guys that made up the background of the picture. I was the guy that you agree to go to homecoming with after you found out that the guy you really wanted had already asked another girl. I was okay with that. In fact, I think that good looks would have been wasted on me. Don't get me wrong, I had my share of dates in high school, but, by design, I never dated anyone for more than a couple months—except Phyllis.

Phyllis was my first girlfriend. She had curly brown hair that sprayed out from her head like the tentacles of a sea anemone. I thought she looked peculiar until the day we shared our first kiss. After that her hair struck me as daring and avant-garde. We were high-school freshmen, following the well-worn path of juvenile courtship, testing boundaries, hiding behind corners to steal a kiss, holding hands under the table in the cafeteria, all the things that seemed so wonderfully exciting to me. Then one day, she insisted that I introduce her to my mother.

"Are you ashamed of me?" Phyllis asked. "Am I just someone you mess around with when it's convenient?" Try as I might, I could not convince her that my intentions were honorable unless I brought her to my house for a formal introduction. Looking back now, I should have simply broken up with her and let her think I was a jerk.

I told my mother that I would be bringing Phyllis by after school that day. I talked about the visit as often as I could that morning, hoping to get across to my mother that she needed to be on her best behavior for that one hour of that one day. All she had to do was be cordial, sober, and normal for one hour. Sometimes I ask too much.

As we strolled up the front walk, I could smell food, or the remains of food, burning in the kitchen. Phyllis had been smiling for the entire walk from school to my house, nervously folding her fingers together as we got closer. I stopped at the front door, hearing my mother scream at some guy named Kevin. I didn't know any Kevin.

"God dammit, Kevin, I can't pay you right now." I could hear the slur in her words.

"That's just great," a male voice hollered back. "I bend over back-ward to help you out and when I need the money you fuck me over."

"It's not my fault you can't keep a job," Mom yelled. "Don't be blamin' me."

"No, but it's your fault I got no money," he said. "I ain't got no retard kid to pay my bills like you do. You owe me a hunnerd dollars. I know you get welfare or some shit for that kid. Just pay me outta that."

"Fuck you! You piece of shit. Get outta my house."

"Where's my money?"

"You'll get your fuckin' money. Now get out."

"When? When do I get the money?"

"Get out. My kid's coming home with some little skank, and I need to get ready."

"When do I get my money?"

"Get out before I call the cops and tell 'em you're driving without a license again."

"You fucking bitch."

Kevin slammed his way out the back door about the same time that the smoke detector shrieked to life, fed by the burning food in the kitchen. I looked at Phyllis and saw that she had folded close the shutters of her brain, albeit too late to block out the experience that would surely be the focus of some future therapy sessions. I wanted to apologize, to explain, or better yet, to disappear, slip through the cracks between the porch planks. Instead, I turned Phyllis around by her shoulders, walked her to the corner, and said my last goodbye to her. The following day at school, she made a point of avoiding me in the halls, which was fine by me because I would have avoided her anyway. After that, I never dated any girl for more than two months. I couldn't endure the humiliation of bringing another girl home to my mother.

I thought of Phyllis as I cooked the noodles for my dinner with Lila. For the first time in my life, I would bring a girl home and not worry about what would meet me at the door. But then again, I wasn't bringing a girl home. This wasn't a date, despite the amount of time I spent getting ready, combing my hair just so, applying a little extra deodorant and a tiny hint of cologne, picking out clothes that said both "look at me" and "I don't care." I even made Jeremy take a shower in my bathroom across the hall. All this effort for a girl who threw a cold shoulder at me with the force of a middle linebacker. But damn, she was cute.

Lila arrived at seven, wearing the same jeans and sweater that she'd worn that morning when she left for class. She said hello, glanced around the kitchen to see that I had started the water boiling, and then went to Jeremy, who was sitting on the couch.

"What's the movie tonight, handsome?" she said.

Jeremy blushed slightly. "Maybe *Pirates of the Caribbean*," he said.

"Perfect." She smiled. "I love that movie." Jeremy smiled his best goofy smile as he pointed the remote at the television, and Lila pushed the button to start the movie.

I felt a strange jealousy watching Jeremy and Lila on my couch, but that was exactly what I had asked for. I used Jeremy to coax Lila to my home, and she came to see him, not me. I turned back to my spaghetti noodles, glancing over at Lila every now and again to see her attention split between the television and a stack of my homework papers on the coffee table.

"Are you researching the war in El Salvador?" she asked.

"The war in El Salvador?" I said, looking over my shoulder. She was reading the newspaper article I'd copied at the library. "You have an article about the signing of a peace treaty between El Salvador and Honduras."

"Oh, that," I said. "No. Look at the column below that."

"The one about the girl?" she said.

"Yeah, I'm interviewing the guy who killed her."

She went silent for a moment as she read each of the articles I had copied at the library. I watched her face wince as she covered those parts of the story that expounded upon the more gruesome details of Crystal Hagen's death. I stirred the pasta and waited patiently for her response. Then she said, "You're kidding, right?"

"What?"

She flipped through the articles again. "You're interviewing this psychopath?"

"What's wrong with that?" I asked.

"Everything," Lila said. "It amazes me how prison scumbags can sucker people into paying them attention. I knew this girl who got engaged to some creep in prison. She swore he was innocent—wrongfully convicted, waited for him for two years until he got released. Six months later he was back in prison after he beat the crap out of her."

"Carl's not in prison," I said with a sheepish shrug.

"He's not in prison? How could he not be in prison after what he did to that girl?"

"He's dying of cancer at a nursing home. He only has a few months," I said.

"And you're interviewing him because . . ."

"I'm writing his biography."

"You're writing his story?" she said, with more than a hint of condemnation.

"It's for my English class," I said, almost as an apology.

"You're giving him notoriety."

"It's an English class," I said. "One teacher and maybe twenty-five students. I'd hardly call that notoriety."

Lila put the papers back down on my table. She looked at Jeremy and lowered her voice. "It doesn't matter that it's only a college class. You should do a story on the girl he killed, or the girls he would have killed if he hadn't gone to prison. They deserve the attention, not him. He should be disposed of quietly, no grave marker, no eulogy, no memory of the man. When you write down his life's story, you're creating a marker that shouldn't exist."

"Don't hold back," I said. "Tell me what you really think." I pulled a thread of spaghetti from the boiling water and threw it at the refrigerator. It bounced off the fridge door and fell to the floor.

"What the hell are you doing?" she asked, looking at the noodle on the floor.

"Testing the spaghetti," I said, glad to be on a different topic.

"By flinging it around the kitchen?"

"If it sticks to the refrigerator, it's done." I bent down and picked the spaghetti strand off the floor and tossed it into the garbage. "And this spaghetti isn't quite done yet."

When I left Hillview earlier that day, I felt good about my project. Iverson had promised to tell me the truth about the death of Crystal Hagen. I would be his confessor. I couldn't wait for my dinner with Lila, to tell her about Carl. In my imagination at least, Lila would be riveted by what I was doing, sharing my excitement, wanting to know all about Carl. After seeing her reaction now, all I wanted to do was avoid that subject for the rest of the evening.

"Did he tell you what he did, or is he telling you he was framed?" she asked.

"He hasn't said a thing about it yet." I pulled three plates from the cupboard and walked them to the coffee table in the living room where we would be eating. Lila got up and grabbed some glasses from the same cupboard and followed me. I cleaned my backpack, my notes, and the newspaper articles off the coffee table. "We haven't gotten to that point yet," I said. "So far, he's told me about growing up in South St. Paul, an only child. Um ... let's see ... his father managed a hardware store and his mom ..." I paged through my memory, "worked at a deli in downtown St. Paul."

"So when you write this guy's story, you're simply gonna write down whatever he tells you to?" Lila placed the glasses on the table by the plates.

"I also have to get a couple of secondary sources," I said, walking back to the kitchen. "But, when it comes to what he did—"

"And by 'what he did' you mean raping and killing a fourteen-year-old girl and burning her dead body," Lila added.

"Yeah . . . that. When it comes to that, there are no other sources. I have to write what he tells me."

"So he can feed you a line of bull, and you'd tell that story?"

"He's already done his time. Why would he lie?"

"Why wouldn't he lie?" Lila said with an edge of incredulity. She stood at the end of the kitchen counter, her hands flat on the Formica, her arms stiff, her fingers spread. "Put yourself in his shoes. He rapes some poor girl, murders her, spends his time in prison telling every cell-mate, guard, and lawyer who cares to listen to him that he's innocent. He's not gonna quit now. Do you really think that he's gonna admit that he killed that girl?"

"But he's dying," I said, flinging another spaghetti strand at the refrigerator—it stuck.

"That proves my point, not yours," Lila said, with the air of a prac-ticed debater. "He gets you to write your little article—"

"Biography—"

"Whatever. And now he has a written account out there in aca-demia, painting him as the victim."

"He wants to give me his dying declaration," I said, pouring the spaghetti into the strainer to rinse it.

"He wants to give you his what?"

"His dying declaration . . . that's what he called it. It's a statement that's true because you don't want to die with a lie on your lips."

"As opposed to dying with a murder under your belt?" she said. "You see the irony, don't you?"

"It's not the same thing," I said. I had no argument as to why it wasn't the same thing. I couldn't hack my way past her logic. Every turn presented another blocked path, so I signaled my defeat by carrying the noodles to the coffee table and dishing them onto the plates. Lila picked up the pan of marinara sauce and followed me. As she started to pour the sauce, she stood up and grinned like the Grinch on Christmas Eve. "Oh, do I have an idea," she said.

"I'm almost afraid to ask."

"A jury convicted him, right?"

"Yeah."

"Which means he had a trial."

"I assume so," I said.

"You can look at his file from the trial. That'll tell you exactly what happened. It'll have all the evidence, not just his version."

"His file? Can I do that?"

"My aunt's a paralegal at a law firm in St. Cloud. She'll know." Lila pulled her cell phone from her pocket and scrolled through her contacts until she found her aunt's number. I handed Jeremy a paper towel to use as a napkin so that he could start eating, and then I listened to Lila's end of the conversation.

"So the file belongs to the client not the lawyer?" she said. "How do I find that out?—Will they still have it?—Can you e-mail that to me?—Perfect. Thanks a bunch. I gotta run.—I will. Bye-bye." Lila hung up her phone. "It's easy," Lila said, turning to me. "His old attorney will have the file."

"It's been thirty years," I said.

"But it's a murder case, so my aunt said they should still have it."

I picked up the newspaper articles, paging through them until I came across the name of the attorney. "His name was John Peterson," I said. "He was a public defender out of Minneapolis."

"There you go," she said.

"But how do we get it from the lawyer?"

"That's the beauty," she said. "The file doesn't belong to the lawyer. It belongs to Carl Iverson. It's Carl's file and the lawyer has to let him have it. My aunt's gonna e-mail me a form that he can sign requesting the file, and they have to give it to him or whoever he sends over to get it."

"So all I have to do is get Carl to sign this form?"

"He'll have to sign it," she said. "If he doesn't sign, then you know that he's full of crap. Either he signs it or he's nothing more than a lying, murdering bastard who wants to keep you in the dark about what he really did."

CHAPTER 8

I'd seen my mom wake up in the morning with the remnants of her previous night's binge still smeared in her hair; I'd seen her stumble into the apartment cross-eyed drunk with her shoes in one hand and wadded-up undergarments in the other; but I'd never seen her look as pathetic as she did when she came shuffling into the Mower County Courthouse wearing her jail-orange jumpsuit with her wrists in handcuffs and shackles on her ankles. Three days of no makeup and no showering brought out the burlap in her skin. Her blonde hair with its dark-brown roots hung heavy with dandruff and greasy build-up. Her shoulders slumped forward as though the cuffs on her wrists weighed her down. I had dropped Jeremy off at Mom's apartment before heading to the courthouse to wait for her first appearance.

She entered with three other people also dressed in orange. When she saw me she waved for me to come up to the wooden railing, her on one side, standing beside the attorney's table with its comfy chairs, and me in the gallery with its wooden church pews for seating. A bailiff held out a hand as I approached her, a signal to not get close enough to pass weapons or other such contraband to the people in orange.

"You need to bail me out," Mom said in a frantic whisper. Up close I could see that the stress of her incarceration had hung deep crescent bags of exhaustion under her bloodshot eyes. She looked as if she hadn't slept in days.

"How much are you talking about," I said.

"The jailer said I'll probably need three thousand to bail out. Else I gotta stay in jail."

"Three thousand!" I said. "I need that money for school."

"I can't take jail, Joey." My mother started to cry. "It's full of crazy people. They stay up all night yelling. I can't sleep. I'm going crazy, too. Don't make me go back there. Please, Joey."

I opened my mouth to speak, but nothing came out. I felt sorry for her—I mean this was my mother, the woman who gave me life. But if I gave her three thousand dollars, I would run out of money midway through my next semester. My thoughts of staying in school were colliding with the vision of my mother in her most desperate hour. I was unable to speak. No matter what I said, it would be wrong. I was rescued from my dilemma when a couple of women entered the court through a door behind the judge's bench, and the bailiff called for everyone to rise. I took a deep breath, thankful for the interruption. The judge entered and instructed everyone to sit down, and the bailiff escorted my mother to a seat in the jury box to sit with the other folks in orange.

As the clerk called what she referred to as the "in-custodies" up to the bench, I listened to the dialogue that went back and forth between the judge and the attorney, a female public defender handling all four defendants. It reminded me of a Catholic funeral mass I had attended when one of my high-school coaches died. The litany had been spoken by the priest and the parishioners so many times that the rote presentation seemed toneless to us outsiders.

The judge said: "Is your name . . . ? Do you live at . . . ? Do you understand your rights? Counsel, does your client understand the charges?"

"Yes, your honor, and we waive any further reading of the complaint."

"How do you wish to proceed?"

"Your Honor, we waive the rule-eight hearing, ask that my client be released on his personal recognizance."

The judge would then set bail, giving each inmate the choice between paying a higher bail amount with no conditions or paying lower bail—or no bail at all—provided that they agree to abide by certain conditions set by the judge.

When Mom took her turn before the judge, they went through the same back-and-forth, with the judge setting bail at $3,000, but then he continued with the second option. "Ms. Nelson you can pay the three thousand dollars, or you can be released on your personal promise to appear at all future hearings as well as the following conditions: keep in contact with your attorney, remain law abiding, no possession or consumption of alcohol, and be hooked up to an alcohol monitoring bracelet. Any use of alcohol will bring you right back to jail. Do you understand those conditions?"

"Yes, your honor," my mother said, looking absolutely Dickensian in her role as the pitiful soul.

"That's all," the judge said.

Mom shuffled back to the line of people in orange, all of whom now stood up and started moving in chain-gang fashion toward the door that would lead them back to the jail. As she passed, Mom looked at me with a glare that would have been the envy of Medusa. "Come down to the jail and bail me out," she whispered.

"But mom, the judge just said—"

"Don't argue with me," she hissed as she left the court room.

"And . . . she's back," I muttered under my breath. I walked out of court, pausing on the sidewalk to ponder which way to turn, left to the jail and my mother or right to my car. The judge said she could leave; I heard him. All she had to do was not drink. A bad feeling crept through my veins, like poison from a snake bite. I wrestled with my decision, eventually turning left, overruling my urge to run.

Entering the jail, I gave my driver's license to a lady behind bullet-proof glass who directed me to a small room where another glass window separated me from the cubicle where they would bring my mother. A couple minutes later they brought my mother to the cubicle, now free of her handcuffs and shackles. She sat in a chair on the other side of the glass, picking up a black phone on the wall. I did the same thing, grimacing as I drew the phone up to my face, imagining the multitudes of unfortunates who had breathed into that receiver before me. It felt sticky.

"Did you pay the bail?"

"You don't need me to pay bail; you can get out on your own. The judge said so."

"He said I could get out if I did that monitor thing. I'm not doing no damn monitor."

"But you can get out for free; you just can't drink."

"I ain't doin' no damn monitor!" she said. "You have enough money. You can help me out for once in your life. I can't take another minute in here."

"Mom, I barely have enough to make it through the semester. I can't—"

"I'll pay you back for Christ sake."

Now we were getting into our own litany. When I turned sixteen, I got my first job changing oil at a garage in town. When I spent my first paycheck on clothes and a skateboard, Mom threw a fit so fierce that the upstairs neighbors called the landlord and the cops. After she settled down, she forced me to open a savings account; and, because a sixteen-year-old can't open an account without a parent, they put her name on it as well. For the next two years she borrowed money from that account whenever she ran light on the rent or her car needed fixing—always with the empty promise that she'd pay me back but never doing so.

The day I turned eighteen, I opened my own account in my name alone. Without direct access to my money, she had to switch her tactic, moving from theft to blackmail because, after all, living in her house and eating her food entitled her to bleed my account of hundreds of dollars. So I started skimming a little off the top each week, hiding the money in a can under the insulation in the attic—my coffee-can college fund. Mom always suspected that I hid money, but she could never prove it, and she never found it. In her mind the few grand that I secreted away had grown to ten times what actually lay beneath the insulation. Add to that my student loans and the pittance I got in grant money, and in my mother's mind my cache had grown to a small fortune.

"Can't we get a bail bondsman?" I asked. "Then you don't have to pay the full three thousand."

"Don't you think I thought of that? You think I'm stupid? I got no collateral. They won't talk to me without collateral."

Her words cut with an edge I knew well, her mean streak showing through as clear as the dark roots that lined the part in her hair. I decided to come back hard myself. "I can't bail you out, Mom. I can't. If I give you three thousand, I can't afford to go to college next semester. There's just no way to do it."

"Well then..." She leaned back in the plastic chair. "...you'll have to take care of Jeremy while I'm in here, cuz I'm not goin' on no damned monitor."

And there it was: the final card in her hand, proving that she had the royal flush; she had beaten me. I could try bluffing and say that I would leave Jeremy in Austin, but that bluff was naked and my mother knew it. She stared at me with the conviction of a falling boulder, her eyes calm, level, my eyes twitching with anger. How could I take care of Jeremy? When I left him alone for a couple hours, he needed to be rescued by Lila. I had gone to college to get away from all this crap. Now here she was pulling me back, forcing me to choose between my college education and my brother. I wanted to reach through that reinforced glass and choke her.

"I can't believe how selfish you are," she said. "I told you I'd pay you back."

I pulled my checkbook out of my back pocket and started writing the check as a current of rage passed through me. I smiled slightly as I imagined filling out the entire check then holding it up to the thick glass that separated us and tearing it to shreds. But deep down, I knew the truth: I needed her—not as a son needs a mother, but as a sinner needs the devil. I needed a scapegoat, someone I could point at and say, "You're responsible for this, not me." I needed to feed my delusion that I was not my brother's keeper, that such a duty fell to our mother. I needed a place where I could store Jeremy's life, his care, a box that I could shut tight and tell myself it was where Jeremy belonged—even if I knew, deep down, that it was all a lie. I needed that thin plausibility to ease my conscience. That would be the only way I could leave Austin.

I tore the check out and showed it to my mother. She smiled an empty smile and said, "Thank you, sweetie. You're an angel."

CHAPTER 9

I stopped at Hillview on my drive back from Austin, hoping to make some progress on my paper and have Carl sign the release that would allow me to get his file from the public defender's office. I had hoped that a visit with him might distract me from the burn in my chest left there by my mother. I trudged into Hillview, my guilty conscience weighing me down. I felt as if some vacuous force, some inexplicable gravity was sucking me backward, pulling me to the south, to Austin. I thought that running away to college would get me out of my mother's reach, but I was still too close, too easily plucked from the low branch I had chosen. What would it take to wash my hands of my mother—my brother? What price would I need to pay to leave them behind? At least for today, I thought to myself, the price was three thousand dollars in bail money.

Janet smiled at me from her station behind the reception desk as I passed. I walked to the lounge where residents, most of whom were in wheelchairs, gathered in small clusters like chess pieces in a half-finished game. Carl sat in his usual place, his wheelchair facing the picture window, looking out at the laundry hanging from the balcony rails of the apartment building outside. I stopped short of Carl when I noticed that he had a visitor, a man who looked to be in his mid-sixties, with short, peppery hair that spiked and leaned toward the back of his head like pond reeds tipping in a breeze. The man's hand rested on Carl's forearm, and he, too, faced toward the window as they talked.

I walked back to the reception desk, found Janet hovering over some paperwork, and asked her about the visitor. "Oh, that's Virgil," she said. "I can't remember his last name. He's the only visitor Carl's ever had . . . except for you."

"Are they related?"

"I don't think so. I think they're just friends. Maybe they met in prison. Maybe they were . . . you know . . . special friends."

"I didn't get the impression Carl swung that way," I said.

"He was in prison for thirty years. That might've been the only swinging he could get." Janet put her hand to her lips and giggled at the guilty pleasure that had escaped them.

I smiled back at her, more in an attempt to stay on her good side than to join in her joke. "Do you think I should go back? I don't want to disturb them if they're. . ." I trailed off, not sure how to finish the sentence.

"I say go for it," she said. "If you're interrupting, he'll let you know. Carl may be dropping weight like a snowman in a skillet, but don't underestimate him."

I made my way back to Carl, who was now chuckling over something the other man had said. Carl had never smiled in my presence, and the lift it brought to his face shed years. He saw me coming and his smile withered as if he were a child being brought in from play. "There's the pup now," he sighed.

The man with Carl looked up at me with an odd indifference, holding out his hand for me to shake. "Hey, Pup," he said.

"Some folks call me Joe," I said.

"That's right," Carl said, "Joe the writer."

"Actually, it's Joe the college student," I said. "I'm not a writer, it's just an assignment."

"I'm Virgil . . . the painter," the man said.

"Painter, as in Dutch master or Dutch Boy," I asked.

"Mostly Dutch Boy," he said. "I paint houses and such. But I do a little canvas work for my own enjoyment."

"Don't let him buffalo you, Joe," Carl said. "Virgil here's a regular Jackson Pollock. Too bad that's when he's trying to paint houses." Carl and Virgil laughed at that, but I didn't understand the reference. Later I would look up Jackson Pollock on the Internet to see his paintings, which resembled something a toddler could have concocted with a plate full of spaghetti and a temper tantrum; I got the joke.

"Mr. Iverson—" I started.

"Call me Carl," he said.

"Carl, I was hoping I could get you to sign this for me."

"What's that?"

"It's a release. It'll let me see your trial file," I said hesitantly. "I need two collateral sources for the biography."

"Ah, young pup here doesn't believe I'll be truthful with him," Carl said to Virgil. "He thinks I'll hide the monster that lurks inside of me."

Virgil shook his head and looked away.

"I don't mean any disrespect," I said. "It's just that a friend of mine . . . well, not so much a friend as a neighbor, thought I could get a better understanding of you if I took a look at the trial stuff."

"Your friend couldn't be more wrong," Virgil said. "If you really want to know the truth about Carl here, the trial's the last place you'd look."

"It's okay, Virg," Carl said. "I don't mind. Hell, that old file's been collecting dust for thirty years now. Probably doesn't exist anymore."

Virgil leaned forward over his knees then stood up slowly, using his arms to raise himself off the chair, like a man far older than he appeared to be. Brushing the wrinkles out of his slacks, he grabbed the worn handle of a hickory cane that leaned against the wall near him. "I'm gonna grab some coffee. Want some?"

I didn't answer, as I figured he wasn't talking to me. Carl pursed his lips, shook his head no, and Virgil walked away with a practiced but unnatural gait, his right leg bending and snapping straight with mechanical rigidity. I looked closer at the rustle of his pant leg just above his shoe and saw the unmistakable glint of metal where his ankle should have been.

I turned back to Carl, feeling as if I owed him an apology, as if I had called him a liar by wanting to check his story against the file—which is exactly what I planned to do.

"I'm sorry, Mr. Iver—I mean, Carl. I wasn't trying to insult you."

"That's alright, Joe," Carl said. "Virgil can be a bit overprotective of me. We've known each other a long time."

"Are you related?" I asked.

Carl thought for a moment and then said, "We're brothers . . . by fire, not by blood." His eyes turned back to the window, his gaze lost in a memory that robbed his cheeks of their color. After a moment he said, "Got a pen?"

"A pen?"

"To sign that paper you brought." I handed Carl the form and a pen and watched him sign the release, his knuckles poking through his skin, his forearms so slight that I could see the pop and contraction in each muscle as he signed. He handed me back the paper, and I folded it, sliding it into my pocket.

"One thing though," he said, looking down at his fingers, which now rested on his lap. He spoke to me without raising his eyes. "When you read that file, you're gonna see a lot of things in there, terrible things that'll make you want to hate me. It sure made the jury hate me. Just keep in mind, that's not my whole story."

"I know," I said.

"No you don't," he said softly, turning his attention back to the colorful towels flapping on the apartment balcony across the way. "You don't know me. Not yet." I waited for him to finish his thought, but he just stared out the window.

I left Carl to his memory, heading to the front door, where Virgil stood waiting for me. He held out his hand, a business card pressed between two of his fingers. I took the card. *Virgil Gray Painting—Commercial and Residential.* "If you want to know about Carl Iverson," he said, "you need to talk to me."

"Were you in prison with him?"

Virgil seemed to be on the cusp of aggravation, speaking in a tone that I had heard often in the bars when guys talked about their bad jobs or nagging wives—irritated yet resigned to the circumstances. "He didn't kill that girl. And what you're doing is bullshit."

"What?" I said.

"I know what you're doing," he said.

"What am I doing?"

"I'm telling you: he didn't kill that girl."

"You were there?"

"No. I wasn't there. Don't be a smartass."

It was my turn to be irritated. I had just met this man, and he felt that he knew me well enough to insult me. "The way I see it," I said, "only two people know what happened: Crystal Hagen and the person who killed her. Anybody else is just saying what they want to believe."

"I didn't have to be there to know he didn't kill that girl."

"Ted Bundy had people who believed in him, too." I didn't know if that was true, but I thought it sounded good.

"He didn't do it," Vigil snapped. He pointed to the phone number on his card. "You call me. We'll talk."

CHAPTER 10

wasted the better part of a week and eight phone calls trying to pry Carl Iverson's criminal file from the public defender's office. Initially, the receptionist struggled to understand my request, and when she finally did understand, she gave me her opinion that the file had probably been destroyed years ago. "Regardless," she said, "I have no authority to hand over a murder file to any Tom, Dick, or Harry who asks for it." After that she simply passed my calls on to the voice mail of Berthel Collins, chief public defender, where my messages seemed to fall into an abyss. On the fifth day of no return call from Collins, I skipped my afternoon classes and caught a bus to downtown Minneapolis.

When the receptionist told me that the chief was busy, I told her I would wait and took a seat close enough to her desk that I could hear her as she whispered into her telephone. I read magazines to kill time until she finally whispered to someone, telling them that I was lingering. Fifteen minutes later she broke down and ushered me into the office of Berthel Collins, a pale-skinned man with a mop of uncombed hair crisscrossing his head and a nose as big around as a ripe persimmon. Berthel smiled at me and shook my hand as if he wanted to sell me a car.

"So you're the kid that's stalking me," he said.

"I take it you got my phone messages," I said. He looked flustered for a second then motioned me to a chair.

"You gotta understand," he said, "we don't get calls all that often asking us to dig up a thirty-year-old file. We store all that stuff off-site."

"But you do still have the file?"

"Oh, yeah," he said, "We have it. We're mandated to keep murder files indefinitely. I had a runner bring it in yesterday. That's it right there." He pointed to a banker's box sitting against the wall behind me.

I hadn't expected that much stuff. I thought I'd have maybe a binder full of paper, not a box. I calculated the number of hours it would take to read the file and watched as those numbers filled a bucket in my head. I then factored in the homework from my other classes and the tests and the lab projects. I suddenly felt dizzy. How would I ever get this all done. I began to regret my decision to get the file; this was supposed to be a simple English assignment.

I reached into my pocket, pulled out the release, and handed it to Mr. Collins. "So, I can take that with me then?" I asked.

"Not all of it," he said. "Not yet. We have some files ready to go. We have to cull out the notes and work product before we let it go out of this office."

"How long's that gonna take?" I shifted in my chair, trying to find a position where the cushion springs didn't grind into my butt cheeks.

"Like I said, we have a couple files ready today." He smiled. "We have an intern working on it. The rest of the file should be ready fairly soon, maybe a week or two." Collins leaned back in his cushy Georgian wingback chair, which I noticed sat a good four inches higher than any other chair in the room and seemed far more comfortable. I shifted again in my seat, trying to keep blood flowing to my legs. "What's your interest in this case anyway?" he asked, crossing one leg over the other.

"Let's just say I have an interest in the life and times of Carl Iverson."

"But why?" Collins asked with genuine sincerity. "There wasn't much to this case."

"You know the case?"

"Yeah, I know it," he said. "I clerked here that year; it was my third year of law school. Carl's lead attorney, John Peterson, brought me on to do his legal research." Collins paused, looking past me to a blank spot on his wall, recollecting the details of Carl's case. "I met Carl in jail a few times and sat in the gallery during his trial. It was my first murder case. Yeah, I remember him. I remember the girl, too, Crystal something or other."

"Hagen."

"That's right, Crystal Hagen." Collins's face grew cold. "I still see the pictures—the ones we had in the trial. I'd never seen crime-scene photos before. That was my first time. It's not peaceful like you see on TV with their eyes closed, looking like they simply fell asleep. No, it's not like that at all. Her photos were violent and gut-wrenching. To this day, I can still see her." He shuddered slightly, then continued. "He could've gotten a deal you know."

"A deal?"

"A plea bargain. They offered him second-degree murder. He could have been eligible for parole in eight years. He turned it down. The man's facing a mandatory life sentence if he's convicted of first-degree, and he turns down a second-degree plea offer."

"That brings up a question that's been bugging me," I said. "If he gets sentenced to life in prison, how can he ever get paroled?"

Collins leaned forward and rubbed the underside of his chin, scratching a day's worth of scruff. "Life doesn't necessarily mean until you die," he said. "Back in 1980 life in prison meant that you had to do seventeen years before being eligible for parole. Later, they changed that to thirty years. They changed it again so that a murder committed during a kidnapping or a rape gets life without possibility of parole. Technically, they convicted Iverson under the old statute, so he was eligible for parole after seventeen years, but forget that. Once the legislature made it clear that they want murdering rapists locked up for good, Iverson's prospects for parole pretty much evaporated. To tell you the truth, when I got your call, I looked up Iverson's record on the Department of Corrections website and about fell on the floor when I saw that he was out."

"He's dying of cancer," I said.

"Well that explains it," he said. "Prison hospice can be problematic." The corners of his mouth tipped downward, his head nodding in understanding.

"What did Carl say happened on the night Crystal Hagen died?"

"Nothing," he said. "He said he didn't do it—said he drank that afternoon until he passed out and couldn't remember a thing. Honestly, he didn't do much to help with his defense, just kind of sat there and watched the trial like he was watching television."

"Did you believe him when he said he was innocent?"

"It didn't matter what I believed. I was just a law clerk. We put up a good fight. We said that Crystal's boyfriend did it. That was our theory. He was the last to see her alive. He had all the opportunity in the world, and it was a crime of passion. He wanted to screw her—she said no—things got out of hand. It was a decent theory: a silk purse from a sow's ear so to speak. But in the end, the jury didn't believe it, and that's all that matters."

"There are some people who think he's innocent," I said, thinking of Virgil.

Collins lowered his eyes and shook his head, dismissing my comment as if I were some gullible child. "If he didn't do it, then he's one sorry bastard. She was found dead in his shed," he said. "They found one of her fingernails on the steps to his back porch."

"He tore her fingernail off?" I said, shuddering at the thought.

"It was a fake fingernail, one of those acrylic things. She had her nails done up for her first homecoming dance a couple weeks earlier. The prosecutor argued that it broke off when he was dragging her dead body to his shed."

"Do you believe Carl killed her?"

"There was no one else around," Collins said. "Iverson simply said he didn't do it, but at the same time, he said he was too drunk to remember anything from that night. It's Occam's razor."

"Occam's razor?"

"It's a principle that says that all things being equal, the simplest conclusion is usually the correct one. Crimes like murder are rarely tricky, and most murderers are far from clever. Have you met him yet?"

"Who? Carl? Yeah, he signed the release."

"Oh, yeah," Collins furrowed his eyebrows, displeased at missing that obvious conclusion. "What did he tell you? Did he tell you he's innocent?"

"We haven't talked about the case yet. I'm easing up to that."

"I expect he will." Collins ran his thick hands through his hair, scratching loose some dandruff that fell to his shoulders. "And when he does, you'll want to believe him."

"But you don't believe him."

"Maybe I did—back then. I'm not sure. It's hard to tell with guys like Carl."

"Guys like Carl?"

"He's a pedophile, and nobody can tell a lie like a pedophile. They're the best. There's no con artist alive who can lie like a pedophile."

I looked at Collins with a blank expression that urged him to explain.

"Pedophiles are the monsters walking among us. Murderers, burglars, thieves, drug dealers, they can always justify what they've done. Most crimes occur because of simple emotions like greed or rage or jealousy. People can understand those emotions. We don't condone it, but we understand it. Everybody's felt those feelings at one time or another. Hell, most people, if they're honest, would admit to planning a crime in their head, committing the perfect murder, getting away with it. Every person on a jury has felt angry or jealous. They understand the base emotion behind a crime like murder, and they'll punish a guy for not controlling that emotion."

"I suppose so," I said.

"Now think of a pedophile. He has a passion to have sex with children. Who's gonna understand that? You can't justify what you've done. There's no explanation for them; they're monsters, and they know it. Yet they can't admit it, not even to themselves. So they hide the truth, burying it so deep inside that they begin to believe their own lies."

"But some can be innocent, right?" I asked.

"I had a guy once . . ." Collins leaned forward, plopping his elbows on his desk. "He was accused of perping on his ten-year-old kid. This guy had me convinced that his ex-wife planted the story in the kid's head. I mean I believed him completely. I'd prepared a scathing cross-examination to tear that kid up. Then, about a month before trial, the computer forensics came back. The prosecutor called me to his office to show me a video that this dumbass made of the whole thing, exactly what his kid said happened. When I showed the video to my client he cried his eyes out, bawled like a frigging baby, not because he raped his kid and got caught, but because he swore it wasn't him. The prosecutor had the son-of-a-bitch on tape, his face, his voice, his tattoos, and he wanted me to believe it was some lookalike."

"So you assume all your clients charged with pedophilia are lying?"

"No, not all."

"Did you assume Carl was lying?"

Collins paused to give my question some thought. "I wanted to believe Iverson at first. I suppose I wasn't as jaded back then as I am now. But the evidence said he killed that girl. The jury saw it, and that's why Iverson went to prison."

"Is it true what they say about pedophiles in prison?" I asked. "That they get beat up and stuff?"

Collins pursed his lips and nodded. "Yeah, it's true. Prison has its own food chain. My drunk-driver clients will ask 'why are they picking on me? It's not like I robbed somebody.' The thieves and the burglars say 'it's not like I killed somebody.' The murderers will say 'at least I'm not a pedophile; it's not like I raped a child.' Guys like Iverson have nowhere to go. There's no one worse than them, and that puts 'em on the bottom of that food chain. To make things worse, he did his time at Stillwater Prison. That's about as bad as it gets."

I had given up trying to get comfortable in the piece-of-crap chair, realizing that the chair was probably uncomfortable by design—a way to encourage short office visits. I stood up and rubbed the back of my thighs. Collins also stood and walked around the desk. He picked two files out of the box and handed them to me. One was tagged *jury selection* and the other was labeled *sentencing*. "These are ready to go," he said. "I guess I can let you have the trial transcripts, too."

"Trial transcripts?"

"Yeah, first-degree-murder cases get an automatic appeal. The court reporter prepares a transcript of the trial, everything that was said, word for word. They'll have copies of that at the Supreme Court, so you can have our copy today." Collins walked to the box and pulled out six softbound volumes, stacking them one-by-one in my arms, creating a pile of paper well over a foot thick. "That'll keep you busy for a while."

I looked at the books and files in my arms, feeling their weight, as Mr. Collins ushered me out. I turned at the door. "What am I going to find in these books?" I asked.

Collins sighed, rubbed his chin again, and shrugged. "Probably nothing you don't already know."

CHAPTER 11

On my bus ride home, I thumbed through the six volumes of transcripts and cursed under my breath. I had managed to create more reading for this one assignment than I had in all my other classes combined. It was too late to drop the class without screwing my GPA. My interview notes and opening chapter for Iverson's biography were due soon—this on top of all the other homework I had to do—and I could see no way to get through all this material in time.

After the long trek from the bus stop to my apartment, the transcripts in my backpack seemed as heavy as stone tablets. I pulled out my keys and started to unlock my door, but paused when I heard the silk of Spanish guitar music coming from Lila's apartment. The transcripts gave me an excuse to stop in and say hi. They were, after all, her contribution to this quixotic project. Besides, I really wanted to see her again. There was something about her leave-me-the-fuck-alone attitude that hooked me.

Lila answered her door, barefoot, wearing an oversized Twins jersey and shorts that barely showed below the tails of the shirt. I couldn't stop my eyes from going straight to her legs, just a quick glance, but enough that she noticed. She looked at me and raised an eyebrow. No "hello." No "what's up." Just a single raised eyebrow. That flustered the hell out of me.

"I . . . uh . . . went to the attorney's office today," I stammered. "I have the transcripts from the trial." I reached into the backpack and showed her proof of my deed.

She remained planted in her doorway, looking up at me, not inviting me in or responding beyond the raised eyebrow. Instead, she studied me as if to size up my intrusion, shrugged, and walked into her apartment, letting the door creak open behind her. I followed her into her apartment, which smelled faintly of baby powder and vanilla.

"Have you read them yet?" she asked.

"I just got 'em." I dropped the first volume onto her table, letting it slam down to show its heft. "I have no idea where to begin reading these things."

"Start with the opening statement," she said.

"The what?"

"The opening statement."

"That should probably be near the beginning, right?" I asked, grinning. She picked up one of the transcripts and began flipping pages. "How do you know about opening statements and stuff? Are you pre-law?"

"Maybe," she said, in a matter-of-fact tone. "I was in mock trial in high school. The attorney who coached us said that the opening statement should tell the story of the case—tell it like you're sitting around the living room with friends."

"You were in mock trial?"

"Yeah," she muttered, licking her fingers and flipping more pages. "If all goes well, I wouldn't mind going to law school someday."

"I haven't locked into a major yet, but I'm thinking journalism. It's just that—"

"Here it is." She stood up, creasing the pages back so she could hold the transcript in one hand. "You be the jury. Sit on the couch, and I'll be the prosecutor."

I sat in the middle of her couch, spreading my arms out to each side, placing them on the backrest. She stood in front of me and read a few lines to herself to get into character. Then she drew her chest up, pulled her shoulders back, and started to speak. And as she spoke, I watched the pixie in her disappear, and from its shadow stepped a woman with the confidence and poise to command a jury's attention.

"Ladies and gentlemen of the jury, the evidence in this case will show that on October 29, 1980, the defendant," Lila waved her arm with the grace of a game-show model, pointing toward an empty chair in the corner, "Carl Iverson, raped and murdered a fourteen-year-old girl by the name of Crystal Marie Hagen." Lila paced slowly in front of me as she read, looking up from her script as often as she could, making eye contact with me as if I were an actual juror.

"Last year, Crystal Hagen was a happy, vivacious, fourteen-year-old girl, a beautiful child, loved by her family and excited to be on the cheerleading squad at Edison High School." Lila paused and lowered her voice for effect. "But, ladies and gentlemen, you will learn that not everything was wonderful in Crystal Hagen's life. You will see excerpts from her diary where she writes about a man named Carl Iverson, a man who lived in the house next door to Crystal Hagen. You will see, in her diary, where she calls him 'the pervert next door.' She wrote that Carl Iverson would stare at her from his window and watch her as she practiced her cheerleading routines in her back yard.

"From that diary, she will tell you about an incident when she was with her boyfriend, a young man she met in her high-school typing class, a boy named Andy Fisher. One night she and Andy were parked in the alley that passed behind both Crystal's house and Carl Iverson's house. They were parked at the end of the alley, away from prying eyes, making out, as kids will do. That's when the defendant, Carl Iverson, walked up to the car like a monster in a slasher movie and glared into the window at them. He saw Crystal and Andy . . . well let's just say that they were experimenting . . . sexually. Just a couple of kids goofing around. And Carl Iverson saw them; he watched them.

"Now that may not seem all that bad, but for Crystal Hagen, it was like the end of the world. You see, Crystal had a stepfather, a devoutly religious man named Douglas Lockwood. He'll be testifying in this trial. Mr. Lockwood didn't approve of Crystal being a cheerleader. He didn't like the idea of her dating at the age of fourteen. So he set out some rules for Crystal—rules to protect the family's reputation and Crystal's modesty. He told her that if she did not live up to those rules, she would not be allowed to continue as a cheerleader. And if the infraction were serious enough, he would send her to a private, religious school.

"Ladies and Gentlemen, what she did in that car that night with Andy Fisher broke those rules.

"The evidence will show that Carl Iverson used what he saw in the alley that night to blackmail Crystal, to get her to ... well ... do his bidding. You see, shortly after that night in the alley, Crystal wrote in her diary that a man was forcing her to do stuff she didn't want to do—sexual stuff. He told her that if she did not do what he wanted, he was going to expose her secret. Now, Crystal doesn't expressly say that Carl Iverson was the man threatening her, but when you see her words in that diary, it'll leave no doubt in your mind who she's writing about."

Lila slowed the cadence of her speech, lowering her voice to little more than a whisper, giving it a dramatic effect. My arms moved from the back of the couch to my knees as I leaned in to hear her.

"The afternoon of her murder, Andy Fisher drove her home after school. They kissed goodbye, and Andy left. Crystal was all alone in an empty house next door to Carl Iverson. After Andrew drove away, we know that Crystal ended up in Carl Iverson's house. Maybe she went there to confront him. You see, Crystal Hagen met with her school counselor that afternoon and learned that what Carl Iverson was doing to her would send him to prison. Or maybe she went there at the point of a gun because on the morning of Crystal's death, we know that Carl Iverson bought an army-surplus handgun. We're not sure of exactly how she came to be in Iverson's house, but we know that she was there because of evidence that I'll get to in a minute. And once she was there, we know that things went terribly wrong for Crystal Hagen. She had a plan to turn the tables on Iverson—send him to prison if he didn't stop the threats and the abuse. Carl Iverson, of course, had other plans."

Lila stopped pacing, no longer pretending to be the prosecutor. She sat down on the couch beside me, her eyes fixed on the transcript. When she continued, she spoke as if she were struck by some profound sadness.

"Carl Iverson raped Crystal Hagen. And when he was finished with her—after he took everything else he could take from her—he took her life. He strangled her using an electrical cord. Ladies and gentlemen, it takes a long time to strangle a person to death. It is a slow, horrible way to die. Carl Iverson had to wrap that cord around Crystal Hagen's throat and pull it tight and hold it there for at least two minutes. And as every second passed, he had the ability to change his mind. Instead he continued to pull on that cord, keeping it tight around her throat until he was sure that she was not just unconscious, but dead."

Lila stopped reading and looked at me with a pained expression, as though I were somehow an extension of Carl, as though some seed of his monstrous deed lived in me. I shook my head. She went back to reading.

"Crystal fought for her life. We know this because one of her false fingernails broke off during the struggle. That fingernail was found on the steps leading out of Carl Iverson's house. It fell there as Carl Iverson dragged her body to his tool shed. He dumped her body onto the floor of that shed as if she were just a piece of garbage. Then, to try and hide his crime from the world, he set his shed on fire, believing that the heat and the flames would destroy the evidence of what he had done. After he touched a match to that old shed, he went back in his house and drank from a bottle of whiskey until he passed out.

"By the time the fire trucks got there, the shed was completely engulfed in flames. After police found Crystal's body in that smoldering rubble, they knocked on Mr. Iverson's door, but he didn't answer. They assumed nobody was home. Detective Tracer returned in the morning with a search warrant and found Iverson still passed out on the couch, an empty whiskey bottle in one hand and the 45-caliber pistol near the other.

"Ladies and gentlemen, you're going to see pictures that will turn your stomach. I apologize in advance for what you're going to see, but it's necessary so that you understand what happened to Crystal Hagen. The fire burned the bottom half of her body so badly that some parts of her were barely recognizable. The tin from the roof of the shed fell on her, covering her upper torso, protecting that part of her from the worst of the fire. And there, tucked under her chest, you'll see her left hand— unburned. And on the left-hand you'll see the acrylic fingernails that she was so proud of, the nails she had done up for her first homecoming dance with Andy Fisher. You'll see that one of the nails is missing, the nail that broke off during her fight with Carl Iverson.

"Ladies and gentlemen, once you've seen all the evidence in this case, I'll be coming back here to speak with you again, and I'll be asking you to return a verdict of guilty for murder in the first degree against Carl Albert Iverson."

Lila put the transcript on her lap, letting the echo of her words fall silent. "What a sick bastard," she said. "I can't believe you can sit with this guy and not want to kill him. They should've never let him out of prison. He should've rotted away in the darkest, dankest cell they have."

I leaned slightly toward her, imitating her posture and resting one of my hands on the cushion next to her leg. If I had spread my fingers I could have touched her. That thought erased all others in my head, but she took no notice.

"What's it like . . . talking to him?" she asked.

"He's an old man," I said. "He's sick and weak and thin as a whip. It's hard to see him in that stuff you read."

"When you write about him, make sure you tell the whole story. Don't just write about the weak old man dying of cancer. Tell them about the drunken degenerate who burned a fourteen-year-old girl."

"I made a promise to write the truth," I said. "And I will."

CHAPTER 12

The month of October flew by with the speed and tumult of a falling, mountain river. One of Molly's bartenders had to quit because the woman's husband caught her flirting for better tips. Molly had asked me to fill in until she found a replacement. I couldn't refuse because I needed to make up for the three thousand dollars I wasted on my mom's bail. So, for most of the month I worked Tuesday through Thursday nights behind the bar and weekend nights at the door. On top of that I had midterms in my economics and my sociology classes. I fell into the habit of reading only the highlighted lines of my textbooks—used books whose previous owners hopefully had an eye for what was test-worthy.

I found a document in Carl's sentencing file that turned out to be a godsend. It was a report that gave a thorough synopsis of Carl Iverson's life growing up in South St. Paul: his family, his petty delinquencies, his hobbies, his education. It touched briefly upon his military service, mentioning that Carl had been honorably discharged from the army after serving in Vietnam, having been awarded two Purple Hearts and a Silver Star. I made a note to myself to explore Carl's military service in more depth. I visited Carl twice in October, just before my notes and opening chapter were due. I managed to finish the first chapter by blending information from the report with the details from my notes— sprinkled liberally with my own creative license.

After I turned the assignment in to my instructor, I did not go back to Hillview until after Halloween, a holiday I had grown to despise. I dressed up as a bouncer for Halloween, just as I had for every Halloween since I turned eighteen, and worked the door at Molly's. I broke up only one fight that night, when Superman grabbed the ass of Raggedy

Ann—if Raggedy Ann had been a stripper, that is—causing her boyfriend, Raggedy Andy, to beat the man of steel to the floor. I rushed Raggedy Andy out the door. Raggedy Ann followed us out, flashing me a coy smile when she passed, as though the fight had been her plan all along, the kind of validation she had hoped for when she tucked her ample, fleshy parts into that tiny costume. I hated Halloween.

Cold weather arrived in earnest on the first day of November, the day I went back to Hillview. The temperature barely crested thirty degrees; dead leaves gathered in the crooks of buildings and around dumpsters where breezes curled. I called that morning to make sure that Carl would be up for a visit, not knowing exactly how pancreatic cancer progresses. I found Carl in his usual spot, staring out the window. He had an afghan covering his lap, thick wool socks under his cotton slippers, and long johns under his blue robe. He was expecting me and had asked one of the nurses to move a comfortable chair next to his wheelchair. Out of reflex, or habit, I shook his hand as I sat down, his thin fingers sliding from my palm, cold, limp, like dead seaweed.

"Thought you forgot about me," he said.

"It's been a busy semester," I answered, pulling out my small digital recorder. "You don't mind do you? It's easier than taking notes."

"This is your show. I'm just killing time." He chuckled at his own gallows humor.

I turned the recorder on and asked Carl to pick up where he'd left off in our last meeting. As Carl told his stories, I found myself breaking them apart into bits of information, spreading them around like pieces of a jigsaw puzzle on the table. Then I tried to reassemble the pieces in a way that would explain the birth and life of a monster. What was it in his childhood, in his adolescence, that planted the seed that would one day come to define him as Carl the murderer? There had to be a secret. Something had to have happened to Carl Iverson to make him different from the rest of the human race, different from me. He had given me that sermon about honesty the day we first met, and now he was telling me his Leave-It-To-Beaver upbringing, all the while hiding that dark tangent that shifted his world onto an axis the rest of us could never understand. I wanted to cry bullshit. Instead, I nodded and prodded and listened as he painted his world egg-shell white.

It was during the second hour of our interview when he said, "And that's when the US government invited me to go to Vietnam." Finally, I thought, an event that might explain the monster. Carl had grown weak from all the talking he was doing, so he put his hands on his lap, leaned back in his wheelchair, and closed his eyes. I watched the scar on his neck pulse as blood passed through his carotid artery.

"Is Vietnam where you got that scar?" I asked.

He touched the line on his neck. "No, I got that in prison. This psychopathic Aryan Brother tried to cut my head off."

"Aryan Brother? Aren't those the white guys?"

"They are," he said.

"I thought the different races stuck up for each other in prison."

"Not when you're a convicted child molester—which I was. The different gangs have dibs on the sex offenders of their own race."

"Dibs?"

"Sex offenders are the runts of the prison litter. If you get shit on, you take it out on the runt; if you need to earn a tear tattoo, to show you're a tough guy, why not kill the runt; if you need a bitch . . . well, you get the picture."

I cringed inside but kept my composure so that he wouldn't see my revulsion.

"One day, about three months after I got to Stillwater, I was on my way to dinner. That's the most dangerous time of the day. They send two hundred guys at a time to the mess hall. In that crowd, the shivs come out. There's no keeping track of who did what to whom."

"Isn't there a place where you can get out of the general population? Oh . . . what's it called . . . protective custody or something like that?"

"Segregation," he said. "Seg for short. Yeah, I could have asked for seg, but I didn't."

"Why not?"

"Because at that point in my life, living didn't matter all that much to me."

"So how'd you get the scar?"

"There was this big gorilla named Slattery who tried to get me to . . . well, let's just say he was lonely for some companionship. Said he'd cut my throat if I didn't give him what he wanted. I told him he'd be doing me a favor."

"So he cut your throat?"

"No. That's not how it works. He was a boss, not a worker. He had some punk do it, some kid looking to make a name for himself. I didn't even see it happen. I felt a warm liquid running down my shoulder. I put my hand up to my throat and felt the blood spurting out of my neck. Nearly died. After they patched me up, they forced me into seg. Stayed there most of the rest of my thirty years: noisy, surrounded by concrete almost every hour of the day. It could drive a man crazy."

"Is prison where you met your 'brother'?" I asked.

"My brother?"

"Virgil—wasn't that his name?"

"Ah, Virgil." He took in a deep breath, as if to sigh, and a wave of pain jolted him upright in his chair. The blood drained from his fingers as he gripped the sides of his wheelchair. "I think . . ." he said, tapping out a series of short breaths, as if he were giving birth, waiting for the pain to pass. "That story's . . . gonna have to wait . . . for another day." He waved a nurse over, asking her for his medication. "I'm afraid . . . I'm going to be asleep . . . in a very short while."

I thanked him for his time, picked up my backpack and recorder, and headed out. I stopped briefly at the front desk to fish my wallet out of my pocket and find the business card Virgil Gray had given to me. The time had come for me to hear from the one person in the world who believed Carl to be innocent, the sole voice arguing against my conclusion that Carl Iverson had been justly punished. As I dug out the card, Janet leaned across the reception desk and whispered, "He didn't take his pain medication today. He wanted to be clear headed when you came. He'll probably be out of it all day tomorrow."

I didn't respond to Janet. I didn't know what to say.

CHAPTER 13

I t had been a couple weeks since I got the call from the public defender's office telling me that the rest of Carl's file had been readied. I felt bad about that. I felt bad because I still hadn't picked it up. Had Virgil Gray not suggested that we meet downtown, that box would likely have stayed at the public defender's office. My assignment was time consuming enough without having to read a stack of files up to my knee. But when I called Virgil, he suggested that we meet in a small courtyard outside the government center in downtown Minneapolis. And that is where I found him, sitting on a granite bench at the edge of the courtyard, his cane resting against his good leg. He watched me as I crossed the length of the square, not waving or otherwise acknowledging me.

"Mr. Gray." I held out my hand; he shook it with the enthusiasm you might show for leftover broccoli. "I appreciate you meeting with me."

"Why are you writing his story?" Virgil asked bluntly. He didn't look at me when he spoke, his eyes focused on the fountain in the center of the courtyard.

"Excuse me?" I said.

"Why are you writing his story? What's in it for you?"

I sat on the bench beside Mr. Gray. "I told you. It's an English assignment."

"Yes, but why him? Why Carl? You could write about anyone. Hell, you could make up a story. Your teacher would never know the difference."

"Why not Carl?" I asked. "He has an interesting story to tell."

"You're just using him," Virgil said. "Carl's been screwed over more than any man deserves. I don't think it's right, what you're doing."

"Well, if he has been screwed, like you say, wouldn't it be good to have someone tell that story?"

"So that's what you're doing?" he said, his words dripping with sarcasm. "That's the story you're telling? You're writing about how Carl got screwed, about how he was convicted for a crime he didn't commit?"

"I haven't written any story yet. I'm still trying to figure out what the story is about. That's why I came to see you. You said he's innocent."

"He is innocent."

"Well, so far you're the only one saying that. The jury, the prosecutor, hell, I think his own attorney, believed he was guilty."

"That don't make it true."

"You didn't stand up for Carl at his trial. You didn't testify."

"They wouldn't let me testify. I wanted to testify, but they wouldn't let me."

"Who wouldn't they let you testify?"

Virgil looked up at a sky the color of fireplace ash. The trees around the courtyard had stripped down to their winter skeletons, and a cold wind swept across the cobblestone and up the back of my neck. "His attorneys," Virgil said, "they wouldn't let me tell the jury about him. They told me that if I testified, it would be character evidence. I told 'em damn straight it'd be character evidence. They need to know the real Carl, not that pile of lies the prosecutor was shoveling. They said if I talked about Carl's character, the prosecutor could also talk about Carl's character, about how he drank all day, couldn't keep a job, all that bullshit."

"So, what would you have said if you'd testified?"

Virgil turned, looking me in the eye, sizing me up one more time, his cold, gray irises reflecting the gathering clouds. "I met Carl Iverson in Vietnam in 1967. We were dumb kids fresh out of boot camp. Did a tour in the jungle with him—doing things, seeing things that you just can't explain to people who weren't there."

"And in that tour you came to know him well enough to say, without a doubt, that he didn't kill Crystal Hagen? Was he some kind of pacifist?"

Virgil narrowed his gaze as if he were getting ready to punch me in the face. "No," he said. "Carl Iverson was no pacifist."

"So he killed people in Vietnam."

"Yeah, he killed people. He killed plenty of people."

"I can see why the defense attorney didn't want you testifying."

"It was a war. You kill people in war."

"I still don't understand how telling the jury about Carl killing people in a war could've helped. I would think that if I had been in a war and had killed—what was it you said . . . plenty of people—that killing would come easier to me."

"There's a lot you don't understand."

"Then make me understand," I said, getting frustrated. "That's why I'm here."

Virgil thought for a moment and then reached down, his hands pinching the fabric of his khaki pants near his right knee, slid his trousers up, and exposed the shiny metal prosthesis that I had seen the day we first met. The artificial leg extended all the way up to his mid-thigh, a white plastic kneecap covering a spring-loaded hinge the size of a fist. Virgil tapped on his metal shin. "See this?" he asked. "This is Carl's doing."

"Carl's the reason you lost your leg?"

"No," he smiled. "Carl's the reason I'm here to tell you about my missing leg. Carl's the reason I'm alive today." Virgil slid his trouser leg back down, leaning forward, resting his elbows on his thighs. "It was May of 1968. We were stationed at a little firebase on a ridge northwest of the Que Son Valley. We received orders to toss a village, some no-name collection of huts. Intel had spotted Viet Cong activity in the area, so they sent our platoon in to check it out. I was walking point along with this kid . . ." A nostalgic smile crossed Virgil's face. "Tater Davis. Dumb kid used to follow me around like a basset hound." Virgil took a moment more to remember before he continued. "So me and Tater were walking point—"

"Point?" I asked. "Like out in front?"

"Yeah. They put a man or two out ahead of the rest of the column. That's the point. It's a hell of a plan. If things go bad, the army would rather lose those two fellas than a whole platoon."

I looked at Virgil's leg. "I take it things went badly?"

"Yep," he said. "We came over a small rise where the trail cut through a rocky knoll. On the downhill side of the knoll the trees thinned out a bit, enough to see the village ahead. Tater picked up the pace once he saw the village, but something wasn't right. I can't say I saw anything in particular, maybe it was a feeling, maybe subconsciously I saw something, but whatever it was, I knew something wasn't right. I signaled for the platoon to hold up. Tater saw me and put his rifle at the ready. I walked ahead on my own, maybe twenty or thirty paces. I was just about to give the 'all's clear' when the jungle exploded with gunfire. It was something else, I tell you. Ahead of me, beside me, behind me, hell, that jungle lit up with muzzle flashes from everywhere."

"The first bullet I took busted my shoulder blade. About that same time, two rounds caught my leg. One shattered my knee, the other busted my femur. I dropped without firing a single shot. I heard my prick of a sergeant, this piece of shit named Gibbs, ordering the platoon back over the knoll to take up defensive positions. I opened my eyes to see my buddies scampering away from me, jumping behind rocks and trees. Tater was running with all his might to make it back to the platoon. And that's when I saw Carl, running toward me."

Virgil stopped talking as he watched the past play out through the tears that had welled up in his eyes. He reached into his pocket, pulled out a handkerchief, and dabbed it to his eyes, his hand trembling slightly. I looked away to give Virgil some privacy. People in finely pressed suits crossed the courtyard in front of us, heading to and from the government center, ignoring the one-legged man sitting next to me. I waited patiently for Virgil to compose himself, and when he did, he continued.

"Carl came running up the trail, screaming like a mad man, firing at the muzzle flashes in the tree line. I could hear Sergeant Gibbs screaming at Carl, telling him to fall back. When Tater saw Carl, he stopped retreating and jumped behind a tree. Carl got to me and dropped down on one knee, putting himself between me and about forty AK-47s. He stayed there, firing his rifle until he was about out of rounds."

Virgil took in a slow breath, again on the verge of tears. "You should've seen him. He picked my rifle up with his left hand as he squeezed off the final rounds from his rifle, firing both guns at the same. Then he dropped his M-16 across my chest and went on firing mine. I popped a fresh magazine into his rifle and handed it back to him in time to reload my rifle again.

"Did Carl get hit?"

"He took a bullet through his bicep on his left arm, another one cut a crease in his helmet, and another took the heel off his boot. But he never budged. It was a sight."

"I bet it was," I said.

Virgil looked at me for the first time since he started telling his story. "Have you ever seen those old movies," he said, "where the sidekick gets shot and he tells the hero to go on without him, to save himself."

"Yeah," I said.

"Well, I was that sidekick. I was as good as dead, and I knew it. I opened my mouth to tell Carl to save himself, but what came out was 'don't leave me here.'" Virgil looked at his fingertips, which were folded together on his lap. "I was scared," he said, "more scared than I had ever been in my whole life. Carl had done everything wrong—militarily speaking, that is. He was saving my life. He was willing to die for me, and all I could do was tell him 'don't leave me here.' I've never been so ashamed."

I wanted to say something comforting, or to pat him on the shoulder, to let him know that it was okay, but that would have been an insult. I wasn't there. I had no say in what was or wasn't okay.

"When the battle was at its worst," he said, "the entire platoon was firing to beat hell. The VC were dealing it back in spades with Tater and Carl and me right in the middle of it all. I looked up and watched torn-up leaves and the splinters from the trees falling like confetti, the tracer rounds crisscrossing above us—red from our guns, green from theirs—noise and dirt and smoke. It was amazing, like I was outside of what was happening. The pain was gone; the fear was gone. I was ready to die. I looked over and saw Tater crouched behind a tree, laying down fire as best he could. He emptied his magazine and reached for a new one. Right then, he took a bullet in the face and fell dead. That's the last thing I remember before losing consciousness."

"You don't know what happened after that?" I asked.

"I was told that we had air support hovering above the mission. They dropped a load of napalm on the VC position. Carl covered me like a blanket. If you look closely, you can still see scars on the back of his arms and neck from the burn he took."

"Was that the end of the war for you two?" I asked.

"It was for me," Virgil said, clearing the choke out of his throat. "We got patched up at the firebase first, and then it was off to Da Nang. They sent me to Seoul, but Carl never made it past Da Nang. He spent some time recovering and then went back to the company."

"The jury never got to hear that story?" I said.

"Not a word of it."

"It is an amazing story," I said.

"Carl Iverson is a hero—a true god-damned hero. He was willing to lay down his life for me. He's not a rapist. He didn't kill that girl."

I hesitated before I said my next thought. "But . . . that story doesn't prove that Carl is innocent."

Virgil shot me a cold stare that bore into my temples, his grip on his cane tightening as if he were preparing to beat me with it for my insolence. I didn't move or say a word as I waited for the anger behind his eyes to thaw. "You sit here all warm and safe," he sneered. "You have no idea what it's like to face your own death."

He was wrong. I didn't feel warm; and with his knuckles turning white as he gripped the handle of his cane, I didn't feel particularly safe, although he had a point about the facing death part. "People can change," I said.

"A man doesn't jump in front of a hail of bullets one day and murder a little girl the next," he said.

"But you weren't with him for the rest of his tour, were you? You flew home, and he stayed there. Maybe something happened; something that turned a screw in his head—made him the kind of guy that could kill that girl. You said yourself that Carl was a killer in Vietnam."

"Yeah, he was a killer in Vietnam, but that's different than murdering that girl."

Virgil's words brought back the first conversation that I'd had with Carl, how cryptic he'd been about the distinction between killing and murdering. I thought Virgil might be able to help me understand, so I asked, "Carl said that there's a difference between killing and murdering. What does he mean by that?" I thought I knew the answer, but I wanted to hear it from Virgil before I talked to Carl about it.

"It's like this," he said. "You kill a soldier in the jungle, and you're just killing. It's not murder. It's like there's an agreement between armies that killing each other is okay. It's allowed. That's what you're supposed to do. Carl killed men in Vietnam, but he didn't murder that girl. See what I'm saying?"

"I see that you owe your life to Carl Iverson, and that you have his back no matter what. But Carl told me that he'd done both. He killed and he murdered. He said he was guilty of both."

Virgil looked at the ground, his face softening with some thought that seemed trapped in his head. He rubbed the stubble on his chin with the back of his index finger and then nodded as if he had come to some silent conclusion. "There's another story," he said.

"I'm all ears," I said.

"It's a story I can't tell you," he said. "I swore to Carl that I would never tell anyone. I never have, and I never will."

"But if it helps to clear—"

"It's not my story to tell; it's Carl's. It's his decision. He's never told a soul, not his lawyer, not the jury. I begged him to talk about it at his trial, but he refused."

"It happened in Vietnam?"

"It did," he said.

"And it shows what?" I asked.

Virgil bristled at my question. "For some reason, Carl seems interested in talking to you. I don't understand it, but he seems willing to let you in. Maybe he'll tell you about what happened to him in Vietnam. If he does talk about it, you'll see. There's no way in hell Carl Iverson could have killed that girl."

CHAPTER 14

After my meeting with Virgil, I stopped by the public defender's office to pick up the rest of the file, carrying it home on my shoulder, my mind juggling the competing sides of Carl Iverson. On the one side, Carl was a man kneeling in a jungle, taking bullets for his friend. On the other side was a sick bastard capable of extinguishing the life of a young girl in order to satiate his deviant sexual desires—two sides, one man. Somewhere in the box on my shoulder, there had to be an explanation of how the first man became the second. The box seemed impossibly heavy as I mounted the staircase to my apartment.

As I reached the top step, Lila opened her door, saw me, pointed at the box on my shoulder, and asked, "What's that?"

"It's the rest of Carl's file," I said. "I just picked it up."

Her eyes lit up with excitement. "Can I see it?" she said.

Ever since Lila had read the prosecutor's opening statement in the transcript, Carl's case had become my lure, the key to getting Lila into my apartment so I could spend time with her. I would have been lying if I'd said that my interest in digging deeper into Carl Iverson's story didn't have a lot to do with my attraction to Lila.

We went to my apartment and started digging through the box, which held a few dozen folders of varying thicknesses, each with the name of a different witness or a label like *forensics*, or *photos*, or *research*. Lila pulled out a file labeled *diary*; I pulled out another with the words *autopsy photos* written on the flap. I remembered the prosecutor's warning in his opening statement about the intensity of the photos. I remembered, as well, the words of Carl's public defender, Berthel Collins, and his reaction the first time he saw the photos. I needed to see those photos—not in the sense that I required their viewing for my project; I needed to understand what happened to Crystal Hagen. I needed to put a face to the name, flesh to the bone. I needed to test my mettle, to see if I could handle it.

The autopsy-photo folder was one of the thinnest in the box, containing maybe a couple dozen eight-by-ten pictures. I took a breath, closed my eyes, and prepared myself for the worst. I raised the folder cover quickly, like tearing off a bandage, and opened my eyes to see a beautiful young girl smiling back at me. It was Crystal Hagen's freshman picture. Her long, blonde hair parted in the middle, curled back along the frame of her face, emulated Farrah Fawcett, as did most of the girls of that time. She smiled a perfect smile, white teeth glistening behind soft lips, her eyes sparkling with a hint of mischief. She was a beautiful girl, the kind of girl that a young man would want to love and an old man should want to protect. This would be the picture that the prosecutor would have propped up in front of the jurors to make them feel for the victim. There would be other pictures he would use to make them despise the accused.

I stared at Crystal's picture for several minutes. I tried to imagine her alive, going to school, worrying about grades or boys or the myriad inconsequential anxieties that seem so overwhelming to a teenager and so mundane to an adult. I tried to imagine her as an adult—aging her from the freshman cheerleader with the long, flowing locks to the middle-aged mother with practical hair and a minivan. I felt sorry that she was dead.

I turned to the next picture, gasping as my heart seized up inside my chest. I slapped the file folder closed to wait for my breath to return. Lila was reading her file—the diary entries—so intensely that she didn't notice my jolt. I had only seen the image for a second, long enough for it to become seared on the back of my eyelids. I opened the file again.

I had expected her hair to be gone; it doesn't take much heat to burn hair. What I didn't expect was for her lips to be burned off. Her teeth, bright white in her class photo, now protruded from her jawbone, stained yellow by the fire. She lay on her right side, exposing the melted tissue of what used to be her left ear and cheek and her nose.

Her face was nothing more than a tight black mask of charred skin. As the burning muscles in her neck contracted, her face had twisted around to look over her left shoulder in a grotesque expression that mimicked a scream. Her legs were bent in a fetal position, and the meat of her thighs and calves had fused to the bone, burnt and shriveled like beef jerky. Both her feet had been burned down to stumps. The fingers of her right hand curled into her wrist, which tucked into her biceps and chest. All her joints had knotted up as the heat from the fire shrank the cartilage and tendons.

I could see where a sheet of tin had fallen across her body, protecting part of her torso from the worst of the flames. I swallowed back a gag in my esophagus and turned to the next picture, which showed Crystal rolled onto her back, her body frozen in a curl. The medical examiner held Crystal's left wrist in one of his latex-gloved hands. The skin on her left hand had been better protected, having been trapped under her body. In the medical examiner's other hand, between his thumb and forefinger, he held the broken fingernail by its edges, matching it up with the other fingernails on her left hand. It was the fake nail that they found on the steps leading from Carl's house to his shed.

I closed the file.

Had Crystal's family seen these pictures? They had to have. They attended the trial. These photos were trial exhibits, probably blown up to a size that could be viewed across a large courtroom. What had it been like to sit in that courtroom and see these pictures, the mutilation of their beautiful daughter? How could they not charge over the bar separating the gallery from the defendant and rip out the man's throat? It would have taken more than an old bailiff with a baton to stop me if this had been my sister.

I took a deep breath, opening the file once again to Crystal's school picture. I felt my heart rate mellow, my breathing returning to normal. Wow, I thought. I had never had such a visceral reaction to a picture. The juxtaposition of the pretty, vibrant cheerleader with the charred corpse made me happy that Carl had rotted for decades in prison, and it made me regret that Minnesota forbids putting criminals to death.

If those pictures had that effect on me, they must have had a similar effect on Carl's jury. There was no way Carl was going to walk out of that courtroom a free man. It was the least the jury could do to avenge Crystal's death.

Just then, my cell phone rang, interrupting my thoughts. I recognized the 507 area code from Austin, but not the number.

"Hello?" I said.

"Joe?" came a man's voice.

"This is Joe."

"It's Terry Bremer."

"Hi, Mr. Bremer." I smiled at hearing the familiar name. Terry Bremer owned the duplex where Mom and Jeremy lived, where I used to live. At that thought, my smile faded. "Is something wrong?"

"We had a small incident here," he said. "Your brother tried to heat up a piece of pizza in the toaster."

"Is he okay?"

"He's fine, I think. He set off the smoke detectors. Mrs. Albers from next door came over to check on him because the alarm didn't stop. She found your brother curled up in his room. He's really freaked out here. He's rocking back and forth and rubbing his hands."

"Where's my mother?"

"Not here," Bremer said. "Your brother mentioned something about her going to some meeting yesterday. She hasn't come back yet."

I wanted to hit something. I balled my hand into a fist and drew it back, my eyes focused on a smooth section of wall just itching to be pounded. But I knew that would be nothing but a ticket to bruised knuckles and forfeiture of my damage deposit. It certainly would not make my mother grow up. It wouldn't bring Jeremy back from his panic. I took a deep breath, lowered my head, and unclenched my fist.

I turned to Lila, who was looking up at me with a worried expression. She had heard enough of the conversation to figure out what had happened. "Go," she said.

I nodded, grabbed my coat and my keys, and headed out the door.

CHAPTER 15

Terry Bremer stood on bowed legs and carried a tin of chew in his back pocket, a good ol' boy who owned a bowling alley, two bars, and a couple dozen apartment units in Austin. He was one of those guys who could have been at the helm of a multinational corporation had his wall held the sheepskin of Harvard Business School instead of Austin High School. As landlords go, he was a good guy, affable, responsive. He'd given me my first bouncer job at a little hole-in-the-wall he owned called the Piedmont Club. It happened a couple weeks after I turned eighteen. He had come around for the rent—rent that my mother had blown on a trip to an Indian casino the weekend before. Instead of yelling or threatening to kick us out, he hired me to watch the door, clear off tables, and haul kegs up from the cellar. It was a good deal for me because it put money in my pocket and taught me how to deal with angry drunks and idiots. It was a good deal for him because if my mom blew our rent money, he simply withheld it from my check.

"Is my mother back yet?" I asked when I walked into the apartment.

Mr. Bremer stood just inside the door like a sentinel waiting to be relieved of duty. "No," he said, "and by the looks of things, she hasn't been around since yesterday." He took his cap off and brushed his palm across the smooth skin of his bald head. "I gotta tell ya, Joe, Mrs. Albers was on the verge of calling social services. Jeremy could've burned the place down."

"I know, Mr. Bremer, it won't—"

"I can't be getting sued Joe—your mom leaving him alone like that. If he burns the place down, I'll get sued. Your mother can't leave a retard home alone like that."

"He's not a retard," I snapped. "He's autistic."

97

"I didn't mean nothin' by it, Joe. But you know what I'm saying. Now that you're off at college there's no one around to keep things in line."

"I'll talk to her," I said.

"I can't have this happen again, Joe. If it does, I gotta kick 'em out."

"I'll talk to her," I said again, a little more insistent. Mr. Bremer put on his coat, paused as if to continue the conversation, to make sure he'd made his point, then must have thought better of it and headed out the door.

I found Jeremy in his room. "Hey, Buddy," I said. Jeremy looked up at me, started to smile, but then stopped, his eyes falling to the corner of the room and his brow taking on that worried expression he wore when life didn't make sense to him. "I heard you had a little excitement here tonight," I continued.

"Hi, Joe," he responded.

"Did you try and cook your own supper?"

"Maybe I tried to make some pizza."

"You know you can't make pizza in the toaster, don't you?"

"Maybe I'm not allowed to use the stove when mom is not home."

"Speaking of that, where is mom?"

"Maybe she had a meeting."

"Is that what she said? Did she tell you she had a meeting?"

"Maybe she said she had to go to a meeting with Larry."

"Larry? Who's Larry?"

Jeremy sent his gaze back to the corner of the room. It was his signal that I'd asked a question for which he had no answer. I stopped asking questions. It was getting near ten o'clock. Jeremy liked to be in bed by ten, so I had him brush his teeth and get ready. I waited in the doorway to his bedroom as he changed into his sleeping clothes. When he took off his sweatshirt, I saw the faint shadow of a bruise across his back.

"Hold up there, Buddy," I said, walking over to get a better look at what I thought I'd seen. The bruise, about six inches in length and the width of a broom handle, started just under his shoulder blade and extended to his spinal cord. "What's this?"

Jeremy looked into the corner of the room and didn't answer. Feeling the blood in my cheeks heating up, I took a deep breath to calm myself, knowing that Jeremy would shut down if I became angry. I smiled at him, letting him know that he wasn't in trouble. "How'd you get this bruise?" I asked. He continued to look at the corner of the room, saying nothing.

I sat down with Jeremy on the edge of the bed, resting my elbows on my knees, pausing for a bit to make sure I was calm. "Jeremy," I said. "It's very important that you and I don't keep secrets from each other. I'm your brother. I'm here for you. You're not in any trouble. But you can't keep secrets from me. You gotta tell me what happened."

"Maybe . . ." His eyes darted from one fixed point to another as he struggled to decide what to do. "Maybe Larry hit me."

I clenched my fists, but my face remained calm. "See?" I said, "You didn't do anything wrong. You're not in trouble. How did he hit you?"

"Maybe he hit me with the remote control."

"He hit you with the remote? The TV remote? Why?"

Again Jeremy averted his gaze. I had asked one question too many. I wanted to put my hands on Jeremy's shoulders and let him know that everything was okay, but you can't do that with Jeremy. I smiled at him and told him to get some sleep and have good dreams. I started his movie up, shut off the light, and closed the door. Whoever this Larry was—he and I were gonna have a talk.

CHAPTER 16

The next day was a Saturday. I woke before Jeremy and made pancakes. After we ate, we headed downtown to buy Jeremy a cell phone, one of those cheap ones that let you add minutes when you need them. When we got back to the apartment, I programmed my phone number into his contact list, making my number the only number on his list. I showed him how to call me, how to turn it on, how to find my number, and how to press the send button. He had never had his own phone before, so we practiced. I told him to hide the phone behind his dresser. After that, I let him beat me in two games of checkers to distract him from his new phone. Then I had him find the phone and call me, to make sure he remembered how to do it. He did.

"If anyone tries to hurt you . . ." I said. "If this Larry hits you or does anything like that, you call me. You got a phone of your own now. You call me. Okay, Jeremy?"

"Maybe I will call you with my new phone," he said, smiling with pride.

After lunch we played some more checkers and then turned on a movie: his movie. As Jeremy watched the movie, I watched the street, waiting for my mother to drive up. I also watched the clock; I had to work at Molly's at seven. The last time I'd bailed on Molly, she told me that I would not be getting any more breaks, and if I didn't show up, I would be fired. My mom left her cell phone in her dresser drawer; I know this because that's where it rang when I tried to call her.

With the drive time to the Twin Cities, I would need to leave Austin by 4:30. As I watched the hands of the clock slide past 3 p.m., I asked Jeremy, "Did Mom say when she was going to be back from her meeting?"

Jeremy pulled his attention from the movie and concentrated hard, his eyes moving back and forth slowly as if reading lines on a page. "Maybe she didn't say," he said.

I found a deck of cards and started playing solitaire on the coffee table. I lost three hands in quick succession, unable to focus my attention anywhere other than the driveway. As the clock inched close to four o'clock, I began going through options in my head. I could take Jeremy back to my apartment, but when I was working or in class, he was apt to find trouble there as easily as he would find it here. I could ask Lila to watch him, but he wasn't her responsibility—for that matter he wasn't supposed to be my responsibility. I could leave him here, alone, but one more problem and Bremer would follow through on his threat to kick them out. Or I could cancel on Molly again and lose my job. I reshuffled my cards and started laying out a new hand of solitaire.

At five minutes before four o'clock, my mother pulled into the driveway. I turned up the volume on the television to drown out the yelling that would be coming from the front yard, and I headed out the door.

"Where have you been?" I said through gritted teeth.

I don't know if it was my tone, my presence at her apartment, or her double-vodka lunch that confused her, but she stared at me as though she had just woken up from a deep sleep. "Joey," she said. "I didn't see your car." A tall man with stringy gray hair and a body shaped like a bowling pin stood behind her curling his upper lip in a snarl. I recognized Larry. I had thrown him out of the Piedmont about a year earlier for getting drunk and slapping a woman.

"You left him alone," I said. "He nearly burned the place down. Where the hell you been?"

"Now you just hold on," Larry said, brushing past my mother. "Don't you talk to your mother like—" Larry raised his right hand, as if reaching to poke me in the chest. That was the exact wrong thing to do. Before his finger could touch me, I shot my right hand across my chest, grabbing the back of his hand and curling my fingers around the pinky side of his palm. In one swift motion I ripped his hand away from my chest, twisting it clockwise and dropping Larry to his knees. The move was called a wristlock takedown. One of the regulars at the Piedmont, a cop we called Smiley, showed me that move. It had always been one of my favorites.

With very little torque, I curled Larry into a ball, his face a few inches from the ground, his arm cocked skyward behind his back, his wrist wrenched forward in my hand. It took everything I had not to kick Larry in the teeth. I leaned down over him and grabbed a tuft of his hair. His ears turned red and his features contorted as he winced with pain. Behind me my mother screeched some nonsense about how it was an accident, and how Larry was really a good guy deep down. Her pleading evaporated into the air around me, no more important to me than traffic noise in the distance.

I pressed Larry's nose and forehead into the grit of the sidewalk. "I know what you did to my brother." I said.

Larry didn't respond, so I gave the pressure point in his wrist a tweak and he grunted.

"Let me be very clear about this," I said. "If you ever touch Jeremy again I will come down on you like nothing you've ever known. Nobody touches my brother. Do you understand?"

"Fuck you," he said.

"Wrong answer," I said, lifting his face off the concrete and tapping it back down just hard enough to make a mark and draw some blood. "I said: do you understand?"

"Yes," he said.

I jerked Larry to his feet and shoved him toward the street. He walked down to the curb holding his bleeding nose and forehead, saying something under his breath that I couldn't hear. I turned my attention back to my mother.

"Mr. Bremer called me."

"We just went to the casino," she said. "We were only gone a couple days."

"What were you thinking? You can't leave him alone for a couple days."

"He's eighteen years old now," she said.

"He's not eighteen," I said. "He'll never be eighteen. That's the point. When he's forty he'll still be a seven-year-old. You know that."

"I'm entitled to have some fun too, ain't I?"

"You're his mother, for God sakes." My contempt seethed in my words. "You can't just run off whenever you want to."

"And you're his brother," she shot back, trying to gain some footing in the argument, "but that don't stop you from running off? Does it? Big college boy."

I stopped talking until the boil in my chest dropped to a simmer, my stare falling on my mother as hard and as cold as winter metal. "Bremer said he's kicking you out if he gets another call." I turned to walk to my car, my eye on Larry as I passed him, waiting for an excuse to light into him again.

As I pulled away from the curb, I saw Jeremy standing at the front window. I waved to him, but he didn't wave back. He just stood there watching me. To the rest of the world he would have appeared expressionless, but I knew better. He was my brother and I was his; and only I could see the sadness behind his calm, blue eyes.

CHAPTER 17

The next morning I was pulled from a bad dream by a knock at my door.

In my dream, I was back in high school, wrestling at a tournament, trying to execute a simple escape maneuver. As I ripped the guy's grip from around my stomach, another hand grabbed my chest and yet another hand pulled at my arm. I pried each new hand loose only to create two more hands, like a hydra growing new heads. Soon I could only twist and scream under the onslaught of hands pulling and tearing at me. That's when I heard the noise that woke me. It took a while to purge the cloud of sleep from my head. I sat up in bed, not sure of what I had heard, waiting, listening—then, another knock. I hadn't dreamt it. I threw on a pair of shorts and a sweatshirt and opened the door to find Lila on the other side, holding two cups of coffee and a file folder.

"I read the diary," she said, walking past me, handing me one of the cups of coffee. "You do drink coffee, don't you?"

"Yeah, I drink coffee," I said. I grabbed a baseball cap from a hook on the wall to cover up my bed head and followed Lila to my couch. I had left the box of files with Lila in my apartment two days earlier when I charged out to go to Austin. She took some of the files home, including the one marked *diary* to comb through in my absence.

"I read her diary last night," she said.

"Crystal's?"

Lila looked at me like I was an idiot. In my defense, I was still groggy with sleep. She turned back to her train of thought. "The diary starts out in May of 1980," Lila said, laying her notes on the coffee table in front of me. "The first few months are full of normal teenage crap. She's excited about starting high school one day and scared about it the next. For the most part she's a happy kid. She has fifteen entries about Carl between June and September, usually referring to him as the pervo next door, or Creepy Carl."

"What'd she say about him?" I asked.

Lila had marked some of the pages with yellow tabs. She turned to the first tab in the diary, which was dated June 15:

June 15 – I was practicing in the back yard and saw Creepy Carl watching me from his window. I flipped him off and he just stood there. What a pervo.

"Just like the prosecutor said," Lila commented, turning to the next tab. "'He's watching me again. He stared at me while I did my routines.' There's one . . ." She turned the pages of the diary to another marked passage, "Here it is."

Sept. 8 – Creepy Carl was watching me again from the window. He wasn't wearing a shirt. I bet he wasn't wearing pants either.

Lila looked at me for a response.

I shrugged. "I can see why the prosecutor liked the diary." I think Lila wanted more of a reaction from me, but I moved on. "What else you got?"

"Most of August is tame," Lila said. "When school starts, she meets that guy, Andrew Fisher, in her typing class. She writes all about her plan to get Andy to invite her to homecoming—which he did. Then around mid-September the entries started getting darker. Read this one."

September 19 – Parking in the alley with Andy. Just when things were getting interesting, Creepy Carl walks up and looks in the window like he's Lurch or something. I could have died.

"Again, just like the prosecutor told the jury," I said. "Carl caught 'em getting it on in the alley."

"Two days later she starts writing about something bad happening, but she writes some of it in code."

"Code?"

"Yeah. There're a few passages where Crystal uses a substitution code—you know, writing numbers instead of letters." Lila pulled a stack of diary pages out of the folder. She had marked the coded entries with green tabs. "Look here."

September 21 – Terrible day today. 7,22,13,1,14,6,13,25,17,24,18,11,1.
I am freaking out. This is very very bad.

"What's it mean?" I asked.

"Did I mention it's a code?" Lila said. "Maybe this was Crystal's way of making sure that if her stepdad ever found the diary, she wouldn't get shipped off to private school."

"Yeah, but it's the code of a fourteen-year-old girl," I said. "Did you try matching the numbers up with letters?"

"You mean like: A equals one, and B equals two, that sort of thing?" Lila rolled her eyes and pulled out the notebook pages where she'd been matching up numbers with letters. "I tried the alphabet forward; I tried it backward; I tried shifting so that A started at the number 2, then three, and so on. I tried matching the most frequent number with the letter E or T because those are the most often used letters in the alphabet. I looked for clues in her diary. I came up with nothing but gibberish."

"Did you try online?" I asked. "I think there are websites that can break codes."

"I thought of that, too," she said. "Crystal didn't leave spaces between her words, so it's just strings of numbers. Nothing I found on the internet could solve it. There are eight billion possible combinations of numbers and letters."

"Eight billion?" I said. "Holy crap."

"Exactly. She must have had a key hidden away, or maybe she memorized a pattern to match the letters to the numbers. Either way, I can't figure it out."

Lila spread the pages on the table. "There are only seven coded entries, the last one written on the day she was murdered. I put them together," she said, laying her own list on top of the diary pages.

September 21 – Terrible day today. 7,22,13,1,14,6,13,25,17,24,26,21, 22,19,19,3,19. I am freaking out. This is very very bad.

September 28 – 25,16,14,11,5,13,25,17,24, 26,21,22,19,19,3,19,26, 21,22,19,19,3,19. If I don't do what he wants he'll tell everyone. He'll ruin my life.

September 30 – 6,25,6,25,25,16,12,6,1,2,17,24,2,22,13,25. I hate him. I feel sick.

October 8 – 25,16,12,11,13,1,26,6,20,3,17,3,17,24,26,21,22,19,19,3, 19,9,22,7,8. He keeps threatening me. 2,3,12,22,13,1,19,17,3,1,11,5, 19,3,17,24,17,11,5,1,2.

October 9 – 6,26,22,20,3,25,16,12,2,22,1,2,3,12,22,13,1,3,25. He forced me. I want to kill myself. I want to kill him.

October 17 – 5,16,17,22,25,3,17,3,25,11,6,1,22,26,22,6,13,2,3,12,22, 19,10,11,5,26,2,6,1,2,5, 10,1.

October 29 – 6,1,19,10,22,18,3,25,16,19,10,22,18,6,13,26,17,3. Mrs. Tate said so. She said that the age difference means he'll go to prison for sure. It stops today. I am so happy.

"October 29 is the day she was killed," Lila said.
"How do we know she's talking about Carl?"
"There are dozens of pages where she talks about Carl being the pervert that watched her from his window," Lila said. "He snuck up on her when she was having sex with Andy. It's not a coincidence that the threats began right after that."

"The code could change everything."

"There are other entries that aren't coded," she said. "Look at this one from September twenty-second, the day after the 'terrible day' when she got caught with Andy Fisher."

September 22 – If they find out, it'll destroy me. They will send me to Catholic school. Goodbye cheerleading, goodbye life.

"Don't you think that seems a bit dramatic," I said. "I mean, they have cheerleaders at Catholic schools, too, don't they?"

Lila shot a skeptical glance at me. "You obviously don't understand the brain of an adolescent girl. Everything is the end of the world. They're emotional to the point of being suicidal." She paused, as if distracted by a thought. Then she continued. "Some things can truly seem like the end of the world."

"Who is Mrs. Tate?" I asked, looking at the last entry.

"You didn't read the transcripts, did you?" Lila said, sounding exasperated.

"I sort of read 'em," I said. "But I don't remember Mrs. Tate."

"She was a school guidance counselor." Lila pulled one of the transcripts from the box and started flipping through it until she got to Mrs. Tate's testimony. "Here it is." She handed the transcript to me and I read:

Q: And when you met with Crystal Hagen that day, what were her concerns, what did she talk about?

A: She was real vague. She wanted to know if oral sex was sex. I mean, she wanted to know if someone forced you to have oral sex, could that be called rape.

Q: Did she tell you why she wanted to know?

A: No. She wouldn't say. She kept saying that she was asking for a friend. That happens a lot in my business. I tried to get her to tell me more. I asked her if someone was forcing her to have oral sex. She didn't answer. Then she asked me if it's force if the person was making you do it by threatening to tell a secret about you.

Q: And what did you tell her?

A: I said that it could be considered coercion. Then she asked me, "What if the guy is older?"

Q: And you responded how?

A: As a school counselor, we receive training on the law regarding stuff like this. I told her that given her age, if a man is more than two years older than her, it doesn't matter if there is coercion or not. Consent is not an issue. If an older man is having sex with a fourteen-year-old, it's rape. I told her that if something like that was happening she needed to tell me, or tell the police, or her parents. I told her if something like that was happening, the man will go to prison for it.

Q: And what was her response to that?

A: She just smiled a really big smile. Then she thanked me and left my office.

Q: And you're sure that conversation took place on October 29 of last year?

A: That conversation took place the day that Crystal was killed. I'm sure of that.

I closed the transcript. "So, Crystal went home, wrote an entry in her diary, and then went to Carl's house to confront him?"

"Either that or she took the diary with her to school," Lila said. "It makes sense, doesn't it? Crystal knew that she had the upper hand. It would be his life that got ruined, not hers."

"So the same day she's planning to put an end to it, Carl's out buying a gun?"

"Maybe he was planning on putting an end to it, too," Lila said. "Maybe his plan all along was to kill her that day."

I stared down at the coded pages, their secret knowledge taunting me. "I wish we could break that code," I said. "I can't believe his lawyer didn't work harder to break it."

"He did," she said. Lila pulled a piece of paper out of the file and handed it to me. It was a copy of a letter to the Department of Defense. The date on the letter showed that it was written two months before the trial. It had been signed by Carl's attorney, John Peterson. In the letter Peterson was asking the Department of Defense to help decipher the diary code.

"Did the Department of Defense ever respond?" I asked.

"Not that I could find," she said. "There's no other mention of the code being deciphered at all."

"You would think that they would move heaven and Earth to decipher the code before they went to trial."

"Unless . . ." Lila looked at me and shrugged.

"Unless what?"

"Unless Carl already knew what it would say. Maybe he didn't want the code deciphered because he knew it would be the final nail in his coffin."

CHAPTER 18

I called Janet the next day and made an appointment for that evening to see Carl. I wanted to ask him about the diary and the code. I wanted to know why such an important part of the prosecutor's case went unchallenged. I wanted to see his face when he told me whether or not he knew what Crystal Hagen meant when she wrote in her diary that it "stops today." I wanted to test his honesty. But first I needed to talk to Berthel Collins. It took me several tries, leaving messages each time. And when he finally called me back, I was already on the road driving to Hillview Manor.

"What can I do for you, Joe?" he asked.

"Thanks for calling me back, Mr. Collins," I said. "I came across something odd in the trial file that I wanted to ask you about."

"That was a long time ago, but I'll do my best to give you an answer," he said.

"There was this diary, Crystal Hagen's diary. It had a code. Do you remember that?"

Collins paused on the other side of the line and then, in a low, somber tone, said, "Yeah, I remember it."

"Well, I found a letter to the Department of Defense where Mr. Peterson tried to get it deciphered. What happened with that?"

Another pause, then Collins answered. "Peterson signed that letter, but I wrote it. That was one of my contributions to the case. We didn't have personal computers back in 1980, at least nothing like we have today. We figured that the Department of Defense would have the technology to break the code, so Peterson assigned me the task of contacting the DoD. I spent hours trying to find someone to take my call. After a couple weeks of trying I found this guy who said he would see what he could do."

"So what happened? Did you ever get an answer?"

"No. Things were moving at the speed of light on our end, but dealing with the DoD. was like swimming in jelly. I don't know if you saw this in the file, but Iverson demanded a speedy trial."

"A speedy trial? What's that mean?"

"A defendant can request that his case be brought to trial within sixty days. We rarely do that because the longer a case lingers, the better it gets for the defense. We get more discovery; we have time to do a thorough investigation of our own; witnesses become less reliable. There was no reason for Iverson to demand a speedy trial, but he did. I was there when Peterson tried to convince him to back off the demand. We needed time to prepare. We needed to hear back from the DoD. Iverson didn't care. Remember how I said he didn't help with his case, like he was watching it on television? That's what I'm talking about."

"So what happened with the Department of Defense? Why didn't they break the code?"

"We weren't a priority to them. This was before you were born, but that year, 1980, the Iranians were holding fifty-two Americans hostage. That was also an election year. Everyone was focused on the crisis, and I couldn't get anyone to talk to me or call me back. The packet I sent them disappeared into some black hole. After the trial I called them to tell them that it was too late, that they didn't need to work on our code anymore. They had no idea what code I was talking about."

"Did the prosecutor ever try to break the code?"

"I don't think so. I mean, why would he? The inferences all pointed toward Iverson. He didn't need the code to be deciphered. He knew that the jury would read into it what he told them to read into it."

I pulled into the parking lot of Hillview and parked my car, laying my head against the headrest. I had one last question, but I hesitated to ask it. A part of me wanted to believe that he was not the monster that the prosecutor talked about. But I wanted the truth. "Mr. Collins, a friend of mine thinks that Carl didn't want the diary to be deciphered. She thinks that he knew that it would have pointed at him. Is that true?"

"Your friend is perceptive," he said, thoughtfully. "We had that same discussion thirty years ago. I think John Peterson agreed with your friend. I got the feeling that John didn't really want the code solved, that's why he gave it to me to do. I was a lowly clerk at the time. I think John wanted to document that we tried, but he didn't really want to receive the results because . . . well . . ." Collins took in a deep breath and sighed. "The truth is, it can be hard sometimes, to give it all you got defending a man that you know murdered his victim."

"Did you ever ask Carl about the diary code?"

"Certainly. Like I said, John tried to convince Carl to back off the speedy-trial demand. That was one of our arguments—that we might get some good evidence from deciphering the code."

"What did Carl say?"

"It's hard to explain. Most guys who are guilty will take a plea bargain. He refused a second degree. And, most guys who are innocent will delay trial for as long as it takes to get their case prepared. He demanded a speedy trial. We were trying to decipher the code, and it seemed like he was working against us. I gotta tell you, Joe, it seemed to me like Carl Iverson wanted to go to prison."

CHAPTER 19

I walked over to Carl and sat down in the lounge chair beside him, his slight sideways glance being the only acknowledgement of my arrival. Then, after a moment, he said, "Beautiful day."

"It is," I replied. I hesitated before launching into our interview. I wasn't going to pick up where we left off—talking about the day he got his draft notice. Instead, I wanted to talk about why he wanted the speedy trial, and why he seemed to not want the diary deciphered. I suspected that my choice of topic would spoil the rest of Carl's day, so I tried to ease into the conversation. "I talked to Berthel Collins today," I said.

"Who?"

"Berthel Collins, he was one of your attorneys."

"My attorney was John Peterson," he said. "And he died years ago, or at least that's what I heard."

"Collins worked as a law clerk on your case."

Carl thought for a moment, apparently trying to remember Collins, then he said," I seem to remember a kid sitting in the room on some of the visits. That was so long ago. Is he a lawyer now?"

"He's the chief public defender in Minneapolis," I said.

"Well good for him," he said. "And why did you talk to Mr. Collins."

"I'm trying to figure out what those coded messages in Crystal Hagan's diary meant."

His gaze never shifted from the apartment balcony across the way. He seemed unmoved by my bringing up the diary, treating my announcement with the insignificance of a burp. "So," he said, "you're a detective now, are you?"

"No," I said, "but I do like a good puzzle. And this one seems to be a real challenge."

"You want an interesting puzzle?" he said. "Take a look at the pictures."

That was not where I wanted our conversation to go. "I saw the pictures," I said, as the images of Crystal Hagen's corpse flashed across my memory. "They almost made me throw up. I have no interest in looking at them again."

"Oh . . . no. Not those pictures," he said, turning his body so that he faced me for the first time since I arrived. A sickly pallor washed over his face. "I . . . I'm so sorry you had to see those pictures." I could tell by his face that he could still see the trial photos in his mind after all these years, his features giving way to a thirty-year-old gravity. "Those pictures were terrible. Nobody should have to look at them. No, I'm talking about the pictures taken of the fire, before the police arrived. Have you seen those?"

"No," I said. "What about them?"

"You ever read a *Highlights* magazine when you were a kid?"

"Highlights?"

"Yeah, you'd find them in dentist offices and doctor's waiting rooms. They're magazines for kids."

"Can't say I've seen one," I said.

Carl smiled and nodded. "Well, they have these pictures in them, two pictures that appear to be identical, but there are small differences. The game is to find the differences, find the anomalies."

"Sure," I said. "I did those kinds of things in grade school."

"If you like solving puzzles and riddles, find the pictures that were taken before and after the fire department arrived and look at them. Play that game. See if you can spot the anomaly. It's hard to see. It took me years to notice it—but then again, I didn't have the head start you'll have. I'll give you a hint, what you're looking at might be looking at you."

"You had the pictures in prison?"

"My attorney sent me copies of most of the stuff in the file. Had all the time in the world to read it after they convicted me."

"Why didn't you take more of an interest in your case before they convicted you?" I asked. Carl looked at me like he was eyeing an unusual chess move. Maybe he saw where I was going with my question—my not-so-subtle segue.

"What do you mean?"

"Collins said that you demanded a speedy trial."

He thought for a moment and said, "That is true."

"Why?"

"It's a long story," he said.

"Collins said they wanted more time, but you pushed to go to trial."

"Yes. I did."

"He thinks you wanted to go to prison."

Carl said nothing, setting his gaze back toward the window.

I pressed on. "I want to know why you didn't fight harder to stay out of prison."

He hesitated before answering. Then he said, "I thought it would silence the nightmare."

Now we're getting somewhere, I thought. "The nightmare?"

I watched as he paused his breathing and swallowed hard. Then, in a low, calm voice, a voice that came from somewhere deep in his soul, he said, "I've done things . . . things that I thought I could live with . . . but I was wrong."

"This is your dying declaration," I said, trying to jump into his thoughts, hoping to grease the skids of his catharsis. "This is why you're telling me your story, to get this off your chest." I saw the surrender in his eye, the desire to tell me his story. I wanted to scream at him to confess, but I whispered my words instead, hoping not to frighten him away. "I'll listen to you. I promise I won't judge."

"Came here to bring me absolution, did you?" He spoke barely above a whisper.

"Not absolution," I said. "But telling me what happened might help. They say that confession is good for the soul."

"They say that, do they?" His attention shifted slowly toward me. "And do you agree with what they say?" he asked.

"Sure," I said. "I think that if you have something that is troubling you . . . telling someone about it can be a good thing."

"Should we try that," he said. "Should we test that idea?"

"I think we should," I said.

"Then tell me about your grandfather," he said.

I felt a thump in my chest that stunned me. I looked away from him while I tried to calm my thoughts. "What about my grandpa?" I said.

Carl leaned in. Still speaking in that soft voice, he said, "That first day that we met, I mentioned him, just in passing. I asked how he died, and you froze. Something heavy came over you. I could see it in your eyes. Tell me what happened to him?"

"He died when I was eleven years old. That's all."

For a long while, Carl said nothing, letting the heaviness of my hypocrisy settle onto my shoulders. Then he sighed and shrugged. "I understand," he said. "I'm just a school project."

An unsettling voice began to bounce around inside my head, fed by my own guilt, a voice that whispered to me, urging me to tell Carl my secret. Why not tell him, the voice said. He would take my secret to the grave in a matter of weeks. Besides, it would be my good-faith payment to him for the confession that he would give to me. But then another voice, a quieter voice, told me that good faith had nothing to do with why I needed to tell Carl my secret. I wanted to tell him.

Carl looked down at his hands as he continued. "You don't have to tell me," he said. "That was never our deal—"

"I watched my grandpa die," I blurted. The words escaped my brain and shot out of my mouth before I could stop them. Carl looked at me, startled by my interruption.

Like a cliff diver leaving the safety of his perch, that single moment of courage or recklessness started an action I could not reverse. I stared out the window now, as I had seen Carl do so many times, and I gathered the details of my memory to me. When my thoughts were clear enough, I spoke again. "I've never told anybody this," I said, "but it was my fault he died."

CHAPTER 20

What I remembered most about my Grandpa Bill were his hands, powerful bulldog paws with stubby fingers as thick as lug nuts, fingers that pulsed with agility as he worked on the small engines that he repaired. I remembered him holding my hand in his when I was little, and the feeling it gave me that everything would be okay. I remembered how he moved through the world with utter patience, giving attention and purpose to every task he performed, whether it was cleaning his glasses or helping my mother through a bad day. He had been there for her in my earliest memories, his whispers drowning out her shouts, his hand on her shoulder able to tame a storm. She had always been bipolar—that's not a condition you can suddenly catch like the flu—but when my Grandpa Bill was alive, the waves never grew into whitecaps.

He used to tell me stories about fishing the Minnesota River, up near Mankato where he grew up, hauling in catfish and walleye by the boatload, and I would dream of the day when I might go fishing with him. Then, when I was eleven years old, that day came. My grandpa borrowed a boat from a friend of his and we launched at the landing at Judson to float down the river with its slow yet powerful current, the plan being to end up at a park in Mankato before nightfall.

That spring, the river had overflowed its banks with the snow runoff, but by July, when we went fishing, it had settled down. The flood had left behind a scattering of dead cottonwood trees jutting up from the river bottom, their branches breaking the water's surface like skeletal fingers. Grandpa Bill kept the motor of the little fishing boat idling so we could maneuver around the trees when we needed to. Occasionally, I would hear the screech of wood on aluminum as a branch, hiding just below the surface, scraped against the hull. The sound frightened me at first, but Grandpa Bill acted like it was as natural as the breeze rustling the leaves around us. That made me feel safe.

I caught my first fish within the first hour, and I lit up like it was Christmas. I had never caught a fish before, and the feel of catching that fish, the twitching of my rod, seeing him lift out of the water flipping and flopping, thrilled me. I was a fisherman. The day meandered beneath a clear blue sky with him catching a few fish and me catching a few more. I think he fished without bait some of the time just to let me get ahead.

By noon we had a decent stringer of fish. He told me to drop the anchor so that we could keep our lines in the water as we ate our lunch. The anchor, which was attached to the boat at the bow—where I sat— dragged along the bottom of the river for a ways until it finally caught and brought our boat to a halt in the middle of the river. We washed our hands with water from a canteen, and Grandpa Bill pulled ham-and-cheese sandwiches out of a plastic grocery bag. We ate the best sandwiches I'd ever tasted, washing them down with bottles of cold root beer. It was a glorious lunch, eaten in the middle of a river at the apex of a perfect day.

When my Grandpa finished his food, he folded his sandwich bag into a small wad and carefully placed it in the grocery bag, which had now become our trash bag. Then, when he finished his root beer, he put his empty bottle in the bag, using the same deliberate motion. He handed the bag to me so that I could follow his lead. "Always keep the boat clean," he said. "Don't leave trash lying around or the tackle box open. That's how accidents happen." I listened with one ear as I sipped my root beer.

Once I drained the last of my drink, Grandpa Bill told me to pull up the anchor—another thing I had never done before. He had turned his attention to the motor, pumping a little ball in the gas line to get it ready to start. He wasn't watching as I laid my empty bottle on the floor of the boat. I would throw it away later, I told myself. I gripped the nylon rope that tethered us to the anchor and pulled. The anchor did not budge. I pulled harder and felt the boat edge upstream, the anchor still not moving. The boat had a flat stem plate for a bow, so I braced my feet against the stem and pulled hand over hand, pulling the boat slowly toward the anchor until my progress ground to a halt. Grandpa Bill saw my struggles and coached me to pull left and right, to work the anchor loose, but the thing would not come up.

Then, behind me, I heard Grandpa Bill stir in his seat. I felt the boat rock. When I looked over my shoulder, I saw him making his way forward to help me. As he stepped over a bench seat that separated us, he put his foot down on my empty bottle. His ankle twisted, curling his foot sideways. He tilted and fell backward, his thigh crashing against the side of the boat, his arms swinging at the air, his torso wrenching around to face the river as he hit. The splash drenched me as the river swallowed my grandpa.

I screamed his name as he disappeared into the murky water. I screamed twice more before he popped to the surface, grabbing for the boat, his hand missing the edge by the width of a penny. His second attempt wasn't even close. The current had him, and it pulled him away from me as I sat there holding on to that stupid anchor rope, never realizing that if I had let go of the rope, the boat would have floated downstream alongside my grandpa, at least for twenty feet or so. By the time he righted himself, he had moved well beyond the reach of the boat, even if I had released the anchor rope.

I yelled and prayed and begged for him to swim. It all happened so fast.

Then everything soared to a whole new level of bad. Grandpa Bill began to thrash around in the water, his arms flailing, clutching at the surface of the river, his leg pinned in place by something hidden in the wet darkness. Later, the sheriff would tell my mother that his boot caught on the branch of a dead cottonwood tree just beneath the surface of the river.

I watched him struggle to keep his face above the water as the current pushed him under. He didn't have his lifejacket zipped shut. It pulled at his arms, tangling them above his head, his upper body tugging against the trapped boot. It was only then that it dawned on me to release my rope. I let it go and paddled with my hand until the rope snapped tight about thirty feet upstream of my grandfather. I could see him scratching and tearing to pull free of the life jacket. I couldn't move. I couldn't think. I just stood there and watched and yelled until my grandfather stopped moving and floated limp in the current.

I told Carl my story, choking back my tears, pausing repeatedly to let my chest settle. It wasn't until I finished that I noticed that Carl had laid his hand on my arm in an attempt to comfort me. To my surprise, I didn't pull away from him.

"You know, it wasn't your fault," he said.

"I don't know that at all," I said. "That's the big lie I've been trying to tell myself for the past ten years. I could have put the bottle in the trash bag. I could have let go of that rope when he fell in. I had a knife in the tackle box; I could have cut the boat loose and saved him. Believe me, I've gone over it a million times. I could have done a hundred things differently. But I didn't do anything."

"You were just a kid," Carl said.

"I could have saved him," I said. "I had the choice to try or to watch. I chose wrong. That's all there is to that."

"But—"

"I don't want to talk about it anymore," I snapped.

Janet tapped me on the shoulder and I turned with a jerk. "I'm sorry, Joe," she said, "but visiting hours are over." I looked at the clock on the wall and saw that it was ten minutes past eight. I had been talking for the entire visit, and I felt drained. My mind spun as the memory of that terrible day swirled and bounced unfettered in my head, cut loose from its moorings by Carl Iverson. I felt cheated because we had never gotten around to talking about Carl. And, at the same time, I felt a sense of relief for having told my secret to someone.

I stood and apologized to Janet for overstaying my permitted time. Then I nodded to Carl in place of saying goodbye and made my way out. As I walked out of the lounge, I paused to look back at Carl. He sat motionless, facing his reflection in the dark glass, his eyes closed tight as though holding back a deep pain, and I found myself wondering if it was the cancer again or if this time it was something else.

CHAPTER 21

To calm down, I cranked rock classics from my car's beat-up speakers on the drive home. I sang along with a string of one-hit wonders until I managed to force the dark thoughts out of my head, replacing them with thoughts of the puzzle that Carl had mentioned. Sure, the idea of a puzzle intrigued me, but it was the notion that I had another excuse to spend time with Lila that made me feel better about things. When I got back to the apartment, I dug through the box and found two files that held pictures taken of the burning shed. I spent half an hour making sure I had the right pictures then I packed the files under my arm and headed to Lila's apartment.

"You like games?" I said to Lila.

"That depends," she said. "What ya got in mind?"

Her response caught me off guard, and for a second there I thought that I detected a flirty smile. It nearly made me forget why I came. I smiled back and stumbled over myself. "I got some pictures," I said.

She looked a bit confused, then showed me to her dining-room table with a nod of her head. "Most guys bring flowers," she said.

"I'm not most guys," I said. "I'm special."

"No argument there," she said.

I spread out a series of photographs, seven pictures in all. Of the seven, the first three showed the fire raging out of control with no fire-fighters on the scene yet. Those pictures were poorly framed, haphazard in the use of lighting, and one of them was terribly out of focus. The second set of photos showed the firefighters working the blaze and had been taken by a better photographer. The first of these showed the firefighters pulling a hose off the truck, the shed burning in the background. Another showed the water from the fire hose as it first hit the shed. Two more showed the firefighters spraying water on the fire from two different angles. One of these last two pictures was the one I'd seen in the newspaper article at the library.

"So what's the game," she said.

"These pictures here . . ." I said, pointing at the first three pictures. "They came from the file of a witness named Oscar Reid. He lived across the alley from Carl and the Lockwoods. He saw the flames and called 911. While he waited for the cavalry to arrive, he grabbed an old instamatic and snapped a few pictures."

"Instead of—oh, I don't know—grabbing a water hose?"

"He told the detective that he thought he might be able to sell a picture to the newspaper."

"A real humanitarian," she said. "And these?" She pointed at the other four pictures.

"These were taken by an actual newspaper photographer, Alden Cain. He heard the fire call over a scanner and ran over there to get some shots."

"Okay," she said. "So what am I looking for?"

"Remember in grade school, the teachers used to give out pictures that looked alike but weren't? And you had to spot the differences between them?"

"That's the game?" she said.

"That's it," I said, lining the pictures up side by side. "What do you see?"

We studied them carefully. In the early photos, flames shot out of a shed window that faced the alley and the photographer. The roof of the shed was intact, and thick black smoke rolled out of spaces where the two-by-four rafters rested on the walls. In the later photographs, the fire rose in a twisting swirl, like a whirlwind from a hole in the roof. The firefighters arrived and had just started dousing the flames with water. Cain stood in pretty much the same spot as Reid because the angles and backgrounds of the pictures were very similar.

"I don't see any anomalies," I said, "other than the firefighters moving around."

"Me neither," Lila said.

"Carl said to look at things that should be the same in each picture, so don't look at the fire because that changes as it grows."

We looked more carefully at the pictures, examining the background for any slight alteration. Other than an increase in light from the growing flames, Carl's house looked the same in every photo. Then I looked at the Lockwood house in the Reid photos: a standard two-story, blue-collar home with a small back porch, a set of three windows on the top floor, and a window on either side of the back door. I looked at the Lockwood house in the Cain photos. Again, it was brighter because of the flames, but otherwise nothing had changed. I went back and forth from one picture to another, wondering if Carl had played a joke on me.

Then Lila saw it. She lifted two pictures off the table, one by Cain and one by Reid and inspected them. "There," she said, "in that window to the right of the back door of the Lockwood house."

I took the pictures from her and looked at the window, going back and forth between the Reid photo and the Cain photo until I finally saw what she saw. The window to the right of the back door had a set of mini-blinds covering it from top to bottom. In the Reid picture the blinds fell to the bottom of the window. In the later picture, the one taken by Cain, the blinds had been lifted a few inches. I pulled the image closer and saw what looked like the shape of a head and maybe a face peering through the gap.

"What the hell?" I said. "Who is that?"

"That's a good question," she said. "It looks like someone peeking out the bottom of the window."

"Someone was in the house?" I said. "Watching the fire?"

"That's what it looks like to me."

"Who?"

I could see Lila reaching back into her memory to conjure up the testimony of the Lockwood family. "There're only a handful of possibilities."

"More like a shop teacher's handful," I said.

"A shop teacher's handful?" Lila asked, looking puzzled.

"You know...he's missing some fingers...so there're fewer options." I forced a chuckle.

Lila rolled her eyes and went back to work. "Crystal's stepfather, Douglas Lockwood, said that he and his son were at his car dealership that evening. He was doing paperwork and Danny was detailing a car. He said that they didn't get home until after the fire had been put out."

I added what I remembered. "Crystal's mom worked the late shift at Dillard's Café," I said.

"That's right," Lila added, as if showing off her superior grasp of the details. "Her boss, Woody, confirmed it."

"Her boss, Woody? You're making that up."

"Look it up," she smiled.

"That leaves the boyfriend, what's-his-name?"

"Andrew Fisher," she said. "He testified that he brought Crystal home after school, drove through the alley, dropped her off, and left."

"So where does that leave us?" I said.

Lila thought for a minute and then counted on her fingers. "I see four possibilities: first, that's not really someone peeking out the window, but I have to believe what I see, so I'm discarding that one.

"I see a peeker, too," I said.

 "Second, it's Carl Iverson—"

"Why would Carl kill her at his house and then watch the fire from the Lockwood house?"

"I didn't say these were probabilities—just possibilities. It is possible that Carl went to the Lockwood's house after he started the fire. Maybe he knew about the diary and wanted to find it. Although it makes no sense for him to start the fire before looking for the diary."

"No sense at all," I said.

"Third, there's a mystery man, someone who the police never thought about, someone who isn't anywhere in this box of files."

"And fourth?"

"And fourth, someone lied to the police."

"Someone like...Andrew Fisher?"

"It's a possibility," Lila said with a defiant exhale. I could tell that she wanted to hold firm to her belief that Carl Iverson murdered Crystal Hagen, but I could also see her trying on these new clothes, slipping into the possibility that something had gone terribly wrong thirty years ago. We sat in silence for a while, unsure of what to make of this revelation, neither of us mentioning the tremor we felt pulse through the ground beneath our feet. It was as though we both saw the crack in the dam take shape, but we didn't understand its ramifications. It would not be long before that crack gaped open, releasing its torrent.

CHAPTER 22

By the time I returned to Hillview, I had fully recovered from my confession about my grandfather's death, and I felt rejuvenated by the mystery of the photographs. Carl owed me a confession—at least that is how I saw it. I beat myself up telling him my story, and now he had to answer some real questions.

He looked healthier than I had ever seen him look. He wore a red flannel shirt in place of the dull blue robe, and his hollow cheeks sported a fresh shave. He smiled a tepid smile, the kind of smile you put on when you run into an ex-girlfriend at a party. I think he knew where we were going to go. It was his turn to open up. My writing assignment had a mid-term paper coming due; I had to write about a major turning point in Carl's life, and I needed to have it to the professor in a week. The time had come to unbury his dead, and he knew it.

"Hello, Joe." Carl waved me to the chair beside him. "Look at that," he said, pointing out the window. I scanned the random balconies of the apartment across the way, seeing nothing had changed.

"What?" I asked.

"Snow," he said. "It's snowing."

I'd seen the snow falling lightly on my drive down, but I'd taken no notice other than to wonder if my car would last through another Minnesota winter. My car's body had gotten so perforated from decay that water from the wet street soaked the carpeting in the trunk after every rain, filling the car with the smell of stale washcloths. Luckily for me, there hadn't been enough snow to accumulate yet. "You're happy because it's snowing?" I said.

"I spent thirty years in prison, much of that time in segregation. I rarely got to watch the snow fall. I love snow." He followed individual flakes as they floated past the window, rose in a curving breeze, and then fell again, disappearing into the grass. I gave him a few minutes of peace and allowed him to enjoy the snowfall for the moment. Eventually, it was Carl that started our conversation.

"Virgil stopped by this morning," he said. "He tells me you and he had quite a talk."

"We did."

"And what did Virgil have to say?"

I pulled the small recorder out of my backpack and placed it on the arm of my chair, close enough to pick up Carl's voice. "He says you're an innocent man. He says you didn't kill Crystal Hagen."

Carl pondered that statement for a moment and then asked. "Do you believe him?"

"I read your court file," I said. "I read the trial transcript and Crystal's diary."

"I see," Carl said. He stopped looking out the window and instead stared at the dingy carpet in front of him. "Did Virgil tell you why he believed so strongly in my innocence?"

"He told me the story of how you saved his life in Vietnam. He said you ran headlong into a barrage of enemy bullets—knelt down between him and the people trying to kill him. He said you stayed there until the VC were pushed back."

"You gotta love that Virgil." Carl chuckled under his breath.

"Why?" I asked.

"He'll go to his grave believing that I'm innocent because of what happened that day, even though he's got the story all wrong."

"You didn't save his life?"

"Oh, I suppose I did save his life, but that's not why I charged that position."

"I don't understand."

Carl's smile turned a shade more melancholy as he thought about that day in Vietnam. "I was Catholic back then," he said. "My upbringing forbade suicide. It was one of those sins that could never be forgiven. The priest said that if you killed yourself you went straight to hell, no questions asked. The Bible also says that there's no greater sacrifice than to give one's life for one's brother. And Virgil was my brother."

"So when you saw Virgil go down that day—"

"I saw it as my chance. I would get in front of Virgil and take the bullet that was meant for him. It was kind of like killing two birds with one stone. I could save Virgil's life and end mine all at the same time."

"It didn't quite work out, did it?" I said, prodding him on.

"That's the messed up part of it all," he said. "Instead of getting my head shot off they gave me medals, a Purple Heart and a Silver Star. Everyone thought I was being brave. I just wanted to die. You see, Virgil's belief in me, his loyalty to me, is based on a lie."

"So the only person who believes that you are innocent is wrong?" I asked, sliding into my intended conversation with an easy subtlety. The snow outside had grown from a light flurry into a snowfall worthy of a snow globe, large wet flakes the size of popcorn kernels swirling in circles. I had asked the question I wanted to ask and received silence instead of an answer. So I watched the snow, determined not to speak again, giving Carl the time he needed to sort through his thoughts and find my answer.

"You're asking me if I murdered Crystal Hagen," he said finally.

"I'm asking if you murdered her, or killed her, or in any way caused her to no longer be alive. Yes, that's what I'm asking."

I could hear a clock somewhere behind me ticking away the seconds as he paused again. "No," he said, his voice barely more than a whisper. "I didn't."

I dropped my head in disappointment. "The day I met you—the day you preached all that bullshit about being honest—you told me you were both a killer and a murderer. Remember? You said killing people was not the same as murdering them and you had done both. I thought this was your dying declaration, your chance to come clean. And now you're telling me that you didn't cause her death in any way?"

"I don't expect you to believe me," he said. "Hell, no one's believed me, not even my own lawyer."

"I read the file, Carl. I read the diary. You bought a gun that day. She called you a pervert because you were always watching her."

"I am well aware of the evidence, Joe," he said, speaking his words with the patience of a glacier. "I know what they used against me in court. I've relived the telling of that story every day for the past thirty years, but that doesn't change the fact that I didn't murder her. I have no way to prove that point to you or anyone else. I'm not even going to try to prove it. I'm going to tell you the truth. You can believe it or not. It doesn't matter to me."

"What about the other story from Vietnam?" I asked.

Carl shot me a look of faint surprise, then, as if to call my bluff, he said, "What story would that be?"

"Virgil said it's your story to tell. He said it proves you didn't kill Crystal Hagen."

Carl sank back into his wheelchair. He put his fingers to his lips, his hand trembling slightly. There was another story; I could see that now, so I pressed on. "You said you'd tell me the truth Carl. It can't be the truth unless it's the whole story. I want to know everything."

Once again, Carl looked past the window, past the snow, and past the apartment balconies. "I'll tell you about Vietnam," he said. "You can decide what it proves or doesn't prove. But I promise you, it will be the truth."

For the next two hours I didn't speak; I barely breathed. I listened to Carl Iverson go back in his memory—back to Vietnam. When he had finished, I stood, shook his hand, and thanked him. Then I went home and wrote that part of Carl Iverson's story that marked the turning point of his life.

CHAPTER 23

Joe Talbert
English 317
Biography: Turning point assignment

On 23 September, 1967, Pfc. Carl Iverson stepped foot on foreign soil for the first time in his life, stepping off the Lockheed C-141 troop transport in Da Nang, Republic of Vietnam. In a temporary barrack used to house replacement troops, he met another FNG—Fucking New Guy—by the name of Virgil Gray from Baudette, Minnesota. With Carl hailing from South St. Paul, they were practically neighbors, never mind that the distance between Baudette and South St. Paul was the equivalent of driving through six states on the east coast. As luck would have it, they were assigned to the same platoon and sent to the same fire base, a dusty hilltop with the aesthetics of a baboon's ass, on the northwest edge of the Que Son Valley.

Carl's squad leader, a short, foul-mouthed E-6 named Gibbs hid some serious psychological scars behind a mask of cruelty. He seethed with contempt for officers and enlisted men alike, criticizing orders and treating FNGs like plague-carrying rats. He reserved the

brunt of his brutality for the Vietnamese:
the gooks. They were the source of all things
bad in Gibbs's world, and the half measures
taken by the brass toward their eradication
picked at Gibbs.

When Carl and Virgil arrived at their new
home, Gibbs took them aside to explain that
President Johnson's war of attrition meant
that "we had to kill more of them than they
could kill of us." It was a strategy that
relied upon body counts. The generals winked
at the colonels, who gave a nudge to the
majors and the captains, who whispered to
the lieutenants, who gave a nod to the ser-
geants, who, in turn, gave standing orders to
the grunts. "If you see a gook running away,"
Gibbs said, "they're either VC or a VC sympathizer. Either way, don't stand there with
your dick in your hand. You shoot the little
bastard."

After four months in country Carl had seen
enough war to last a lifetime. He'd set up
ambushes, watched VC soldiers dissolve into a
vapor of blood when he clicked the detonator
of a Claymore mine, and held the hand of a
guy, whose name he didn't know, as the man
cried out his last breath, his legs ripped
away from his waist by a Bouncing Betty.
Carl had grown used to the constant buzz of
mosquitoes, but not the random mortars that
Charlie liked to throw at them in the middle
of the night. He celebrated his first snow-
less Christmas crawling down the throat of a
spider hole.

The crack in Carl Iverson's world, one that would cause him to want to die in Vietnam, began on a peaceful winter morning in early February 1968. Light clouds covered the horizon in advance of the sunrise, the stillness of the surrounding valley belying the ugliness of coming events. The brilliance of that sky reminded Carl of a morning he'd spent at his grandfather's cabin in the north woods, a morning long ago when the notion of killing or being killed held no place in Carl's life.

The fighting had weighed Carl down, made him feel old. He leaned back against a pile of sandbags, tossed a cigarette butt into a shell casing the size of a thermos, lit another cigarette, and watched the sunrise.

"Hey, Hoss," Virgil said as he tromped down the dirt path.

"Hey, Virg." Carl kept his eyes on the horizon, watching the amber slowly sift out of the sky.

"Whatcha lookin' at?"

"Lake Ada."

"Come again?"

"I saw that same sunrise coming up over Lake Ada when I was sixteen. I was sittin' on the back porch of my grandpa's cabin. I swear it was the same red sky."

"You're a long ways from Lake Ada, Hoss."

"Roger that. In every way possible."

Virgil sat down next to Carl. "Don't let it get to you, man. We're wheels up in eight months. That's gonna be no time. Then we're outta here. We'll be di di mau."

Carl settled back on his sandbags and took a drag off his cigarette. "Can't you feel it, Virg? Can't you feel things slipping?"

"Feel what slipping, Hoss?"

"I don't know how to explain it," Carl said. "It's like every time I go into that jungle I feel like I'm standing on a line, a line I know I shouldn't cross. And there's this screaming in my head, like some banshee whirling around me, pulling me, taunting me to step over that line. I know if I cross it, I become Gibbs. I'd say fuck 'em, they're just gooks, so fuck 'em all."

"Yeah," Virgil said. "I know. I feel it, too. The day Levitz bought the farm, I wanted to lay waste to every butter head in the province."

"Levitz?"

"The guy that got cut in half by that Betty."

"Oh . . . that was his name? I didn't know."

"But Hoss, once you go there you don't come back," Virgil said. "That sixteen-year-old kid on Grandpa's porch, watching the sunrise, won't be there no more."

"Sometimes I wonder if he's there now."

Virgil turned his face so that Carl could see the seriousness in his eyes. "We don't have a vote on being here," Virgil said, "and for the most part we don't have a vote on how we leave. But we do have control of how much of our soul we leave behind in this mess. Don't ever forget that. We do still have some choices."

Carl held out his hand, and Virgil gripped

it tightly. "You got that right partner," Carl said. "We need to get outta here with our shit intact."

"That's all we need to do," Virgil said.

Another pair of boots kicked down the path from the latrine toward their pile of sandbags. "Hey guys," hollered Tater Davis.

Davis, a true Tennessee volunteer, had joined the company just after Christmas and had attached himself to Virgil like an orphaned duck. A little fellow, Tater had peach skin blotted with freckles and ears that stuck out on the side of his face like one of those Mr. Potato Head toys. His parents had named him Ricky, but Virgil called him Potato Head. It stuck throughout the platoon, until one day when Ricky held his ground in a bad firefight, after that he became simply Tater.

"Cap'n say we're fixin' to di di soon," he said.

"Don't worry, Tater, they won't leave without you," Carl said.

"Yeah," Virgil added, "Cap knows they can't win the war without you."

Tater grinned a goofy, high-cheeked smile. "Whad Cap'n mean when he says we're fixin ta go ta Injun country today?" Tater asked.

Carl and Virgil exchanged a knowing glance. "Didn't you study history in school?" Virgil said.

"I dropped outta school. Tweren't nuttin they had to say that I cared to hear."

"You ever heard of General Sheridan or Mackenzie?" Carl asked.

Tater gave a blank stare.

"What about Custer before he had that unfortunate incident at Little Bighorn?" Virgil added.

Nothing registered.

Carl said, "Well let's just say that before the west was won, there was this whole other group of people living there, and we had to get them to leave."

"Yeah, but what's that got to do with Vietnam?" Tater said.

"Well, the Colonel decided that we need to expand our free-fire zone," Vigil said. "The only problem with that is there's this village—we're calling it Oxbow—we gotta move that village so it's outside the free-fire zone. I mean you can't have a village inside of a free-fire zone. The whole point of a free-fire zone is to be able to shoot anything that moves."

"So we're fixin' to move 'em out?" Tater said.

"We're encouraging them to find a better location for their village," Carl said.

"Kinda like we did with the Indians," Virgil added.

Carl took a last drag from his cigarette, dropped it into the 105 casing, and stood up. "We probably ought not keep the big dogs waiting." The three men hoisted rucksacks onto their backs, slung their M16s over their shoulders, and headed toward the sound of the first helicopter rotors breaking the morning calm.

The Hueys made quick work of getting the soldiers to the landing zone, sweeping in fast and low, skidding to a stop at the edge of a field where water buffalo mixed shoulder to shoulder with yellow cows. About a hundred yards upstream stood a small hooch with a lean-to for a manger. Another hundred yards beyond that was the collection of huts that made up the hamlet code-named Oxbow.

"You two on me." Gibbs pointed at Carl and Virgil. "The rest of first squad take to the road. Clear out everything on the way. Assemble the gooks in the center of Oxbow and wait for Lieutenant Maas."

Gibbs led Carl and Virgil toward the hooch in the field, the one with the manger, while the rest of the squad headed down the dirt road that led to Oxbow. As they reached the halfway point between the LZ and the hooch, a patch of elephant grass at the edge of the field shook with life. Carl readied the stock of his weapon against his shoulder and drew down on the moving grass.

"Fire, Iverson!" Gibbs called out.

Carl squeezed his finger against the trigger but then eased up. A bulb of black hair bounced through the tall grass running toward the hooch.

"He's evading!" Gibbs yelled. "God dammit fire!"

Carl squeezed the trigger again, but again released it as a teenage girl charged out of the elephant grass and scrambled for her home.

"It's just a girl, Sarge," Carl said, lowering his weapon.

"I gave you an order."

"She's civilian."

"She's evading, so that means she's VC."

"Sarge, she's running home."

Gibbs charged at Carl. "Iverson, I gave you a goddamn order. You ever disobey my command again, I'll put a bullet through your head. You hear me?" Tobacco juice dripped from the corners of his mouth as he spat his fury at Carl. The girl, of no more than fifteen years, made it to her hooch, and Carl could hear her talking to someone inside in that strange broken Vietnamese tongue he had heard so many times, like a familiar song with indiscernible lyrics. Gibbs turned his attention to the hooch and considered it for a moment.

"You two go shoot those cows," Gibbs yelled. "Then burn the barn. I'll handle the hooch."

Virgil and Carl looked at each other. There were some pages of the field manual that were worthless in the field, except maybe to wipe your ass with. But there were some instructions that demanded respect. One of those rules to respect was to never clear a hut alone.

"Sarge?" Virgil asked.

"Now, dammit!" Gibbs barked at Virgil. "I ain't gonna have trouble with you, too, am I? I gave you an order. Now go shoot those cows."

"Yes, Sir."

Carl and Virgil walked to the field, raised their rifles, and started firing into the heads of the unsuspecting beasts. In less than a minute the cows were dead, and Carl turned his attention toward the hooch. In the distance he could see the rest of the squad rousting villagers from their huts, marching them down the dirt road, herding them toward the center of the village. Gibbs was nowhere to be seen.

"Somethin' ain't right," Carl said.

"Where's Sarge?" Virgil answered.

"That's what I mean. It shouldn't take this long."

The two men moved toward the hooch, their M16s at the ready. Virgil took up a position to cover Carl as Carl crept up to the door, being careful to step on soft grass to avoid the crunch of sand on the hard-packed dirt. He steadied his breathing, listening to muffled grunting coming from the other side of the thatched wall. Carl nodded to himself as he counted down from three and charged through the door.

"Jesus Christ!" Carl slid as he stopped his charge, pulling the muzzle of his rifle up, and almost stumbling backward through the opened door. "Sarge! What the hell?"

Gibbs had the girl pinned down, her knees on the plank floor, her torso pressed down on a rickety bamboo bed, most of her clothing ripped away. Gibbs knelt behind her, his fatigues bunched down around his thighs, his hairy, pale butt cheeks flexing with each thrust.

"I'm interrogating a VC sympathizer," he said over his shoulder.

Gibbs had her arms wrenched behind her back, holding her wrists with one hand, leaning on her, holding her against the bed with his weight. She struggled to breathe as his girth flattened her lungs. In the corner of the hut, an old man lay lifeless on his side, a rut the size of a rifle butt cutting across his nose and left cheek bone, blood trickling from his empty eye socket.

With an angry flourish, Gibbs finished his irruption and pulled his pants back up. The girl did not move.

"Your turn," he said to Carl.

Carl couldn't speak. He couldn't move.

Gibbs took a step toward Carl. "Iverson, I'm tellin' you to interrogate this VC sympathizer. That's an order."

Carl fought to keep from retching. The girl lifted her head enough to turn and look at Carl, her lips trembling with fear, or rage, or both.

"Did you hear me?" Gibbs shouted, pulling his service revolver from its holster and ratcheting a round into the chamber. "I said that's an order."

Carl stared at the girl's face, at the hopelessness in her eyes. He heard Gibbs chamber the round in his 45, but Carl paid it no heed. He would defy the banshee. He would leave Vietnam with his soul, or die with it intact.

.

"No, sir," Carl said.

Gibbs's eyes went red. He stabbed the muzzle of the gun into the side of Carl's head. "You disobeyed a direct order. You're a dead man."

"Sarge, what are you doing?" Virgil yelled from the doorway.

Gibbs looked at Virgil, then back at Carl.

"Sarge, this ain't the way to handle it," Virgil said. "Think it through."

Gibbs held the gun against Carl's temple, huffing through his flared nostrils like a horse ridden hard. He stepped back from Carl, the gun still aimed at Carl's head. "You're right," he said. "There is a better way to handle this." He holstered his side arm and pulled a knife from the scabbard strapped to his thigh. He turned to the girl, who still lay naked, half on the bed, half on the floor. Grabbing a fistful of her hair, he yanked her to her knees.

"Next time I give you an order to shoot a gook . . ." He pulled the knife across her throat, cutting deep into the gristle and tissue, the blood spurting onto Carl's boots. "You'd better goddamn obey me." The girl jerked and twitched as blood filled her lungs. Her eyes rolled up into her forehead, and Gibbs let her limp body fall to the floor. "Now burn this hooch." Gibbs stepped over the body and put his face into Carl's face. "That's an order."

Gibbs left the hut, but Carl couldn't move.

"C'mon, Hoss." Virgil pulled Carl backward

out of the hooch. "This ain't our Alamo. We gotta keep our shit intact. Remember?"

Carl rubbed his eyes on the sleeves of his shirt. Virgil headed to the manger with his cigarette lighter in his hand.

To the north, the entire village had been set aflame; a line of villagers, now refugees, marched like condemned prisoners down the dirt road that would lead them out of the free-fire zone. Carl pulled his zippo from his pocket and touched it to the dried palm fronds and elephant grass of the hut. Within a couple seconds, flame engulfed the thatch roof, the smoke rolling off as thick as water.

Carl stepped back from the hut as the ravenous fire licked down from the roof, covering the two bodies on the floor. That's when he saw something that filled his chest with ice. The girl's hand opened; her fingers reached out, beckoning to Carl. They trembled as the girl strained to reach out. Then they curled back into her palm as the fiery roof crashed down on top of her.

CHAPTER 24

I watched Lila as she read my assignment, her face wincing as she read about Gibbs raping the girl, her eyes looking up at me in disbelief after reading about the girl's hand moving as the burning hut fell in on her.

"You can see why Virgil was so adamant that Carl is innocent," I said.

"Is this true?" she held up my assignment.

"Every word," I said. "Virgil confirmed it. He was there. Said Carl was never the same after that day."

"Wow," Lila whispered. "Did you notice that the girl in Vietnam was burned in her hut just like Crystal was burned in that shed?"

"That's what you got out of that?" I said.

"It seems more than coincidental, don't you think?"

"His sergeant put a gun to his head. He was willing to die rather than rape that girl. That's what the story is about. How could that man in Vietnam be the same man who killed Crystal Hagen? If he's really a rapist and a murderer, he would have given in to the dark side when he was in Vietnam."

"You think he's innocent?" Lila asked, her tone more inquisitive than condemning.

"I don't know," I said. "I'm starting to. I mean, it's possible, isn't it?"

Lila considered my question for a long time before answering, rereading the last part of my assignment, the part where Carl refused Gibbs's order. Then she put the paper down. "Let's just assume, for the sake of argument, that Carl is not the killer. What does that mean?"

I thought about her question for a moment. "It means that someone else did it."

"Of course it means that," she said. "But who?"

"It could be anyone," I said. "It could be some random guy walking by that saw her home alone."

"I don't think so," she said.

"Why not?"

"The diary," she said. "I suppose it's possible that some random guy killed her. But if the diary holds any meaning, Crystal was being threatened. Some guy was forcing her to do stuff. That means that Crystal knew her attacker."

"If it's not Carl," I said, "and it's not some random guy, then . . ."

"If it is not Carl," Lila said, "and that's a big if, then that leaves Doug the stepfather, Danny the stepbrother, and Andy the boyfriend." She counted the names off on her fingers. "It could still be someone we don't know, someone that Crystal knew but didn't name in her diary—unless it's in code."

"We have the file," I said. "We have all the evidence in the case. Maybe we can figure it out."

Lila turned on the couch to face me, curling her feet up under her butt. "This case was investigated by cops, detectives, people who do this for a living. We're not gonna figure anything out. It's been thirty years."

"Hypothetically speaking," I said." If we were going to look into Crystal's murder, where would we begin?"

"If it were me," Lila said, "I'd begin with the boyfriend."

"Andy Fisher?"

"He was the last person to see her alive."

"What would we ask him?"

"You keep saying *we*," Lila said, an incredulous smile crossing her face. "There is no *we*. This is your firing squad."

"I don't know if you've picked up on this, but you're the smart one here," I joked.

"So, that would make you the pretty one?" she said.

"No, you're that one, too," I said, watching for her reaction—a smile, maybe a wink, some sign that she heard my compliment. Nothing.

I'd been dancing around Lila ever since I first saw her in the hallway, trying to get past the wall she had put up, the wall that kept me at arm's length, the one she tore down for Jeremy the first day they met. I wanted to see her laugh and have fun with me like she did with Jeremy. But all my subtle compliments and attempts at humor fizzled like wet firecrackers. I had been contemplating a more direct approach, one that would ensure a response one way or another; I was going to ask Lila out on a date. As I joked about her being pretty, it dawned on me that now would be as good a time as any. I stood and walked to the kitchen, having no reason to do so other than to execute a cowardly delay tactic. Once I had a little distance between us, I stumbled into my speech.

"You know . . . I've been thinking . . . I mean . . . I think we should go out." I blurted it out, catching her by surprise, her lips parting as if to speak, then pausing, as if she was unsure of what to say.

"Like, on a date?" she said.

"We don't have to call it a date."

"Joe, I'm not . . ." She looked down at the coffee table, her shoulders slumping forward, her fingers picking at the material of her sweatpants. "This was supposed to be just a spaghetti dinner, remember? Nothing more than that."

"We can go to an Italian restaurant. It'll still be just a spaghetti dinner."

Silence filled the room. I noticed that I was holding my breath as I waited for Lila to respond. Finally, she looked at me and said, "I can get extra credit if I go see a play for my American Lit. class. It's playing the weekend of Thanksgiving. I can get two tickets for that Friday. This is not a date; it's just extra credit. That's the deal. Are you okay with that?"

"I love plays," I said. In truth, I had never actually seen a play other than skits and vignettes that the drama club put on at the pep rallies back in high school. "What's the play called?"

"*The Glass Menagerie*," she said.

"Great," I said. "It's a date . . . I mean . . . it's not a date."

CHAPTER 25

W e found Andy Fisher through an alumni directory on his high school's Facebook page. Andy, who now went by the more adult name of Andrew, had inherited an insurance agency from his father, operating an office in a strip mall on the east side of Golden Valley, Minnesota.

Andrew Fisher had not aged well. His boyish locks were gone, replaced by a monk-like bald spot that covered most of his crown, spreading from the back of his head to the front, leaving a thin wisp of hair that curved along the top of his forehead like an old picket fence. His waistline bulged against an overworked leather belt, and dark lines formed permanent crescents under his eyes. He sat in a cheaply paneled office, its walls lined with undersized hunting and fishing trophies.

When we walked in, Andrew came into the empty reception area to greet us, his hand thrust out in front of him to shake mine. "What can I do you for?" he said, with the gusto of a salesman. "No wait, let me guess." He glanced out the plate glass window at my rusted Accord and smiled. "You're looking to buy a new car and need an insurance quote."

"Actually," I said, "we were hoping you'd talk to us about Crystal Hagen."

"Crystal Hagen?" The smile vanished from his face. "Who are you?"

"I'm Joe Talbert. I'm a student at the U., and this is . . . um . . ."

"I'm his classmate, Lila," she said.

I continued, "We're doing a story on Crystal's death."

"Why?" he said. "That was so long ago." He looked almost sad for a moment, then he shook the memories away. "I've put that all behind me. I don't like talking about it."

"It's important," I said.

"How can it be important?" he said. "It's ancient history. They caught the guy: Carl Iverson. He lived next door to her. Now I think you should leave." He turned his back on us and started walking into his office.

"What if we told you that we think Carl Iverson might be innocent," Lila said, blurting out the words without any forethought. We glanced at each other, and she shrugged. Fisher stopped in the doorway to his office, took a deep breath, but didn't turn toward us.

"All we want is a little bit of your time," I said.

"Why won't this ever go away?" Andrew whispered to himself as he walked the rest of the way into his office. We didn't leave. He sat at his desk, surrounded by dead animal heads, not making eye contact with us. We waited. Then, without looking up, he lifted two fingers and waved us in. We entered and sat in the client chairs across the desk from him, not sure how to begin the conversation. Then he spoke. "I still have nights when I see her in my dreams, the way she was back then—sweet . . . young. Then the dream turns dark, and we're at the cemetery. She's sinking into the ground and calling my name. That's when I wake up in a cold sweat."

"She calls your name?" I said. "Why? You didn't do anything wrong? Did you?"

He looked at me coldly. "That case messed up my life."

I know I should have been more sympathetic, but to hear this guy moan "poor me" kind of rubbed me the wrong way. "It kinda messed up Crystal Hagen's life, too," I said. "Don't you think?"

"Son," Andrew held up his finger and thumb to mark an inch. "You're about this close to getting your butt kicked out of here."

"That must have been a terrible time for you," Lila interrupted, speaking in a comforting tone, cognizant that honey will better attract the bear.

"I was sixteen years old," Andrew said. "It didn't matter that I didn't do anything wrong. People treated me like a leper. Even though they arrested that Iverson guy, there were all these rumors floating around that I killed her." The muscles in Andrew's jaw twitched as a flash of emotion passed through his cheeks. "The day they buried her, I went to toss a handful of dirt on the coffin . . . after they lowered her casket down. Her mother shot me a cold stare that froze me in my tracks—like Crystal's death was my fault." The corners of Andrew's mouth dipped down as if he were going to start crying. He took a moment to gather himself. "I've never forgotten that look—the accusation in her eyes. It's what I remember most when I think about the day we buried Crystal."

"So people thought you killed Crystal," I said.

"People are idiots," he said. "Besides, if I was gonna kill anybody, it would've been that damned defense lawyer."

"The defense lawyer?" I said.

"He's the one who fed the rumor that I killed her. He told the jury that I did it. That son of a bitch. It was in the papers. I was sixteen for god's sake."

"You were the last one to see her alive," I said. Andrew narrowed his gaze at me and for a second I thought I had blown it. "We read the trial testimony," I added.

"Then you know that I dropped her off at her home and drove away," he said. "She was alive when I left."

"That's right," Lila said. "You dropped her off, and if I recall, you said she was home alone."

"I never said she was alone; I said I didn't think anyone else was home. There's a difference. The place seemed empty to me, that's all."

"Do you know where her stepfather was?" Lila asked. "Or her stepbrother?"

"Now how would I know that?" he said.

Lila looked at her notes, pretending to refresh her memory. "Well, according to Doug Lockwood's testimony—that's Crystal's stepfa-ther—he and Danny were at his used car dealership when Crystal was being murdered."

"That sounds right," he said. "The old man ran a used car lot. He licensed Crystal's mom and Danny both as dealers so that they could drive any car on the lot. All they had to do was put dealer plates on the car."

"Danny was a dealer, too?"

"Only on paper. As soon as he turned eighteen he got his dealer's license. He was one of those kids on the cusp. His birthday was near that cutoff where he could either be the youngest kid in his class or they could hold him back a year and he'd be the oldest kid in his class. They held him back." Andrew leaned back in his chair. "Personally, I always thought Danny was an ass."

"Why?" I asked.

"Well, to begin with, that family argued a lot. Crystal's mom and stepdad were constantly yelling at each other, and it was usually about Danny. Danny didn't like his dad marrying Crystal's mom. The way Crystal told it, Danny treated her mom like shit—kind of went out of his way to cause fights. And then there were the cars."

"Cars?" Lila asked.

"Because Danny's old man ran that car lot, Danny got to pick any car on the lot to drive to school. When Danny was a senior his dad flat out gave him a car—this cherry Grand Prix—as an early Christmas present. It was a great car, but . . . I mean . . . it's one thing to act cool in a car you bought and fixed up yourself, because that says something about you. It's your car—you earned it. But he drove around like he was hot shit in a car that his daddy gave him. I don't know. He was just an ass that way."

"What was the stepdad like?" Lila asked.

"A real wing nut," Andrew said. "He used to act all religious, but it seemed to me that he used the Bible to back any argument he wanted to make. There was this one time when Crystal's mom found out that the old man had been visiting a strip club. He tells her about how Jesus hung out with prostitutes and tax collectors—like that made it okay for him to be tucking dollar bills into G-strings."

"How did he and Crystal get along?" I asked.

Andrew gave a polite shudder like he'd just bit into an under-cooked trout. "She hated him," he said. "He used to belittle her using lines from the Bible. Most of the time, she had no idea what he was saying. One time, he told her that she should be thankful that he was not Jephthah. We looked that one up."

"Jephthah . . . That's from the Bible?"

"Yeah, from the Book of Judges. He sacrificed his daughter to God so that he could win a battle. I mean, who the hell says stuff like that to a teenaged girl?"

"Did you ever talk to Danny or to Doug about what happened that day?" Lila asked.

"I never talked to anyone about it. I gave a statement to the cops and then I tried to pretend it didn't happen. I didn't talk about it again until the trial."

"Did you watch the trial?" I asked.

"No. I did my testimony and left." He looked down at the desk the way Jeremy looks away from me when he doesn't want to answer a question.

"You didn't go back to watch any of it?" I pressed.

"I saw the closing arguments," he said. "I skipped school to watch the end of the trial. I thought the jury would have a verdict right away like they do on TV."

I tried to remember if I'd read the closing argument in the transcript. "I assume the prosecutor talked about Crystal's diary in his closing."

The blood suddenly drained from Andrew's cheeks, his face turning the color of plumber's putty. "I remember the diary," he said, his voice now lowered to a whisper. "I didn't even know Crystal kept a diary until that day when the prosecutor summed everything up for the jury."

"The prosecutor argued that Mr. Iverson was making Crystal do things to him . . . sexually, because he caught you two . . . you know."

"I remember," Andrew said.

"Did Crystal ever talk to you about that?" I asked. "About getting caught or Mr. Iverson threatening her? I mean that never made much sense to me. The prosecutor went on and on about it. The jury bought it, but you were there. Is that what happened?"

Andrew leaned forward, rubbing his palms into his eyes, his fingers extending up to his bald head. He slowly dragged his fingers down his face, over his eyes, down his cheeks; then he folded them together to form a steeple on his lips. He looked back and forth between Lila and me, contemplating whether to tell us what weighed so heavily on his mind. "Remember me telling you about waking up in cold sweats," he said finally.

"Yeah," I said.

"It's because of that diary," he said. "The prosecutor got it wrong. He got it all wrong."

Lila leaned forward. "Tell us," she said in a sweet, consoling voice, coaxing Andrew to unburden his soul.

"I didn't think it was important; I mean... it shouldn't have been important. I didn't know until I went to the trial and watched the closing argument, what they said about Mr. Iverson catching us: Crystal and me..." Andrew stopped talking. He was still looking in our direction, but he averted his eyes as if he was ashamed of whatever secret he had been keeping.

"What about Crystal and you?" Lila said.

"It's true," Andrew said. "He did catch us. Crystal was creeped out by it. But at the trial the prosecutor made such a big deal out of it, saying that Crystal thought her life would be ruined because of us getting caught having... well, you know. He told the jury that she made a diary entry on September twenty-first, saying that she was having a very bad day. He said she was freaking out because Mr. Iverson was blackmailing her or something. That entry had nothing to do with us getting caught having sex."

"How do you know that?" I asked.

"The twenty-first of September was my mother's birthday. Crystal called me that night. She wanted me to meet her. I didn't. I couldn't. We were having a party for my mom's birthday. Crystal was going out of her mind."

"Crystal told you why she was freaking out?" I asked.

"Yes." Andrew stopped talking, turned his chair around, pulled a tumbler and a small bottle of Scotch out of the buffet behind him, poured three fingers of liquor into the glass, and drank half of it. Then he put the glass and bottle down on his desk, folded his hands together, and continued.

"Crystal's stepdad had some really great cars on his lot, one in particular: a 1970 Pontiac GTO, bronze with a spoiler on the back. It was a beautiful car." He took another drink of his Scotch. "One night around the middle of September, Crystal and me were talking about that car. I was telling her how I wished I could drive a car like that, how unfair my life was. You know, normal high-school stuff. And she says that we should take the GTO for a ride. She knew where her stepdad kept the spare keys to the office and where the car keys were kept in the office. All we had to do was return everything to where it was. So we take my crappy Ford Galaxy 500 to her stepdad's lot, and it was just like she said. We found the keys to the GTO and took it for a spin."

"You were a sophomore?" Lila said.

"Yeah. I'm also one of those cusp babies, like Danny. I got my license that August after I turned sixteen."

"Car theft?" I said. "That's what she was upset about?"

"It gets worse," he said. He took another deep breath, letting it go with a sigh. "Like I said, I only had my license for about a month, and I never drove a car with that much power. I couldn't help racing from stoplight to stoplight. We were having a great time until . . ." He finished his drink, licking the last few drops from his lips. "I was flying down Central Avenue, probably doing seventy miles an hour—God, I was stupid. The tire blew out. I tried to hold it together, but we crossed lanes and skidded into the side of a car: a police squad car—empty— parked in front of a deli. Later, I read in the paper that the cops were in the back of the deli dealing with a break-in, so they had no idea we smashed into their car."

"Did anyone get hurt?" Lila asked.

"We weren't wearing seatbelts," Andrew said. "We both hit pretty hard. I bruised my chest on the steering wheel and Crystal went face first into the dashboard. She broke her glasses—"

"Glasses?" I said. "Crystal wore glasses? I saw the trial pictures. She wasn't wearing glasses."

"She usually wore her contacts. But sometimes her eyes would get irritated, and then she wore her glasses instead. And that's the terrible thing that freaked her out. One of her lenses popped out in the accident. We didn't realize it until later. She just grabbed her glasses from the floor after the accident, and we ran as fast as we could. By the time we realized the lens was gone, it was too late to go back. It took us about an hour to walk back to my car. I came up with an idea to break a window at the car lot to make it look like someone broke in and stole the keys to the GTO. The next day the story was on the radio and on TV. It was a big deal because we hit a cop car."

"That's what Crystal was freaking out about?" I said. "They found her lens?"

"Not just that," Andrew said. "Crystal hid the broken eyeglasses. We were going to buy her a new pair and we wanted to make sure that we got identical frames. But that day when she called me up— my mom's birthday—Crystal said that her eyeglasses were missing. She thought somebody found the proof that we stole the car and did a hit and run. That's why she was freaking out."

"Where'd she hide them? Home? School?"

"I honestly don't know. She never said. She got weird after that, sad and distant. She didn't seem to want to be around me." He paused to take another breath, to calm the emotion swelling up in his chest. "I didn't realize until I heard the closing argument—until I heard the words from her diary—that she was being . . . well . . . you know."

"And you didn't mention to anybody about the diary being misread?" Lila said.

"No." Andrew lowered his eyes.

"Why didn't you tell his attorney?" I said.

"That prick dragged my name through the mud. I'd just as soon spit on him than talk to him. You can't imagine what it was like to open a newspaper to see some defense attorney accusing you of raping and murdering your girlfriend. I had to go to therapy because of that bastard. Besides, I lettered in three sports in high school. I was good enough to get a baseball scholarship to Mankato State. If I had told anyone about stealing that car, I would've been arrested, suspended from school, kicked out of sports. I would have lost everything. That whole thing fucked me up pretty bad."

"Fucked you up?" I said, my anger bubbling through. "So let me get this straight. Rather than ruin your letter jacket, you let the jury believe a lie."

"There was a ton of evidence against that Iverson guy," Andrew said. "What'd it matter if they misunderstood the diary? I wasn't gonna stick my neck out for him. He killed my girlfriend . . . didn't he?"

Andrew looked back and forth between Lila and me, waiting for one of us to answer. We didn't say a word. We watched as he swallowed the dust from his tongue. We waited as his words echoed off the walls and came back to him, tapping his shoulder like Poe's tell-tale heart. Lila and I waited, saying nothing until finally he looked down at the top of his desk and said, "I should have told someone. I know that. I've always known that. I guess I was waiting for the right time to get this off my chest. I thought I might forget about it someday, but I didn't. I couldn't. Like I said, I still have nightmares."

CHAPTER 26

On television, people dressed in nice clothes when they attended the theater, but I didn't have any nice clothes. I had moved to college with a single duffel bag filled with jeans, shorts, and shirts, mostly collarless. So I did a pilgrimage to a second-hand store the week of the play, finding khakis and a button-down shirt to wear. I also found a pair of deck shoes, but the seam above the big toe on the right foot was torn. I poked a paperclip through the holes where the stitching had been and sealed the tear, twisting off the excess.

By 6:30 I was ready to go, although I couldn't get my palms to stop sweating. When Lila opened her door, I was astonished. A red sweater hugged her torso and waistline, showing off curves I didn't know she had, and a shiny black skirt squeezed her hips, sliding down her thighs as smooth as melting chocolate. She wore makeup, which I'd never seen her do before, her cheeks, her lips, her eyes all quietly demanding my attention. It was like washing the dust off a window that you didn't realize was dirty. I fought to keep from grinning. I wanted to grab her and squeeze her and kiss her. More than anything else, I wanted to spend time with her, walking and talking and watching a play.

"Well, don't you look nice," she said.

"Back at you." I smiled, pleased that my hand-me-downs had passed muster. "Shall we?" I said, motioning down the hall. It was a beautiful night for a walk, at least for Minnesota in late November—forty degrees, clear, no wind, no rain, no sleet, no snow—which was a good thing, since it was a ten-block walk to the Rarig Center for the play. Our path took us across Northrop Mall, the oldest and grandest part of campus, and then across the footbridge that spanned the Mississippi River.

Most of the students had gone home for the Thanksgiving break. I thought about going home to see Jeremy, but the downside always seemed to outweigh the upside. I had asked Lila why she wasn't going home for the holiday. She simply shook her head and didn't answer. Even I knew that meant to leave it alone. Besides, I chose to look at the positive—with the campus so empty, it made our walk seem all the more private, more like a date. I walked with my hands in my coat pocket, my elbow cocked out to the side just in case Lila decided to link her arm with mine. She didn't.

I didn't know a thing about *The Glass Menagerie* before that night. If I had, I might not have gone—even if that would have meant missing out on my date with Lila.

In the very first scene, this fellow named Tom walked onto the stage and started talking to us. Our seats were right in the middle of the theatre, and he seemed to pick me as a focal point for his attention from the get-go. At first, I thought that was cool, this actor saying his lines as though he was talking to me personally. As the play progressed, we met his sister, Laura, whose debilitating introversion seemed oddly familiar to me, and his mother, Amanda, who lived in a fantasy world waiting for some outside savior—a gentleman caller—to arrive and save them from themselves. I felt a trickle of sweat bead on my chest as visions of my own screwed-up little family moved on that stage.

As the first act came to an end, I heard my mother on stage as Amanda, chastising Tom, saying, "Self, self, self, is that all you ever think of?" I could see Tom pacing in his cage, the apartment, trapped there by his affection for his sister. The theatre grew warmer with each line. At intermission, I needed to get some water, so Lila and I walked to the lobby.

"Well . . . what do you think about the play so far?" she asked.

I felt a little sick in my chest, but I smiled politely. "It's marvelous," I said. "I don't know how they do it, memorizing all those lines. I could never be an actor."

"There's more to it than just memorizing lines," she said. "Don't you love the way they pull you in, make you feel the emotions?"

I took another drink of water. "It's amazing," I said. I had a lot more to say about that, but I kept those thoughts to myself.

As the lights went down for the second act, I put my hand on the armrest between us, my palm up, hoping that she might want to hold it—a forlorn hope at best. In the play, the gentleman caller showed up, and I held out hope for a happy ending. I was wrong; everything fell apart. It turned out that the gentleman caller was already engaged to marry another woman. The stage erupted in anger and recrimination, and Laura retreated back to her world of tiny glass figurines, her glass menagerie.

The actor playing Tom walked to the front of the stage, pulled the collar of his pea coat up around his neck, lit a cigarette, and told the audience how he left St. Louis, leaving his mother and sister behind. I felt my throat and chest tighten and my breath stumble. Tears began to well up in my eyes. These are just actors, I told myself. It's just a guy saying lines that he memorized. That's all. Tom lamented about how he still hears Laura's voice and sees her face in the colored glass of perfume bottles. As he spoke, I could see Jeremy looking out the front window at me the last time I drove away, not moving, not waving goodbye, his eyes accusing me, begging me not to leave.

Then the son of a bitch onstage looked directly at me and said, "Laura, I tried to leave you behind me, but I am more faithful than I intended to be."

I couldn't stop the tears from falling down my face. I didn't raise my hand to wipe them away; that would have drawn attention to my state. So I let them fall, unfettered. That's when I felt Lila's hand gently wrap into my fingers. I didn't look at her; I couldn't. She didn't look at me either. She just held my hand until the man on stage stopped talking and the pain in my chest subsided.

CHAPTER 27

After the play, Lila and I walked to Seven Corners, a hub of taverns and eateries on the West Bank of campus, named for a particularly confusing cluster of intersections. On the way there, I told her about my trip to Austin, about leaving Jeremy with my mother and Larry, and about the bruise on Jeremy's back and the blood on Larry's nose. I felt that I needed to explain why the play messed me up the way it did.

Lila said, "Do you think Jeremy's safe?"

"I don't know," I said. But I think I did know. That was the problem. That was the reason that last scene of the play tore me up the way it did. "Was I wrong to leave home?" I asked. "Was I wrong to go to school?"

Lila didn't answer.

"I mean, I can't stay home forever. No one can ask me to do that. I have a right to live my own life, don't I?"

"You are his brother," she said. "Like it or not, that means something."

That wasn't what I wanted to hear. "Does it mean I have to give up college and everything I want in my life?"

"We all have our own baggage to deal with," she said. "Nobody gets through life unscathed."

"That's easy for you to say," I said.

She stopped walking and looked at me with an intensity normally reserved for a lover's quarrel. "That's not easy for me to say," she said. "That's not easy at all." She turned and started walking again, her cheeks getting rosy from the November chill. A cold front was on its way—one that would usher in the deep freeze of winter. We walked on in silence for a while and then she linked her arm through mine and gave my arm a squeeze. I think it was her way of telling me that she wanted to change the subject, which was fine with me.

We found a bar with a few open tables and music playing at a decibel level that would allow us to talk. I scanned the room, looking for the quietest table, and found a booth for us far from the noise. After we sat, I dug around for a topic of small talk.

"So, are you a junior?" I asked.

"No, I'm only a sophomore," she said.

"But you are twenty-one, right?"

"I took a year off before coming to college," she said.

The waitress came by to get our drink order. I ordered a Jack and Coke, and Lila ordered a 7 Up. "Oh, you're hitting the hard stuff are you?" I said.

"I don't drink," Lila said. "I used to, but not anymore."

"I feel kind of strange, drinking alone."

"I'm not a temperance chick," she said. "I have nothing against drinking. It's just a choice I made."

As the waitress set our drinks on the table, a loud roar erupted from the corner of the bar where a table full of drunks were competing with one another to be heard in some inane debate about football. The waitress rolled her eyes. I looked over my shoulder at the group of guys pushing and jostling in that good-natured way that so often turns into a brawl after one too many drinks. The bouncer at the door had his eye on them as well. I settled back down into my booth.

After the waitress left, Lila and I launched into a discussion of the play, with Lila doing most of the talking. She was a big fan of Tennessee Williams. I sipped my drink and listened to Lila talk and then laugh. I had never seen her so animated, so passionate about anything. Her words rose and purled in a graceful arabesque and then kicked with jazz. I hadn't realized how lost I had become in our conversation until Lila abruptly stopped talking in mid-sentence, her eyes fixed on something over my left shoulder. Whatever it was, it had stunned her into silence.

"Oh, my God," came a voice from behind me. "It's Nasty Nash."

I turned to see one of the guys from the loud table standing a few

feet from our booth, his left hand holding a beer that shook as he tee-
tered. He pointed at Lila with his other hand, and in a booming voice,
called her out.

"Nasty Nash. I don't fucking believe it. Remember me?"

Lila's face had gone pale, her breathing shallow. She stared at her
glass, which she held with trembling fingertips.

"Huh? Don't remember? Maybe this will help." He put a hand
down in front of his crotch area, his palm turned down as if he were
holding a bowling ball. Then he started pumping his hips. He screwed
his face up, biting his lower lip, tipping his head back. "Oh yeah! Oh
yeah! Doing the nasty."

Lila began to shake—whether with rage or fear, I couldn't tell.

"What do you say we take a trip down memory lane?" the slob said,
looking at me and smiling. "I don't mind sharing, just ask her."

Lila stood and ran from the bar. I didn't know whether to chase
after her or give her some space. That's when the slob spoke again, this
time to me. "You better get her, dude. She's a sure thing." I felt my right
hand tighten into a fist. Then I relaxed it.

When I first started working at the Piedmont Club, a fellow
bouncer named Ronnie Gant showed me a move that he called Ronnie's rope-a-dope, which, like a magician's illusion, relied upon misdi-
rection. I rose from my seat, looked at the slob, and smiled a big hearty
smile. He was three steps away from me. I walked toward him, taking
my three steps at a casual pace, just a couple guys saying hello, my arms
outstretched in a friendly gesture. He smiled back, as if we were sharing
an inside joke. *Get him to drop his guard.*

I gave him a thumbs-up on my second step, joining him in a laugh,
my smile disarming him, distracting him. He was taller than me by
three or four inches, and he probably outweighed me by forty pounds,
which he stored mostly in his ample gut. I kept his eyes focused on
my face, his beer-addled brain focused on our apparent connection. He
didn't see my right hand slink down to my waist, cocked at the elbow.

With my third step I invaded his personal space, planting my right
foot squarely between his feet. I shot my left hand up under the slob's

right armpit, grabbed the shirt behind his shoulder blade, cocked my right arm back, and jammed my fist into his stomach with all the force I could muster. My punch landed in that soft catfish belly that every man has just below his ribcage. I hit him so hard that I could feel his rib bones wrap around my knuckles. The breath shot from his chest, his lungs exploding like a balloon. He wanted to double over, but I clutched his shirt and shoulder blade with my left hand and pulled him into me. His knees started to buckle, and I could hear the squeaking of his lungs as they fought for air.

The key to Ronnie's rope-a-dope was subtlety. If I had clocked him in the jaw, he would have fallen back making a huge fuss. His buddies at the loud table would have been on me in a flash. A couple of his friends were already watching me. But to an outsider, I looked like a Good Samaritan helping a drunk to a seat. I walked the slob to the booth where Lila and I had been sitting and plopped him down just in time to watch him puke.

His two friends started making their way toward their buddy. The bouncer also took notice of me. I mimed the international sign for drinking too much: thumb and pinky stretched out to simulate the handle of a beer stein and a wave up and down with the thumb near the lips. The bouncer nodded and started over to deal with the vomiting drunk. I wiped my sweaty palms across the thighs of my pants and walked out the door, calmly and orderly, as if I had become bored with the evening.

Once outside, I started running. The slob would soon be breathing enough to tell his friends what happened. They would, no doubt, come after me in numbers far from fair. I headed for the Washington Avenue footbridge that connected the West Bank of campus to the East Bank. Before I could turn a corner, two guys came out of the bar and saw me. I had about a one-block head start. One of the guys was built like an offensive tackle, big and powerful and slow as mud. His friend, however, had some legs, a tight end maybe or a linebacker in high school. He might be trouble. He screamed something that I couldn't make out over the whistling of wind and pounding of blood in my ears.

I saw right away that I wouldn't make it across the footbridge; the tight end would catch me in that long straightaway for sure. Besides, Lila would be on the footbridge by now. If they saw her in the bar, they might recognize her and go after her instead. I ran for a cluster of buildings around Wilson Library, reaching the first building, the Humphrey Center, with only a couple hundred feet between me and the tight end. I had been holding back just a bit as I ran, letting him think I could only run so fast. When I turned the first corner, I poured it on, twisting and twining around every building I came to: around Heller Hall, then Blegen Hall, then around the Social Sciences Building and Wilson Library. By the time I made my second pass around the Social Sciences Building, I could no longer see the tight end behind me nor hear his footsteps.

I found a parking lot and ducked behind a pickup truck to wait, my lungs heaving and burning as they shoveled oxygen in and out. I lay on the asphalt to breathe and recover from my escape, peering under the truck across the mostly empty parking lot and watching for my pursuers. After ten minutes, I saw the tight end about a block away, walking up Nineteenth Avenue, making his way back toward Seven Corners and the bar. When he had gone, I took a deep breath, stood and brushed the dirt and grit from my body, and headed for the footbridge and Lila's apartment, where, hopefully, she would be waiting for me.

CHAPTER 28

I could see a dim light falling from Lila's apartment as I approached the building. I paused on the front stoop to collect myself and catch my breath after my jog home. Then I walked up the narrow staircase and down the hall to knock gently on Lila's door. No answer. "Lila," I said, through the door. "It's me, Joe." Still nothing.

I knocked again, and this time heard the unmistakable click of the deadbolt being turned back. I waited for the door to open but it didn't, so I opened the door a few inches and saw Lila sitting sideways on her couch, her back to me and her knees tucked up to her chest. She had changed out of the sweater and skirt and into a gray sweatshirt and matching sweatpants. I stepped inside her apartment, carefully closing the door behind me.

"You okay?" I asked. She didn't answer. I walked to the couch and sat behind her, putting one hand on the back of the couch, my other hand gently touching her shoulder. She shuddered slightly under my touch.

"Remember," she said, her voice shaky and weak, "how I told you I took a year off before starting college?" She took a deep breath to try to settle herself before continuing. "I went through a bad spell. Some stuff happened in high school, stuff I'm not proud of."

"You don't have to—"

"I was kind of . . . wild in high school. I used to get drunk at parties and do stupid shit. I wish I could tell you it was because I fell in with a bad crowd, but that wouldn't be true. At first it was silly stuff like dancing on tables or sitting on the guys' laps. You know—flirting. I guess I liked how they looked at me." She paused to gather up her courage, taking in a breath that fluttered as she exhaled. "Then . . . it

became more than flirting. By the time I was a junior, I had lost my vir-
ginity to a guy who told me I was beautiful. Then he told everybody
that I was easy. After that there were more guys and even more stories."

Her trembling grew to an uncontrollable shake. I wrapped my
arms around her and pulled her into me. She didn't protest, but instead
turned her face into my sleeve and cried hard. I laid my cheek against
her hair and held her while she cried. After a while the trembling subsided, and she took another deep breath.

"When I was a senior, they started calling me Nasty Nash. Not
to my face, but I heard them. And the sad thing is . . . it didn't stop
me. I'd go to parties and get drunk and wind up in some guy's bed, or
in the backseat of some piece-of-shit car. And when they were done,
they would just kick me to the curb." She rubbed the top of her arm,
kneading it the way Jeremy sometimes rubs his knuckles when he's
upset. She paused again to calm her trembling voice before going on.

"Then, on the night of my graduation, I got messed up at a party.
Somebody put something in my drink. I woke up the next morning
in the backseat of my car, out in the middle of a bean field. I didn't
remember a thing. Nothing. I hurt. I knew that I'd been raped, but I
didn't know who did it or how many there were. The police found a
drug called Rohypnol in my system. It's a date-rape drug. It makes it so
that you can't fight back, and then it wipes out your memory. Nobody
else remembered anything either. No one from the party would say
how I left, or who I was with. I don't think they believed me when I
said I was raped.

"A week later someone e-mailed a picture from a phony e-mail
account." Lila started to shake again, and her breathing turned
shallow. She gripped my arm as if to steady herself. "It was a picture of
me . . . and there were two guys . . . their images were scrambled . . . and
they were . . . they . . ." she broke down, crying uncontrollably.

I wanted to say something to take the pain away, a task that I knew
I could not achieve. "You don't have to say any more," I said. "It doesn't
matter to me."

She wiped her tears on her sleeve and said, "I have to show you something." She nervously reached up, gripped the oversized collar of her sweatshirt, and pulled it down, exposing six thin scars—straight striations from a razor blade—cutting across her shoulder. She brushed her fingers over the scars to draw my attention to them. Then she lowered her head into the back of the couch, as if to turn her face as far away from me as she could. "That year that I took off before starting college . . . I spent that time in therapy. You see, Joe," she said, her lips twitching upward into a frightened smile, "I have issues."

I brushed my cheek against the soft tickle of her hair, then I wrapped one arm around her waist, the other under her tucked-up knees, and lifted her off the couch. I walked her to her bedroom, laid her in bed, rolled a comforter up to her shoulders, and bent down and kissed her cheek, which creased with a slight smile.

"I'm not afraid of issues," I said, letting the words settle on her before I stood up to leave—although leaving was the last thing I wanted to do. That's when I heard her say, in a voice barely loud enough to reach me, "I don't want to be alone."

I swallowed my surprise, hesitating only a moment before walking around to the other side of the bed. I slipped off my shoes, lay down on the bed, and gently wrapped my arm around Lila. She squeezed my hand, pulling it up to her chest, holding it like she would hold a teddy bear. I lay behind her, breathing in her scent, savoring the faint beating of her heart against my fingertips, curling my body around her body. And although my presence in her bed came about because of her pain and sadness, it filled me with an odd sense of happiness, a sense of belonging, a feeling I had never felt before, a feeling so exquisite that it bordered on agony. I reveled in that feeling until I fell asleep.

CHAPTER 29

I woke the next morning to the sound of a hair dryer whirring in Lila's bathroom. I was still in her bed, still wearing my khakis and shirt, still not sure where things stood between us. I sat up, checked the corners of my mouth for drool, climbed out of her bed, and followed the scent of fresh coffee brewing. Before I got to her kitchen, I stopped in front of a framed poster to check my appearance in its glass. Tufts of hair stuck out of my head in all directions, like I'd been cow-licked by a drunken heifer. I splashed some water from the kitchen faucet onto my bed head to tame my hair a bit, just as Lila came out the bathroom.

"I'm sorry," she said. "Did I wake you?" She had changed into another oversized jersey and a pair of silky pink pajama bottoms.

"Not at all," I said. "Did you sleep okay?"

"I slept great," she said. She walked up to me, put one hand on my cheek, raised up on her tiptoes, and kissed my lips, a soft, slow, warm kiss, so tender it hurt. When she finished, she eased back a couple steps, looked into my eyes, and said, "Thank you."

Before I could say a word, she turned around to the cupboard, casually picking up two coffee mugs. She handed one to me and twirled the other on her finger as we waited for the coffeemaker to finish its magic. Could she tell that the taste of her kiss still lingered on my lips, that my cheek tingled where her fingers had touched it, that the scent of her skin pulled me toward her like gravity? She seemed unaffected by the current that had left me paralyzed.

The coffeemaker dinged its success, and I filled our mugs, first hers then mine. "So, what's for breakfast," I said.

"Ah, breakfast," she said. "Here at Chez Lila we have a terrific breakfast menu. The specialty du jour is Cheerios. Or I could have the chef whip up an order of Special K."

"What, no pannekoekens?" I asked.

"And if you want milk with your Cheerios, you're gonna have to run to the store and get some."

"Do you have an egg?" I asked.

"I have a couple of them, but no bacon or sausage to go with them."

"Bring your eggs to my place," I said. "I'll whip us up some pancakes."

Lila grabbed the eggs from the fridge and followed me to my apartment. As I got the mixing bowl and ingredients out of the cupboard, she went to the coffee table where the Carl Iverson project lay sorted into piles.

"So, who do we track down next?" Lila said as she flipped through the piles, not looking at anything in particular.

"I think we should track down the bad guy," I said.

"And who's that?"

"I don't know," I said, as I measured pancake mix into a bowl. "When I look at that stuff my brain hurts."

"Well, we know Crystal died sometime between when she left school with Andrew Fisher and when the fire department got there. And we know that the diary entries were about a stolen car and not about Carl seeing Crystal and Andy Fisher in the alley. So whoever was blackmailing Crystal had to know about them crashing the GTO."

"That has to be a pretty short list."

"Andrew knew, of course," she said.

"Yeah, but he wouldn't have told us about it if he was the one in the diary. Besides, the diary suggests that someone else figured it out."

"Daddy Doug ran the car lot," she said, "Maybe he didn't buy the whole car-theft hoax."

"It's also possible that Andrew bragged to someone, maybe let it slip that he and Crystal were the ones that crashed into that cop car. I mean if I pulled a stunt like that, I would've been itching to tell my buddies. He'd have been king shit at school."

"Nah, I don't buy the coincidence."

"Yeah, me neither," I said.

"There's gotta be something in these piles that points the way."

"There is," I said.

"There is?" She leaned forward on the couch.

"Sure. We just gotta solve the code."

"Very funny," she said.

A knock at the door interrupted our conversation, and I turned the heat down on the pancakes. My first thought was that the slob from the night before, or one of his friends, had tracked me down. I pulled a flashlight from the kitchen drawer. Holding it in my right hand, I planted my foot behind the door, giving it six inches of leeway. Lila looked at me as if I had lost my mind. I hadn't told her about ripping into that guy at the bar, or about the two friends that charged after me. I opened the door to find Jeremy in the hall.

"Hey, Buddy, what . . ." I let the door swing wider and saw my mother around the side. "Mom?"

"Hi, Joey," she said, giving Jeremy a light shove through the door. "I need you to watch Jeremy for a couple days." She made a slight movement, as if turning to leave, but stopped when she saw Lila sitting on my couch, wearing what looked to be pajamas.

"Mom! You can't just show up here—"

"Now I get it," she said. "I see what's going on." Lila stood up to greet my mother. "You're shacking up with little miss thing here, leaving your brother and me to fend for ourselves." Lila wilted back onto the couch. I grabbed my mother, who was halfway into the apartment, and forced her back into the hallway, shutting the door behind us.

"Where do you come off—" I started.

"I'm your mother."

"That doesn't give you the right to insult my friend."

"Friend? Is that what they call 'em these days."

"She lives next door and . . . and I don't owe you an explanation."

"Fine," she shrugged. "You do whatever you want, but I need you to watch Jeremy."

"You can't just show up here and drop him off like this. He's not an old shoe you can toss around."

"That's what you get for not taking my calls," she said, turning to leave.

"Where're you going?"

"We're heading to Treasure Island Casino," she said.

"We?"

She hesitated. "Larry and me." She headed down the stairs before I could chew her out for still being with that asshole. "I'll be back on Sunday," she hollered over her shoulder. I took a deep breath to calm down and then went back into the apartment with a smile—for Jeremy's sake.

I finished making pancakes for all three of us, and we ate them in the living room. Lila joked with Jeremy, calling me Jeeves the Butler as I served them their breakfasts. Although the thought of my mother dumping Jeremy off without warning pissed me off, I couldn't deny the joy of having him here, sitting with Lila and me, especially after the guilt trip of the play. I used to roll my eyes when people told me they were homesick. The thought of missing my mother's dank apartment was as incomprehensible as driving a nail through my ankle for the fun of it. But that morning, as I watched Jeremy laughing with Lila, calling me Jeeves, eating my pancakes, I realized that a large part of me was homesick, not for the apartment but for my brother.

After breakfast, Lila went to her apartment to retrieve her laptop to do some homework. I didn't have any DVDs, or even a checkerboard, so Jeremy and I played Go Fish with a modified deck of playing cards, sitting on the couch, using the cushion between us as a tabletop.

At one point, Lila was tapping away on her computer with the speed of a concert pianist. Jeremy stopped playing cards to watch her, seemingly mesmerized by the flutter of keystrokes. After a few minutes, Lila looked up from her keyboard and stopped typing.

"Maybe I think you're a good typer, Lila," he said.

Lila smiled at Jeremy. "Why thank you. That's a very sweet thing to say. Do you know how to type?"

"Maybe I took a keyboarding class with Mr. Warner," Jeremy said. "Do you like typing?" she asked.

"I think Mr. Warner was funny." Jeremy smiled a big smile. "Maybe Mr. Warner made me type 'the quick brown fox jumps over the lazy dog.'" Jeremy laughed and Lila laughed, which made me laugh.

"That's right," Lila said. "That's what you have to type. The quick brown fox jumps over the lazy dog." Jeremy laughed even harder when Lila said it.

Lila went back to work on her laptop, and Jeremy returned to our game of Go Fish, asking for the same card over and over until I would draw it from the deck. Then he would go to the next card and do the same.

After a few minutes Lila stopped typing, her head snapping up like she had been bitten by a bug or hit square in the face by an epiphany. "It has every letter of the alphabet in it," she said.

"What has what?" I said.

"The quick brown fox jumps over the lazy dog. They use that sentence in keyboarding class because it has every letter of the alphabet in it."

"Yeah?" I said.

"Crystal Hagen started using her code in September 1980 . . . her freshman year of high school . . . when she was taking a typing class with Andy Fisher."

"You don't think . . ." I said.

Lila pulled out a notepad and wrote the sentence down, crossing out the second time that a letter would appear. Then she put a number under each letter.

T	H	E		Q	U	I	C	K		B	R	O	W	N		F	x	X
1	2	3		4	5	6	7	8		9	10	11	12	13		14		15

J	x	M	P	S		x	V	x	x		x	x	x		L	A	Z	Y		D	x	G
16		17	18	19			20								21	22	23	24		25		26

I found Crystal's diary and handed Lila the first page of code that I came to, September 28. Lila started replacing the numbers with letters. D-J-F-O . . . I shrugged my shoulders; another dead end

I thought . . . U-N-D-M . . . I sat up a little straighter, spotting at least one complete word . . . Y-G-L-A-S-S-E-S.

"DJ found my glasses!" She yelled, thrusting her notes at me. "It says DJ found my glasses. We did it—Jeremy did it. Jeremy, you solved the code." She jumped to her feet and grabbed Jeremy's hands, pulling him off the couch. "You solved the code, Jeremy!" She jumped up and down, which caused Jeremy to jump up and down, laughing, not knowing why he was excited.

"Who is DJ?" I said.

Lila stopped jumping, and we both reached into the file box at the same time, pulling out transcripts. She grabbed the transcript with Douglas Lockwood's testimony and I grabbed Danny's. At the beginning of each witness's testimony, they were asked to give their full name, date of birth, and the spelling of their last name. I frantically flipped through the pages until I found Danny's direct examination.

"Daniel William Lockwood," I read. I closed my transcript and looked at Lila. "His middle name's William. It's not Danny," I said.

"Douglas Joseph Lockwood," she said, her face beaming, barely able to contain her excitement. We looked at each other, trying to grasp the enormity of what we had just learned. Crystal Hagen's stepfather had the initials DJ. DJ is the person who found Crystal Hagen's glasses. The person who found Crystal's glasses was forcing her to have sex. And the person forcing her to have sex was the person who killed her. It was simple deduction. We had found our murderer.

CHAPTER 30

ecause we needed to take care of Jeremy, Lila and I waited until
Monday before we took our information to the police. In the
meantime, the three of us celebrated our own little Thanksgiving, complete with mashed potatoes, cranberries, pumpkin pie, and Cornish
game hens, which we told Jeremy were mini-turkeys. It was probably the
best Thanksgiving he or I had ever experienced. By Sunday evening, my
mom had run out of money at the casino and came to pick up Jeremy.
I could tell that he didn't want to go. He sat on my couch ignoring
our mother until she finally turned stern and ordered him to stand up.
After they left, Lila and I organized the diary notes and the transcript
pages that we would take to the police the next day after class. We were
barely able to contain our excitement.

The Minneapolis Police Department's Homicide Division has
an office at Minneapolis City Hall, an old castle-like building in the
heart of the city. Ornate archways gave the building's entrance a brief
taste of classic Richardsonian architecture before dissolving into cor-
ridors more reminiscent of a Roman bathhouse than Romanesque
Revival. Five-foot marble sheets lined the walls. Above that, someone
had painted the plaster a color that seemed to combine fuchsia with
tomato soup. The hallway ran the length of the block, turned left, and
ran another half block or so before passing room 108, the office of the
Homicide Division.

Lila and I gave our names to a receptionist who sat behind bullet-
proof glass, then we took a seat to wait. After about twenty minutes,
a man entered the waiting area, a Glock nine-millimeter on his right
hip and a badge clipped to his belt on the left. He was tall with a thick
chest and biceps like he pumped iron in a prison yard. But he had com-

passionate eyes that softened his tough appearance and a gentle voice, a notch or two softer than I expected. Lila and I were the only two people in the waiting area. "Joe? Lila?" he asked, extending his hand.

We each shook it in turn. "Yes, sir," I said.

"I'm Detective Max Rupert," he said. "I was told you have information on a homicide case?"

"Yes, sir," I said. "It's about the murder of Crystal Hagen."

Detective Rupert looked away as if reading names from a list in his head. "That name doesn't ring a bell."

"She was killed back in 1980," Lila said.

Rupert blinked hard a couple times, cocking his head to the side like a dog hearing an unexpected sound. "Did you say 1980?"

"I know you may think we're a couple of crackpots, but just give us two minutes of your time. If you think we're full of crap after two minutes, we'll leave. But if we make sense, even a little bit, then there may be a murderer running free."

Rupert looked at his watch, sighed, and gave a flick of his fingers, waving us to come with him. We walked through a room full of cubicles and turned into a room with a simple metal table and four wooden chairs. Lila and I sat on one side of the table and opened up our red-rope folder.

"Two minutes," Rupert said, pointing at his watch. "Go."

"Um . . . Uh," I didn't think he would take me literally about the two minutes, and it flustered me at first. I gathered my thoughts and began. "In October of 1980, a fourteen-year-old girl named Crystal Hagen was raped and murdered. Her body was burned in a tool shed belonging to her next-door neighbor Carl Iverson, who was convicted for her murder. One of the key pieces of evidence was a diary." I pointed at the red-rope folder, and Lila pulled the diary out.

"This is Crystal's diary," Lila said, laying her hand upon the pages. "The prosecutor used certain passages from the diary to suggest that Carl Iverson was stalking Crystal and forcing her to have sex with him. He used those diary entries to convict Iverson. But there were a few coded lines in the diary." Lila opened the diary to the first coded message.

"Where'd you get that?" Rupert picked up the diary pages and flipped through them. "See these numbers?" He pointed to a number stamped on the bottom of each page. "These pages are Bates stamped," he said. "This was evidence in a case."

"That's what we're telling you," I said. "We got them from Iverson's attorney. They're from his trial."

"Look at this code," Lila said, showing Rupert the pages with the code. "In September of 1980 Crystal started writing in code. Not a lot, just every now and again. They never deciphered the code for the trial."

Rupert read through the diary for a bit, lingering on the pages with coded entries. "Okay . . . And?" he said.

"And . . ." I looked at Lila. "We broke the code. Well actually, she broke the code." I pointed at Lila, who pulled a page from her folder with all of the coded entries listed, followed by the decoded text. She slid the paper in front of Detective Rupert.

September 21 – Terrible day today - 7,22,13,1,14,6,13,25,17,24,26,21, 22,19,19,3,19. I am freaking out. This is very very bad.

September 21 – Terrible day today – can't find my glasses. I am freaking out. This is very very bad.

September 28 – 25,16,14,11,5,13,25,17,24,26,21,22,19,19,3,19. If I don't do what he wants he'll tell everyone. He'll ruin my life.

September 28 – DJ found my glasses. If I don't do what he wants he'll tell everyone. He'll ruin my life.

September 30 – 6,25,6,25,25,16,12,6,1,2,17,24,2,22,13,25. I hate him. I feel sick.

September 30 – I did DJ with my hand. I hate him. I feel sick

October 8 – 25,16,12,11,13,1,26,6,20,3,17,3,17,24,26,21,22,19,19,3, 19,9,22,7,8. He keeps threatening me. 2,3,12,22,13,1,19,17,3,1,11,5, 19,3,17,24,17,11,5,1,2.

October 8 – DJ won't give me my glasses back. He keeps threatening me. He wants me to use my mouth.

October 9 – 6,26,22,20,3,25,16,12,2,22,1,2,3,12,22,13,1,3,25. He forced me. I want to kill myself. I want to kill him.

October 9 – I gave DJ what he wanted. He forced me. I want to kill myself. I want to kill him.

October 17 – 25,16,17,22,25,3,17,3,25,11,6,1,22,26,22,6,13,2,3,12, 22,19,10,11,5,26,2.6,1,2,5,10,1.

October 17 – DJ made me do it again. He was rough. It hurt.

October 29 – 6,1,19,10,22,18,3. 25,16,19,10,22,18,6,13,26,17,3. Mrs. Tate said so. She said that the age difference means he'll go to prison for sure. It stops today. I am so happy.

October 29 – It's rape. DJ is raping me. Mrs. Tate said so. She said that the age difference means he'll go to prison for sure. It stops today. I am so happy.

"What's this about lost glasses?" Rupert asked.

I explained our conversation with Andrew Fisher, about how he and Crystal stole the car, wrecked it, and left behind proof of their deed in the form of the lens from Crystal's glasses. "You see," I said, "whoever found those glasses must have known about the stolen car and the lens. He knew he had something to hold over her, leverage to make her . . . you know, comply."

Rupert leaned back in his chair, looking up at the ceiling. "So this Carl guy gets convicted based, in part, on this diary?"

"Yes," I said. "The prosecutor told the jury that Iverson caught Crystal in a compromising position and was using that to force Crystal to have sex with him."

Lila added. "Without breaking the code, there would be no way to know for sure who was raping her."

"Do you have an idea who DJ is?" he asked.

"It's the girl's stepfather," Lila said. "His name is Douglas Joseph Lockwood."

"And you think it's him because his name is Douglas Joseph?" Rupert said.

"That," I said, "and the fact that he managed the car lot where Crystal stole the car, so he would have known about the lens. The cops investigating the theft must've mentioned it when they came by the lot."

"We also have these pictures," Lila said and pulled out the picture showing the closed blind and the second one that showed someone peeking out the window when no one should have been in the house.

Rupert studied the pictures, pulling a magnifying glass out of a drawer to look closer at each. Then he put the pictures down on the table, put his hands together, fingertip to fingertip, and tapped them as he spoke. "Do you know which prison Iverson is in?" he asked.

"He's not in prison," I said. "He's dying of cancer, so they paroled him to the nursing home in Richfield."

"So you are not trying to get this guy out of prison?"

"Mr. Rupert," I said. "Carl Iverson's going to be dead in a matter of weeks. I'd like to clear his name before he dies."

"It doesn't work like that," Rupert said. "I don't know you. I don't know this case. You walk in here with the story of a diary and a code, and you want me to absolve this Iverson guy. I'm not the Pope. Someone's got to dig our file out of the basement, go through it, and verify that what you're saying is even close to being true. And then, even if it is true, who's to say you're right about this DJ person. I have no idea what other evidence there might be. Maybe the diary doesn't matter. Maybe there's an explanation for this picture. You're asking me to reopen a thirty-year-old investigation where the guy was convicted by a jury, beyond a reasonable doubt. Not only that, but the guy's not in prison anymore; he's sitting in a nursing home."

"But if we are right," I said, "there's a murderer who went free thirty years ago."

"Have you been reading the papers?" Rupert asked. "Do you know how many homicides we've had this year?"

I shook my head.

"We've had thirty-seven so far: thirty-seven homicides this year. We had nineteen homicides all of last year. We don't have enough manpower to solve murders that happened thirty days ago much less thirty years ago."

"But we've solved the case already," I said. "All you have to do is verify it."

"It's not that easy." Rupert started stacking the papers together as if to indicate that our meeting was over. "The evidence has to be strong enough to convince my boss to reopen the case. Then my boss has to convince the County Attorney that they screwed up and convicted the wrong man thirty years ago. After that, you have to go into court and convince a judge to undo the conviction. Now you said this Iverson guy only has a few weeks to live. Even if I did believe you—and I'm not saying I do—there's no way to undo his conviction before he dies."

I couldn't believe what I was hearing. Lila and I were so excited when we broke the code. The truth jumped off the page and screamed at us. We knew Carl was innocent. I suspected that Detective Rupert knew the truth as well, which made his "we're too busy" excuse all the harder to swallow. I knew Carl's file well enough to know the massive resources they threw into this case when they thought Carl was guilty. But now—now that we could prove his innocence—the entire system became rusted. It seemed so unfair. Rupert handed the stack of papers back to me.

"This ain't right," I said. "I'm not some nut job coming in here and telling you he's innocent because I saw a vision in my cereal bowl or talked to a dog. We brought proof. And you're not going to do anything because you're understaffed? That's bullshit."

"Now, hold on—"

"No. You hold on," I said. "If you thought that I was full of crap and kicked me out, I would understand. But you're not going to look into this because it's too much work?"

"That's not what I said—"

"So you are gonna look into it?"

Rupert held his hand up to stop me from talking. He considered the folder in front of me. Then he put his hand down and leaned onto the table. "Let's do this," he said. "I got a friend who works at the Innocence Project." Rupert reached into his pocket, pulled out one of his business cards, and wrote a name on the back of it. "His name is Boady Sanden. He's a law professor at Hamline Law School." Rupert handed me the card. "I'll dig our old file out of storage, assuming it's still there, and you contact Boady. Maybe he can help. I'll do what I can on this end, but don't get your hopes up. If your guy is innocent, Boady can help get the evidence back into court."

I looked at the card with Rupert's name on one side and Professor Sanden's name written on the other. "Have Boady call me," Rupert said. "I can tell him what we have in the file here, if anything."

Lila and I stood up to leave.

"And Joe," Rupert said. "If this is a wild-goose chase, I'll be calling on you. I don't like getting yanked around. Are we clear?"

"Crystal," I said.

CHAPTER 31

C arl wasn't expecting my visit that day.

After meeting with Detective Rupert, I dropped Lila off at the apartment and drove to Hillview to tell Carl the good news. I expected to find Carl sitting in his wheelchair by the window, but he wasn't. He hadn't gotten out of bed all day; he couldn't. His cancer symptoms had weakened him to the point that he needed to have oxygen and nutrients piped into him through tubes.

Mrs. Lorngren was initially reluctant to let me see Carl, but she relented after I told her about our breakthrough. I even showed her the coded diary entries and their deciphered versions. As I explained Carl's innocence to her, she became sullen. "I'm afraid I haven't been a very good Christian," she said.

She sent Janet back to check with Carl, to see if he would receive me. A minute later they showed me to his door. Carl's room consisted of a bed, an end table, a wooden chair, a closet with a built-in dresser, and a single tiny window with no view. The room's moss-colored walls were barren of any decor other than a placard of instructions on good hygiene. Carl lay in his bed, a plastic tube feeding oxygen into his nose and an IV in his arm.

"I'm sorry to drop in on you like this," I said, "but I found something you should see."

"Joe," he said. "It's good to see you. Think it's gonna snow today?"

"I don't think so," I said, peeking out the window at the dead branches of the unkempt lilac bush that blocked his view. "I went to see a detective today."

"I wish it would snow," he said. "One great big one before I die."

"I know who killed Crystal Hagen," I said.

Carl stopped talking and looked at me as if he were trying to change the stream of his thoughts. "I don't understand," he said.

"Remember the diary, the one the prosecutor used to convict you?"

"Oh yes," he said, with a melancholy smile. "The diary. I always thought she was such a sweet girl, practicing her little cheerleading routines in the back yard; and all that time she thought I was a pervert—a child molester. Yeah, I remember the diary."

"Do you remember the lines that had numbers in them? The code? I deciphered it—well, we deciphered it—my brother, me, and this girl named Lila."

"Well I'll be." Carl smiled. "Aren't you clever? And what did it say?"

"All that stuff she was saying, about being forced to have sex and being threatened, she wasn't saying that about you at all. She was saying it about someone named DJ."

"DJ?" he said.

"Douglas Joseph . . . Lockwood," I said. "She was talking about her stepfather not you."

"Her stepfather. That poor girl."

"If I can get the cops to reopen the case, I can exonerate you," I said. "And if they won't look into what really happened—then I'll do it myself."

Carl sighed, let his head sink deeper into his pillow, and turned his attention back toward the tiny window and the dead lilac bush. "Don't do that," he said. "I don't want you risking anything on my behalf. Besides, I've always known I didn't kill her. And now you know. That's enough for me."

His response caught me off guard. I couldn't believe he could be so calm. I would have been howling and jumping in my pajamas. "Don't you want people to know you didn't kill her?" I said. "Clear your name? Let everyone know the prosecutor was wrong for putting you in prison?"

He smiled warmly. "Remember how I told you that I can count my life in hours?" he said. "How many of those hours should I spend worrying about what happened thirty years ago?"

"But you spent all that time in prison for a crime you didn't commit," I said. "That's just wrong."

Carl turned to me, his pale tongue licking his chapped lips, his eyes settling on mine. "I can't regret getting arrested, getting sent to prison. If they hadn't arrested me that night, I wouldn't be here today."

"What do you mean?" I asked.

"You know that gun I bought the day Crystal was killed. I bought that gun to use on myself, not to use on that poor girl."

"On you?"

His voice became thin, and he cleared his throat before continuing. "I didn't mean to pass out that night. That was an accident. I put the gun up to my temple two or three times but didn't have the guts to pull the trigger. I got a bottle of whiskey out of the cupboard. I was just gonna have a bit of it before I used the gun—just a nip to give me some courage. But I drank too much. I guess I needed more courage than I thought. I passed out. When I woke up, two big cops were hauling me out of my house. I would have finished the job had they not arrested me."

"You didn't kill yourself in Vietnam because you didn't want to go to hell. Remember?"

"By the time I bought that gun, God and I weren't exactly on speaking terms. I was already in hell. I didn't care anymore. It didn't matter. I couldn't live with what I had done. I couldn't live with myself one more day."

"All that because you couldn't save that girl in Vietnam?"

Carl looked away from me. I could see his breath grow shallow in his chest. He licked his lips again with a dry tongue, paused to compose his thoughts, and said, "That's not all. That is where things started, sure, but that's not the end of the story."

I said nothing. I watched him in silence, waiting for him to explain. He asked me to pour some water for him, which I did. He sipped it to wet his lips.

"I'm going to tell you something," he said, his voice soft and level. "Something I've never told anyone, not even Virgil. I'm telling you this because I promised I'd be honest with you. I said I would not hold anything back." He settled back into his pillow, his eyes staring at the ceiling. I watched as the pain of a jagged and dreadful memory crossed his face. Part of me wanted to save him that pain—tell him that he could keep his secret to himself—but I couldn't. I wanted to hear it. I needed to hear it.

He summoned his strength and continued, "After that fight, the one where Virgil and I both got shot, they sent Virgil home, and I spent a month recuperating in Da Nang before getting sent back to my unit. Vietnam was tolerable when I had Virgil and Tater there, but without them . . . well, I can't think of a word to describe how low I got. And then, just when I thought it couldn't get worse, it did."

His eyes lost their focus as he once again went back to Vietnam. "We were on a routine search and destroy mission in July of '68, tossing some little no-name village, looking for food and ammo: the usual. It was a hell of a hot day, 'bout as hot as a man can stand, with mosquitoes as big as dragonflies that liked to suck your blood dry. Made you wonder why anyone would live in such a godforsaken place, or why in the hell anyone would be fighting over it. As we were rousting this village, I see a girl run down a trail and into a hut, and I see Gibbs watching her, following her, heading that way all by himself. It was Oxbow all over again."

Carl's lips quivered as he took another drink of water before continuing. "At that moment, the war around me seemed to disappear. All the crap, the screaming, the heat, all the right and wrong of it—it all melted away, leaving just me and Gibbs. The only thing that mattered to me was stopping Gibbs. I couldn't let Oxbow happen again. I went to the hooch, and Gibbs had his pants down. He had beaten the girl bloody and had a knife against her throat. I pointed my rifle at him, right between the eyes. He looked at me, spit tobacco juice on my boot, and said he'd deal with me in a second. I told him to stop what he was doing, but he didn't. 'Shoot me you fucking coward,' he says to me. 'Shoot me and they'll stand you up in front of a firing squad.'

"He was right. I was ready to die in Vietnam—sure—but not like that. When I put my rifle down, Gibbs laughed at me, that is, until he saw me draw my knife. His eyes were as big as chicken eggs when I stabbed him, stuck him right through his heart, watched him bleed to death in my hands. He looked so surprised, so disbelieving." Carl's voice leveled out, smooth and calm like a plane pulling out of a storm. "You see, Joe, I murdered Sergeant Gibbs. Murdered him in cold blood."

I didn't know what to say. Carl stopped talking. He had come to the end of his story. He had told me the truth. The silence that followed pressed and squeezed at my chest until I thought my heart would stop, but I waited for Carl to continue.

"I helped the girl put her clothes back on, shoved her out the door, and told her to run away—to *di di mau*—into the jungle. Then I waited a bit and fired a few shots into the air to call in the cavalry. I told them I saw someone running toward the jungle." He paused again and then he looked at me. "So, you see Joe, I am a murderer after all."

"But you saved that girl's life," I said.

"I had no right to take Gibbs's life," Carl said. "He had a wife and two kids back in the states, and I murdered him. I killed a great many men in Vietnam . . . a great many, but they were soldiers. They were the enemy. I was doing my job. I murdered Gibbs, and as far as I'm concerned I murdered that girl in Oxbow. I didn't pull the knife across her throat, but I murdered her just the same. When they arrested me for the murder of Crystal Hagen . . . well, I think part of me figured it was time to pay my debt. Before I went to prison, I used to fall asleep every night seeing the face of that poor Vietnamese girl. I would see her fingers begging me to come to her, to help her. No matter how much whiskey I drank, I could never dim that memory." Carl closed his eyes and shook his head as he remembered. "God, how I drank. I just wanted the pain to stop."

I could see the energy drain from Carl's face as he spoke, his words falling loose and frayed from his lips. He took another sip of water and waited until his breath stopped trembling. "I thought that by going to prison, I might silence my ghosts—bury that part of my life, those things I did in Vietnam. But in the end, there's no hole deep enough." He looked up at me. "No matter how hard you try, there are some things you just can't run away from."

Something in his eyes told me that he could see my own yoke of guilt. I shifted uncomfortably in my seat as the silence of Carl's pause moved around me. Then Carl closed his eyes, clutched his stomach, and winced in pain. "Jesus, this cancer crap can hurt like a son of a bitch."

"Want me to get somebody?" I asked.

"No," he said, eking the words out through gritted teeth. "It passes." Carl twisted his hands into a ball and lay still until his breathing returned to a calm, shallow rhythm. "You want to know the real kicker?" he said.

"Sure," I said.

"After all that time I spent wanting to die, trying to die, it took prison to make me want to live."

"You liked prison?" I said.

"Of course not," he chuckled through his pain. "No one likes prison. But I started reading, and thinking, and trying to understand myself and my life. Then one day, I was lying on my bunk, contemplating Pascal's gambit."

"Pascal's gambit?"

"This philosopher named Blaise Pascal said that if you have a choice of believing in God or not believing in God, it's a better gamble to believe. Because if you believe in God and you're wrong—well, nothing happens. You just die into the nothingness of the universe. But if you don't believe in God and you're wrong, then you go to hell for eternity, at least according to some folks."

"Not much of a reason to be religious," I said.

"Not much at all," he said. "I was surrounded by hundreds of men waiting for the end of their lives, waiting for that something better that comes after death. I felt the same way. I wanted to believe there was something better on the other side. I was killing time in prison, waiting for that crossover. And that's when Pascal's gambit popped into my head, but with a small twist. What if I was wrong? What if there was no other side. What if, in all the eons of eternity, this was the one and only time that I would be alive. How would I live my life if that were the case? Know what I mean? What if this was all there is?"

"Well, I guess there'd be a lot of disappointed dead priests," I said.

Carl chuckled. "Well, there's that," he said. "But it also means that this is our heaven. We are surrounded every day by the wonders of life, wonders beyond comprehension that we simply take for granted. I decided that day that I would live my life—not simply exist. If I died and discovered heaven on the other side, well, that'd be just fine and dandy. But if I didn't live my life as if I was already in heaven, and I died and found only nothingness, well . . . I would have wasted my life. I would have wasted my one chance in all of history to be alive."

Carl drifted off, his eyes locked on a chickadee flitting on a naked branch outside. We watched the bird for several minutes until it flew away, bringing Carl's attention back to me. "I'm sorry," Carl said. "I tend to get philosophical when I think about the past."

He grabbed his stomach again, a slight squeal of agony escaping his lips. He squeezed his eyes shut and gritted his teeth. Instead of passing, this one grew. He had suffered spells before, but I'd never seen one this bad. I waited a few seconds, hoping the pain would pass, Carl's face contorting, his nostrils flaring as he tried to breath. Was this how it would end? Was he dying now? I ran into the hall and yelled for a nurse. She came running to his room with a syringe in her hand. She cleaned the port in Carl's IV and injected him with morphine, and in a few seconds his muscles began to loosen, his jaw unclenched, his head rolled back onto his pillow. He was a mere waif of a man, completely drained of his strength. He looked barely alive. He tried to stay awake but couldn't.

I watched over him as he slept, and I wondered how many more days he had left—how many more hours. I wondered how much time I had left to do what I needed to do.

CHAPTER 32

When I got home, I pulled Max Rupert's card out of my wallet, the one with Professor Boady Sanden's name on it, and placed a call. Professor Sanden sounded nice on the phone and made time to see me the next day at 4:00. My last class on that Tuesday was economics, and I didn't get out until 3:30. If I had known that the lecture that day would be verbatim from the textbook, I would have skipped class and gotten to Hamline University sooner. By the time the bus dropped me off in St. Paul, I had nine blocks to go and only six minutes to get there. I ran the first seven blocks and walked the last two with my coat open, letting the cold winter breeze evaporate my sweat. I arrived at Professor Sanden's door exactly on time.

I expected the law professor to be old, with receding gray hair, a bowtie, and wearing a camel's-hair jacket, but Professor Sanden met me at the door to his office in carpenter-blue jeans, a flannel shirt, and loafers. He sported a thin beard, had a touch of gray in the temples of his otherwise brown hair, and shook my hand with the grip of a construction worker.

I had brought the folder of materials with me—the one that I'd shown to Detective Rupert. Professor Sanden cleared a space on his cluttered desk and offered me a cup of coffee. I liked him right off. I didn't tell Professor Sanden that Carl had been paroled from prison, remembering how that information stunted Max Rupert's enthusiasm. I didn't want Professor Sanden dismissing my argument simply because Carl was no longer in prison. I started my presentation with the photos of Lockwood's window. "Interesting," he said.

"It gets better," I said, pulling the diary pages out of the file, laying them out in front of him, leading him through the progression of diary entries, explaining how the prosecutor used them to paint a false picture and convict Carl Iverson. Then I showed him the deciphered entries, with the name of the killer spelled out. He cocked his head and smiled as he read about DJ.

"DJ: Douglas Joseph. That makes sense," he said. "How did you figure out the code?"

"My autistic brother," I said.

"Savant?" Professor Sanden asked.

"No," I said. "Just lucky. Crystal Hagen had a typing class that fall and she based her code on that sentence . . . you know, the one that has every letter of the alphabet in it."

Professor Sanden rolled back through his memory. "Something about a lazy dog, right?"

"That's the one," I said. "That was her code: her enigma machine. Once we discovered the key to the code, the answer appeared in black and white. The way we figure it, Doug got Danny to go along with the lie about them being at the dealership. Danny hated his stepmom, and we know that the marriage was rocky. Maybe Doug told Danny that he was covering for something else."

"Like what?" Sanden asked.

"According to Andrew Fisher, Crystal's boyfriend at the time, Mr. Lockwood used to go to strip clubs behind his wife's back," I said. "Maybe Doug got Danny to go along with the lie because Danny thought he was protecting his dad from getting in trouble for something like that. Besides, no one suspected Doug. The police locked on to Carl Iverson right away. Everyone thought Carl did it."

"It makes sense that it was the stepfather," he said.

"Why's that?"

"He was close to her—in the same house. They're not related by blood, so he can justify his impulses toward her. He used the secret that he discovered to gain power and control over his victim. One of the keys to being a successful pedophile is to isolate the victim, make her feel like she can't tell anyone. Get her to believe that it'll destroy her and her family, that everyone will blame her. That's what he was doing.

He starts with the glasses, using the threat of that crime to get leverage over her, to get her to touch him. Then he has her do more, crossing each new boundary with small steps. The sad thing here is that Crystal's salvation, her learning that she could turn the tables on her stepfather, ensured her death. There was no way he would let her have that kind of power."

"So how do we get this guy?" I asked.

"Were there any bodily fluids in evidence? Blood, saliva, semen?"

"The medical examiner testified that she was raped; they found traces of semen inside her."

"If they still have the sample in evidence, we might be able to get DNA. The only problem is: this was thirty years ago. They didn't have DNA evidence back then. They may not have saved the specimen, and if they did, it might be so deteriorated that we can't use it. Moist specimens don't store well. If a bloodstain stays dry the DNA will last for decades." Professor Sanden punched the speakerphone button and dialed a number. "Let's just give Max a call and see what he has over there."

"Boady!" Boomed the voice of Max Rupert. "How's it hanging?"

"You know me, Max, still fighting the good fight. How about yourself?"

"If I get another murder case, I'm gonna kill somebody," he said, laughing.

"Max, I got you on speakerphone. I'm here with a kid named Joe Talbert."

"Hi, Joe." The words popped out of the speakerphone like we were old friends.

"Hi . . . Detective."

"I've been looking at Joe's evidence here," Professor Sanden said, "I think he has something."

"You always do, Boady," Rupert said. "I brought our file up from the basement and took a look through it."

"Any fluids?" Sanden asked.

"The girl's body was burned in a tool shed or garage or something like that. Her legs were mostly burned off; the fluids in her had boiled.

The lab could ascertain the presence of sperm, but the sample was too far gone to get anything beyond that. The killer was a non-secretor, so there was no blood in the semen. As far as I can tell, there were no slides preserved. I called the BCA, and they don't have anything either."

"BCA?" I said.

"Bureau of Criminal Apprehension," Professor Sanden said. "Think of it as our version of CSI." He turned his attention back to the phone. "No blood stains? Saliva?"

"Every shred of her clothing burned up in the fire," Max said.

"What about the fingernail?" I said.

"Fingernail?" Professor Sanden sat up in his chair. "What fingernail?"

Suddenly I felt as if I were part of the conversation. "The girl's fake fingernails. They found one on Carl Iverson's back porch. Doug must have put it there to frame Carl."

"If the victim lost her fingernail during a fight, there may be skin cells on it," Sanden said.

"There's no fingernail in the file," Rupert said.

"It'll be in the B-vault," Sanden said.

"B-vault?" I asked.

"It's where the court stores evidence that's been admitted in trials," Sanden said. "This is a murder case, so they'll have kept it. We'll send a runner to get a swab from Iverson and get a court order to have the fingernail tested. If there is DNA on that fingernail, it'll either prove Iverson's guilt or give us ammunition to reopen the case."

"I'll fax the evidence inventory sheet over for your motion," Rupert said.

"I appreciate the help, Max," Sanden said.

"Don't mention it, Boady," Max said. "I'll get it ready."

"See you at poker Friday?" Sanden said.

"Yep, see you then."

Professor Sanden cut the connection. I thought I understood what would happen next, but I wanted to confirm it. "So, Professor Sanden—"

"Please, call me Boady."

"Okay, Boady, if this fingernail has skin cells on it—they can get DNA from that?"

"Absolutely, and probably some blood as well. It sounds like it's been kept dry. There's no guarantee they'll find DNA, but if they do— and it's not Carl Iverson's—we should have enough here with the diary and stuff you found to get our foot in the door and maybe vacate his conviction."

"How soon will we know?"

"We're probably looking at four months to get the DNA test back, then a couple more months to get into court."

My heart sank and I dropped my head. "He doesn't have that long," I said. "He's dying of cancer. He may not be alive in four weeks, much less four months. I need to exonerate him before he dies."

"Is he a relative?"

"No. He's just some guy I met. But I need to do this." Ever since Lila broke the code, the memory of my grandfather in the river had been visiting me in my sleep, kicking through my mind whenever I let my thoughts rest. I knew that nothing I could do would change that past, but it didn't matter. I needed to do this. For Carl? For my grandfather? For me? I didn't know. I just needed to do it.

"Well, that may be tricky." Professor Sanden tapped his fingers on the desk as he thought. "We could use a private lab, which might be faster than the BCA, but even with that, there's no guarantee." He tapped some more. "I can try and pull in some favors, but don't get your hopes up." He frowned at me and shrugged his shoulders. "I guess, all I can say is, I'll do what I can."

"Short of the DNA test, is there anything we can do, maybe just with the diary?" I asked.

"The diary is great," he said, "but it won't be enough. "If this Lockwood guy jogged into court and confessed his sins we could move faster, but short of that, all we can do is wait for the DNA results."

"Confession . . ." I said the word quietly to myself as a thought began forming, a dark and reckless thought, a thought that would follow me home and poke at me with the persistence of a petulant child. I stood and reached across the desk to shake Boady's hand. "I can't thank you enough."

"Don't thank me yet," he said. "A lot of stars have to align for this to work."

For the next few days, as I struggled to catch up on homework in my other classes, I remained distracted by two thoughts that turned in my head, flipping back and forth like a tossed coin. On the one side, I could wait. Professor Sanden had pulled the chocks out from under the wheels of Carl's case and things were moving. The fingernail would be sent in for DNA testing. If Crystal fought with her attacker, the DNA would belong to Doug Lockwood, and that evidence, along with the diary, would exonerate Carl. But that path would take time—time that Carl Iverson didn't have. I saw Professor Sanden's efforts as a Hail-Mary pass at best. If he could not get the DNA results back in time, Carl would die a murderer—and I would have failed.

On the other side of that flipping coin lived a rash idea. I needed to know that I did everything that I could to help Carl Iverson die an innocent man in the eyes of the world. I could not stand by and watch him die a murderer knowing that I might have changed that. This was no longer about getting an A on my project. It wasn't even about my naive belief that right and wrong should balance out in the end. This had somehow become about me, about when I was eleven and watched my grandfather die. I could have done something, but I didn't. I should have at least tried. Now, faced with the choice to act or to wait, I felt I had no choice. I had to act. Besides, what if there was no DNA on the fingernail? Then all the time spent waiting would have been wasted.

A thought as small as a strawberry seed began to grow in my mind, a seed accidentally planted there by Professor Sanden. What if I could get Lockwood to confess?

I turned on my laptop, searched the Internet for the name Douglas Joseph Lockwood, and found a police blotter announcing his arrest for DUI and another site with the minutes from a County Board of Commissioner's meeting where a Douglas Joseph Lockwood had been given notice of being a public nuisance for having junked cars on his property. Both websites gave the same address in rural Chisago County, just north of Minneapolis. The DUI entry gave his age, which fit. I wrote the address down and laid it on the kitchen counter. For three days I watched it pulse like a beating heart while I talked myself into—and out of—tracking down Doug Lockwood. Finally, it was a weatherman who tipped the scale.

I turned on the news to have some background noise while I did homework, and I heard the weatherman announce that a record snowfall was on its way to bitch slap us—my words, not his—with up to twenty inches of snow. The talk of snow made me think of Carl, how he yearned to see a big snowstorm before he died. I wanted to go see him, to see the joy in his eyes as he watched the snow. I decided that before I went to see Carl, I would track down Douglas Lockwood and take a shot at getting him to confess.

CHAPTER 33

approached my plan to meet Douglas Lockwood the way someone might approach a sleeping bull. I paced a lot, thinking and rethinking the idea and trying to screw up my courage. My legs twitched as I sat in my classes that day. My mind drifted, unable to pay attention to the lecture.

I went to Lila's apartment after class, to tell her about my decision to drop in on Lockwood and maybe to give her a chance to talk me out of it. She wasn't home. My last act before I left was to call Detective Rupert. My call went to voicemail, and I hung up and put my phone in my backpack. I told myself that I would simply drive out to Lockwood's house—drive past it to see if he still lived there. I could then report back to Rupert, although I strongly suspected that Rupert would not care enough to act on what I learned. He would want to wait for the DNA results. He would go by the book and get nowhere until after Carl Iverson was dead. So, armed with my digital recorder, my backpack, and absolutely no semblance of a plan, I headed north.

I listened to loud music on the drive, letting the songs drown out my doubts. I tried not to think about what I was doing as the six lanes of blacktop turned into four lanes, then two, and eventually I turned onto the gravel road leading to Douglas Lockwood's house. In the thirty minutes it took me to drive there, I went from skyscrapers and concrete to farm fields and trees. Thin gray clouds draped across the late-afternoon sky, and the weak December sun had already started its descent in the west. A light drizzle had turned to sleet, and the temperature dropped sharply as a northerly wind heralded the coming of the winter storm.

I slowed as I passed Lockwood's place, an old farmhouse that leaned with age and had wood siding rotting from the ground up. The grass in the front yard had not been mowed all summer, looking more like a fallow field than a lawn, and an old Ford Taurus with a sheet of plastic for a back window sat decaying in the gravel driveway.

I turned around at a field entrance just past the house and doubled back. As I neared his driveway, I saw a figure move in front of a window. A chill ran through me. The man who killed Crystal Hagen walked freely on the other side of that window. A spike of anger boiled up inside of me as I thought about the stain of Lockwood's sin infecting Carl's name. I had told myself over and over that this was going to be a simple drive into the country, a recon mission to find a house. But deep down, I always knew that it would be more than that.

I pulled into Lockwood's driveway at a crawl, the gravel crunching under my tires, my palms sweating where I gripped the steering wheel. I parked behind the busted-down Taurus and turned off the engine. The porch was dark. The interior of the house appeared gloomy as well, the only light coming from deep inside. I turned on my digital recorder, put it into my shirt pocket, and walked to the porch to knock on the front door.

At first, I saw no movement and heard no footsteps. I knocked again. This time a shadowy figure emerged from the lighted room in the back, turned on the porch light, and opened the front door.

"Douglas Lockwood?" I asked.

"Yeah, that's me," he said, sizing me up and down as if I had stepped across some no-trespass line. He stood maybe six-foot-two, with three days' worth of stubble covering his neck, chin, and cheeks. He reeked of alcohol, cigarettes, and old sweat.

I cleared my throat. "My name's Joe Talbert," I said. "I'm writing a story on the death of your stepdaughter, Crystal. I'd like to talk to you if I could."

His eyes went wide for a split second then narrowed. "That's . . . that's all done with," he said. "What's this about?"

"I'm doing a story about Crystal Hagen," I repeated, "and about Carl Iverson and what happened back in 1980."

"You a reporter?"

"Did you know that Carl Iverson got paroled from prison?" I said, trying to distract him and make it sound like my angle was Carl's early release.

"He was what?"

"I'd like to talk to you about it. It'll only take a couple minutes."

Douglas looked over his shoulder at the torn furniture and stain-covered walls. "I wasn't 'specting company," he said.

"I only have a few questions," I said.

He muttered something under his breath and walked inside, leaving the door open. I stepped through the doorway and saw a living room strewn knee deep in clothes, empty food containers, and crap you might find at a bad garage sale. We had taken only a few steps into the house when he suddenly stopped and turned to me. "This ain't a barn," he said, looking down at my wet shoes. I looked at the piles of junk cluttering the entryway and wanted to debate the point, but instead, I removed my shoes and followed him to the kitchen to a table covered with old newspapers, debt-collection envelopes, and about a week's worth of crusty dinner plates. In the middle of the table, a half-empty bottle of Jack Daniel's stood out like a holiday centerpiece. Lockwood sat in a chair at the end of the table. I took off my coat—careful to keep the recorder in my shirt pocket out of Lockwood's sight—and draped my coat over the back of a chair before sitting down.

"Is your wife here?" I asked.

He looked at me as if I'd just spat on him. "Danielle? That bitch? She ain't been my wife for twenty-five years. She divorced me."

"Sorry to hear that."

"I ain't," he said. "It is better to live in a desert than with a quarrel-some woman. Proverbs 21:19."

"Okay . . . I suppose that makes sense," I said, trying to find my way back to my topic. "Now, if I recall, Danielle testified that she was working the night that Crystal was killed. Is that right?"

"Yeah . . . What's that got to do with Iverson getting out of prison?"

"And you said that you were working late at your car dealership, correct?"

He tightened his lips together and studied me. "What are you gettin' at?"

"I'm trying to understand, that's all."

"Understand what?"

It was about here that my lack of planning made itself known, the way a single piano key left out of tune will blare its presence. I wanted to be subtle. I wanted to be clever. I wanted to lay a trap that would pull Lockwood's confession from him before he knew what had happened. Instead, I swallowed hard and threw it out there like a shot put. "I'm trying to understand why you lied about what happened to your step daughter?"

"What the hell?" he said. Who do you think you—"

"I know the truth!" I yelled the words. I wanted to stop any protest he had before the words formed in his throat. I wanted him to know that it was over. "I know the truth about what happened to Crystal."

"Why you . . ." Lockwood gritted his teeth and leaned forward on his seat. "What happened to Crystal was God's wrath. She brought that on herself." He slammed his hand on the table. "'On her head was the name, a mystery: Babylon the Great, the mother of prostitutes and of earth's abominations.'"

I wanted to pitch back into the fray, but his Bible-verse outburst confused me. He was spitting out something he had probably been telling himself for years, something that eased his guilt. Before I could correct my bearings he turned to me, his eyes on fire, and said, "Who are you?"

I reached into my back pocket and pulled out a copy of the diary pages. I laid them in front of Doug Lockwood with the coded version on top. "They convicted Carl Iverson because they thought Crystal wrote these diary entries about him. Do you remember the code, the numbers that she had in her diary?" He looked at the diary page in front of him, then at me, then back at the page. I then showed Lockwood the deciphered version, the ones that named him as being the man forcing Crystal to have sex. As he read the words, his hands started to tremble. I watched his face turn white, his eyes bulging and twitching.

"Where did you get these?" he asked.

"I broke her code," I said. "I know she was writing about you. You were the man making her do those things. You were raping your step-daughter. I know you did it. I just wanted to give you the chance to explain why before I go to the cops."

A thought passed behind his eyes, and he looked at me with a mixture of fear and understanding. "No . . . You just don't understand . . ." He reached toward the center of the table and picked up the bottle of Jack Daniels. I tensed up, waiting for him to swing at me, prepared to block and counterpunch. But instead, he unscrewed the top and took a big drink of the whiskey, his hand shaking as he wiped his mouth on the back of his sleeve.

I had hit a nerve. What I said had knocked him against the ropes, so I decided to push it. "You left your DNA on her fingernail." I said.

"You don't understand," he said again.

"I want to understand," I said. "That's why I came here. Tell me why."

He took another big drink from his bottle, wiped the traces of spittle from a corner of his mouth, and looked down at the diary. Then he spoke in a low, trembling voice, his words coming out monotone and rote, as if he were uttering thoughts that he meant to keep to himself. "It's biblical," he said, "the love between parent and child. And you come here, after all this time . . ." He massaged the sides of his head, pressing hard on his temples as though trying to rub out the thoughts and voices that clattered in his brain.

"It's time to make this right," I said. I greased the skids the way I had seen Lila coax information out of Andrew Fisher. "I understand. I really do. You're not a monster. Things just got out of control."

"People don't understand love," he said, as if I were no longer in the room. "They don't understand that children are a man's reward from God." He looked at me, searching my eyes for a hint of understanding—finding none. He took another drink from the bottle and began to breathe heavily, his eyes rolling up behind a pair of flittering lids. I thought that he might pass out. But then he closed his eyes and spoke again, this time, reaching down and pulling the words from some deep dark cavern inside his body. His words oozed out, viscous and thick, like old magma. "'I do not understand my own action,'" he whispered. "'For I do not do what I want . . . but I do the very thing I hate.'" Tears filled his eyes. His knuckles turned white as he gripped the neck of the whiskey bottle, holding on to it like a life preserver.

He was about to confess, I could feel it. I carefully glanced down at the recorder in my shirt pocket, making sure that nothing covered the tiny microphone. I needed to get Lockwood's words in his own voice admitting to what he had done.

I looked up just in time to see the whiskey bottle before it smashed into the side of my head. The blow sent me reeling off my chair, my head hitting the wall. Instinct told me to run for the front door, but the floor of Lockwood's house began to curl like a corkscrew. My damaged sense of balance threw me to the left, tossing me into a television. I could see the front door at the end of a long, dark tunnel. I fought against the spinning of the room to get there.

Lockwood hit me in the back with a pan or chair—something hard—knocking me to the floor, short of the door. I made one last all-exhausting lunge. I felt the door handle in my hand and threw it open. That's when another blow caught me in the back of the head. I stumbled off the porch, landing in the knee-deep grass, the darkness swallowing me as if I had fallen down a well. I floated in that darkness, seeing above me a small circle of light. I swam for that light, fighting against the abyss that pulled me down, forcing myself to regain consciousness. Once I reached that light, the cold December air filled my lungs again, and I could feel the frosted grass against my cheek. I was breathing. The pain in the back of my head punched through to my eyes and a trickle of warm blood dribbled across my neck.

Where had Lockwood gone?

My arms were stones: useless limbs propped unnaturally at my side. I focused all my energy and consciousness on moving my fingers, willing them to wiggle, then my wrists, then elbows and shoulders. I drew my hands under me, my palms on the cold ground, raising my face and chest out of the weeds. I heard movement behind me, around me, the sound of grass brushing against denim, but I could see nothing through the haze.

I felt a strap, like a canvas belt, wrap around my throat, drawing tight, cutting off my breath. I tried to push off the ground, to get to my knees, but the blows to my head had disconnected something. My body ignored my commands. I reached behind me, feeling his knuckles tightening in a desperate grip as he pulled on the ends of the belt. I couldn't breathe. What little strength I had left drained from my body. I felt myself falling back into that well, back into that endless darkness.

As I went limp, a wave of disgust flashed through my mind, disgust at my naiveté, disgust at not seeing the man's tight grip on the bottle for what it was, disgust that my life would end quietly, unceremoniously, lying face down in the frozen grass. I had let this old man—this whiskey-soaked child molester—beat me.

CHAPTER 34

I came back to life through a dream.

I stood alone in the middle of a fallow bean field, a cold wind whipping at my body. Black clouds rolled above my head, churning with pent-up fury, twisting into a funnel, preparing to reach down to Earth and pluck me away. As I stood firm against the threat, the clouds broke apart and descended in tiny specks, the specks diving toward me, growing in size, sprouting wings and beaks and eyes, becoming blackbirds. They swooped down in hostile disorder, landing on the left side of my body, pecking at my arm, my hip, my thigh, and the left side of my face. I swatted at the birds and began running through the field, but nothing could deter their attack as they tore the skin from my body.

That's when I felt the world bounce. The birds were gone; the field was gone. I struggled to make sense of my new reality, my eyes seeing only darkness, my ears hearing the hum of a car motor and the whining of tires on pavement. Pain throbbed in my head, the entire left side of my body burned as if someone had scaled that part of me like a fish. The inside of my throat felt as if it had been shaved with a dull rasp.

My memory returned as the pain sharpened, and I remembered the whiskey bottle smashing into the side of my head, the belt tightening around my neck, and the stench of his rot in my nostrils. I had been wadded into a fetal position and stuffed into a cold, dark, noisy place. My left arm lay trapped beneath my body, but I could wiggle the fingers on my right hand, feeling them twitch against the cloth of my blue jeans. I felt my thigh. Then I moved my hand over my hip and across the thin shirt covering my chest, feeling for my recorder. It was gone. I reached down to the floor beneath me, touching a nap of carpeting, wet, freezing, biting into my skin along the left side of my body: the blackbirds from my dream. I knew this carpet. It was the mat that covered the floor of my car trunk, eternally wet from the water that sprayed through the rusted holes between the trunk and the wheel well.

Jesus Christ, I thought to myself. I was in the trunk of my car— no coat, no shoes, the left side of my jeans and shirt drenched with icy road spray—and we were moving to beat hell. What was going on? I began to shiver uncontrollably, my jaw muscles clenching so tightly that I thought my teeth would break. I tried to roll onto my back, to give some small measure of relief to my left side, but I couldn't. Something blocked my knees. I reached down carefully, my shaking, brittle fingers probing the darkness, touching the rough surface of a cinder block that leaned against my knee. I reached farther and felt a second block with a log chain connecting the two. I followed the chain as it twisted between my calves and to my ankles, where it was circled twice and hooked.

Cinder blocks chained to my ankles. It didn't make sense, not at first. It took a moment or two to clear away the cobwebs. My hands were not tied, no tape around my mouth, but my ankles were chained to cinder blocks. He must have thought I was already dead. That's the only thing that made any sense. He was taking me somewhere to dump my body, somewhere with water, a lake or a river.

A spectacular fear gripped me, choking my thoughts in a sudden panic. My body shook with terror and cold. He was going to kill me. He believed he already had killed me. A tiny spark of realization came to me, calming my trembling body. He thought I was dead. A dead man can't fight; he can't run; he can't mess up the best laid plans of mice and men. But this was my car. Lockwood had made the mistake of stepping onto my battlefield: I knew my trunk blindfolded.

I remembered the small plastic panels, the size of a paperback novel, that covered the taillights from inside the trunk. I had replaced both my turn signals within the past year. I fumbled in the darkness for a second or two until I found the small latch that allowed me to pull free the panel covering the right-side blinker. With a quick twist

I popped the taillight bulb out of its bracket, flooding the trunk with heavenly light.

I wrapped my hands around the bulb, letting its heat thaw the icy joints of my knuckles. Then I twisted my torso to reach the left tail-light, being careful not to move too suddenly or make any noise that might alert Douglas Lockwood to the fact that his cargo was still alive. I pulled the panel and light out of the left bracket, giving the car no tail-lights and illuminating the trunk like midday.

The chain around my ankles had been secured with a single hook. Lockwood must have used every bit of his strength to cinch it that tightly. I struggled to unhook the chain, my frozen fingers curling into themselves as if crippled by arthritis, my thumb as useless as a flower petal. I gripped the light bulb again, holding it tightly in my hand, feeling it burn, the white-hot light bulb steaming against my frozen skin. I tried to unhook the chain again, and again, but could not loosen it. I needed a tool.

I did not own many tools, but I did own a piece-of-crap car that broke down a lot, so every tool that I owned, I kept in the trunk: two screwdrivers, a small crescent wrench, pliers, a roll of duct tape, and a can of WD-40, all wrapped up in a greasy towel. I grabbed the screw-driver with my brittle right hand, jamming the head between the hook and the chain link, wiggling it, pushing it, working the head in milli-meter by millimeter. Once I felt the screwdriver bite enough chain to give me leverage, I pushed the handle skyward, forcing the link from the hook. The chain dropped to the floor with a clamor that seemed to echo in the small confines of that trunk. I bit my lip as the rush of blood poured back into my frozen feet, hurting so badly I wanted to scream. I held my breath for several seconds, waiting for Lockwood to react. I heard a slight hum of music coming from the radio in the passenger compartment. Lockwood kept driving.

At least ten minutes had passed since I first pulled the taillights from their brackets. If there had been a cop anywhere around, he would have stopped my car by now. The corners and curves we were taking were tighter than those on a freeway, and the occasional bump in the road suggested that we were on some backwoods, county highway, lightly traveled, especially when there is a blizzard on the way.

I went through the options in my head. I could wait for a cop to pull us over, but the percentages were all wrong. I could wait for Lockwood to arrive at his destination, opening the trunk to find me alive and pissed off, but I could just as easily be dead from hypothermia by then. Or I could break out. That's when it dawned on me that trunks are designed to keep people out, not to keep people in. I examined the trunk lid to find three small hex-nuts attaching the trunk's lock in place. I smiled through my locked jaw.

I dug through my tools and grabbed my crescent wrench, the frozen handle burning in my hand as if it were dry ice. I wrapped the wrench with the grease towel and tried turning the worm screw to adjust the wrench. My fingers refused to move. I stuck my right thumb in my mouth to warm the knuckle, holding the taillight in my left hand to warm it up at the same time.

The car slowed, coming to a stop. I gripped the wrench in my right hand and prepared to lunge out of the trunk. I would surprise Lockwood and kill him. But the Accord began to move again, turning right and accelerating until it reached an aggressive speed.

I tried the worm screw on the wrench again. It turned, tightening the jaws of the wrench until they closed on the first hex screw. I held the wrench between the palms of my hands, my fingers curled and wilted by the cold. I had to concentrate my effort as if I were a small child attempting some feat far beyond my abilities, my arms shaking so badly that merely lining the screw up with the jaws of the wrench took forever.

By the time I got the third screw out, my body had stopped shaking. Whether the calm came from my effort and concentration on completing my task or from entering a new stage of hypothermia, I didn't know. As the last screw fell, the trunk opened a crack. Now, the only impediment to my opening the trunk was a wire that connected the trunk latch to the trunk release lever beside the driver's seat, a wire that I could remove with a simple tug from my pliers.

I pushed the trunk lid up a few inches and the interior light of the trunk turned on. I quickly closed the lid. I had forgotten about that light. I waited and listened to see if my mistake had caught Lockwood's attention, but he didn't change his speed. I removed the bulb, covered the other taillight bulbs, and opened the trunk again. The highway passed under me at about sixty miles an hour, disappearing into a darkness that held no other car light, no house lights, no glow of city lights. I wanted out of that trunk, but I didn't want the pain of hitting the pavement at that speed.

My shivering returned, tearing at the muscles in my calves, arms, and back. I needed to act soon or I would be too frozen to do anything—or dead. I tore the grease towel into three equal pieces, folding two of them into rectangles roughly the size of my feet, moving carefully to attach the rags to the bottoms of my feet using the duct tape, wrapping it around and around to make shoes. I wrapped the third section of the grease towel around the handle of the crescent wrench in a wad big enough to choke off the exhaust coming from the tailpipe. I quietly ripped off another piece of tape about three feet long, tying one end to the hole in the trunk lid where the lock used to be. I replaced the taillights so that no light would seep from the trunk as I opened the lid. Then I cut the trunk release wire with my pliers, holding the lid shut with the tape. I tested my escape hatch, pushing it open a few inches with one hand and pulling it back down with the tape in the other. It was time to escape.

I let enough tape loose to allow the trunk to open a foot or so, enough space that I could ease my shoulders through, but hopefully, not so much as to draw Lockwood's attention. I slithered head first over the backside of the car, holding the lid down against my back with the duct tape in my right hand, the towel-wrapped wrench in my left. The frigid air took my breath away.

I shoved the wrench into the tailpipe with all the strength I could muster, the rag stopping the flow of exhaust, the carbon monoxide backing up into the manifolds and heads. I held the stopper against the pressure of the exhaust until the car sputtered, coughed twice, then died, rolling silently toward the shoulder of the road. When it had slowed to a crawl, I leapt from the trunk and ran as fast as I could in my duct-tape shoes, heading for the woods on the side of the road.

As I reached the tree line, I heard the car door slam shut. I kept running. Branches ripped at the flesh of my arms. I kept running. Another few steps and Lockwood yelled something unintelligible. I couldn't understand the words, but I understood the rage. I kept running. A few feet more and I heard the first crack of a gun being fired.

CHAPTER 35

I had never been shot at before. And with the night I was having—getting strangled into unconsciousness, chained to cinder blocks, and nearly freezing to death in a trunk—it never occurred to me that things could get worse. I lowered my head and serpentined as I ran, charging blindly through the woods. The first bullet ripped into the bark of a jack pine ten yards to my right; two more bullets split the cold night air above my head. I looked over my shoulder to see Douglas Lockwood in the glow of the taillight, his right arm raised, pointing a gun in my direction. Before I could worry anymore about bullets, the ground dropped from under my feet, and I tumbled into a gully. Dead branches and scrub brush tore at my frozen skin. I jumped to my feet, clutching a sprig of birch for balance and listening as another gunshot sent a bullet well above my head.

Then silence.

Standing erect, I could see over the bevel of the gully. My car was fifty yards away, its high beams casting a cone of light up the highway. Lockwood aimed his gun toward the sound of my fall, unsure of where I was. He waited for another sound, a breaking twig or the crackle of dead leaves, to hone his aim. He listened; but I stood still, my body shaking violently from the cold now that I had stopped running. Lockwood looked at the back end of my car, bent down, and pulled the wrench from the tailpipe, throwing it into the woods.

He headed for the driver's-side door. With the stopper gone from the tailpipe, the car would start. He had headlights with which he could flood the countryside. I scrambled out of the gully, running deeper into the woods, dodging what I could dodge, and getting scraped and whipped by sticks I could not see. By the time he turned the car around,

I had put a hundred yards of thick forest between us. Barely any light from the headlights seeped through the thicket. I skated down a small hill, and the headlights disappeared behind the horizon.

He would search the wood—at least that's what I would do. He can't let me live. He can't allow me to make it back to civilization to tell what I know. I kept moving, spikes of pain shooting up from my toes with each step, my eyes adjusting enough to the darkness that I could avoid the fallen trees and branches in my way. I stopped to catch my breath, listening for footsteps. I could hear nothing. He had to be out there, somewhere. As I strained to hear, I became dizzy, my thoughts disjointed and thick. Something was wrong. I tried to grab a sapling, but my hand refused to obey my command. I fell.

My skin felt hot. I had learned about this in school. What was it? That's right. People dying of hypothermia will feel hot and shed their clothes. Was I dying? I needed to move, to keep moving, to get blood flowing. I needed to stand up. I pushed against the ground with my elbows, getting on to my knees. I could no longer feel them. I could no longer feel the frozen earth against my skin. Am I dying? No. I won't allow it.

My legs wobbled like a newborn foal, but I got to my feet. Which way was I running? I couldn't remember. Every direction seemed equally foreign, equally foreboding. I must move—or die. The wind had been at my back, hadn't it? I chose a direction and walked—the cold wind pushing me on. For all I knew, I could have been walking right back to Lockwood. It didn't matter. Death by bullet might be preferable to death by hypothermia.

I didn't see the land fall away again, and I fell down a steep grade, bouncing like a gunny sack full of potatoes, landing in the middle of a cart path, two parallel tracks worn bare by truck tires. The sight of the path filled me with resolve. I rose to my feet, randomly stumbling in the direction I faced, my knees buckling and shaking, threatening to give way with every step. When I thought my body had reached its limit, when I got to a point where I could do little more than fall forward, I saw a glint of reflection a few feet ahead of me. I blinked to clear my eyes, believing that my muddled brain had thrown a final taunt at me. But there it was again. A sliver of moonlight piercing the clouds had sailed to Earth like a well-aimed arrow, ricocheting off the dirty glass window of a hunting shack: the promise of shelter, maybe a blanket, or—better yet—a stove.

I found a reserve of strength I didn't know I had, a final gasp of life. I dragged my feet along the cart path. The cabin had a metal door that was locked, but the window next to the door would break easy enough. I found a rock, but my fingers were useless nubs on the ends of my arms, so I picked the rock up using my wrists and forearms. I threw the rock and my body against the glass, shattering a small corner of the window. I slid my arm through the hole, reaching in, trying to grip the door knob firm enough to turn it. My hand flopped impotently against the knob. I was so close to rescue, yet if I could not get in, it meant nothing.

Dizziness washed over me again. My right leg snapped, and I fell against the hut, my left leg struggling to keep me upright. I tipped my head back and drove my forehead into the window, breaking the glass into shards that cascaded to the floor. With my elbows I punched the remaining glass fragments out of the frame and lunged through the opening, falling to the floor, pieces of glass hooking and tearing my stomach as I fell.

I crawled on my knees and elbows across the floor, taking inventory of my new digs as much as the pale moonlight would allow: a sink, a card table with four chairs, a couch, and . . . a wood-burning stove. Jackpot! The hunters had left a small stack of jack-pine logs near the stove, and beside the stack of wood I found an old newspaper and a canister about the size of a soda can with two long-stem matches. I slid a match through my gnarled fingers and struck it against the side of the cast-iron stove. My shakes caused me to drive the head of the match into the stove with such force that it snapped the stick in two, its head falling into the darkness.

"F-F-F-FUCK!" I uttered my first word out loud since I'd been hit with the whiskey bottle. The sound scraped hard against my sore throat as it came out.

I slid the second match into my left hand, pressing my wrist against my abdomen to steady it. I touched the head of the match to the metal of the stove then jerked my torso, causing the match to strike the metal hard enough to light it without breaking it. I turned the match on its side and watched the flame grow. I lit a corner of newspaper, the flame licking the dry paper, climbing quickly toward my hand, the heat from the flame feeding me; and I consumed it with a pauper's gluttony.

As light from the burning newspaper filled the small room, I found strips of pine bark beside the woodpile. Stacking the bark across the burning newspaper, I watched it take to the flame. Soon I had a fire with the authority of wood. The bark led to sticks; the sticks led to logs; and in a matter of minutes, I found myself squatting before robust fire, rotating my body in quarter turns, letting each side heat up to the edge of pain before turning.

As I revolved on my imaginary spit, as my skin thawed, as my senses came back to life, the many cuts on my body found their voice. Gashes covered my arms and feet. I pulled splinters of glass from my abdomen. One particularly large scrape across my shoulder still had pine needles stuck to it. The skin on my neck, where Lockwood's belt had cut off my air, burned a reminder of how close I'd come to dying. I unwrapped the tape from around my feet, the blood chewing its way back into the capillaries and crevices of my toes, setting them on fire. I rubbed the muscles of my calves and chest and jaw where cramping from my shivering still stabbed at me like a spike.

As soon as my joints thawed enough to stand up, I went to the window, fireplace poker in hand, to look and listen for Douglas Lockwood. The wind, which had been at my back as I ran through the trees, had grown to gale force. It whipped the gingham curtain and whistled as it swayed the pines outside. It sounded ominous, but it was a godsend because it carried the smell of smoke away from my pursuer. I saw no sign of Lockwood. I heard no footsteps. He had a gun, but he couldn't shoot what he couldn't find. I tucked the curtain into the window sash, trying to make certain that it covered every inch of the window, preventing the fire's light from bleeding through to the outside. I listened and waited. I would make Lockwood come inside the hut if he wanted to kill me. Now that I was ready for him, he would have a hell of a fight on his hands.

I squatted next to the window for at least an hour, straining to hear footsteps or see the barrel of a gun poke through the curtain where I had smashed the window. And after an hour, I started to believe he would not find me in that hunting shack. As I peeked out to look for any sign of Lockwood, I saw the blizzard that the weathermen had predicted. Snowflakes as big as cotton balls moved sideways in the wind, cutting visibility to near zero. Lockwood would never find me now. He wouldn't be crazy enough to stay in the woods in the middle of a blizzard. I shoved a couch cushion into the window frame to further seal the hole and gave up my vigil.

I looked around the cabin, now lit by a wonderful, blazing fire, and saw it to be a single room about the size of a boxcar—no bathroom, no electricity, no phone. A pair of chest-high fishing waders hung from a hook on the wall near the sink. I walked over the broken glass to the waders, took off my blue jeans, which were wet and frozen, and slipped into the waders, hanging my jeans above the stove on the end of a broom handle. I found two large towels and a fillet knife in a cupboard. I took off my shirt, hanging it with my jeans, and draped the towels across my shoulders, wearing them like a shawl. I picked up the knife, touching its razor-sharp edge with my thumb, holding it in my hand, thrusting it into the shadows, killing Lockwood over and over again in my mind. I had clothes, heat, a couch, and a roof. I felt like a king. I believed in my escape. I believed that I was safe from the crazy man who'd spat Bible verses at me just before he tried to kill me. Yet, as I lay on that couch, I clutched the fillet knife in one hand and the fireplace poker in the other, waiting for one more fight.

CHAPTER 36

That night I slept like a man on a ledge. Every crackle of the fire woke me from my fitful slumber, sending me to the window to scan the woods for signs of Lockwood. As the new day broke, the storm maintained its crescendo with the wind whipping the snow into a blinding wall of white that would make a sled dog think twice. At first light, I stepped outside into twelve inches of snow to look for a water pump. The hut had a sink with a drain, but no faucet. I didn't find a pump, so I melted snow in a pan on the stove. I had enough wood to last a couple days, and as long as I had fire, I would survive.

I changed back into my blue jeans and shirt, both of which had dried overnight, and I spent the morning inspecting the cabin with the benefit of sunlight. The hunters stored very little in the way of food. I found a can of beef stew well past its expiration date, a box of spaghetti noodles, and a few spices—enough to feed me until the storm passed.

I would need a coat for my trip out of the woods, so I gathered all the supplies I could find and set to the task. I made sleeves out of my two towels, turning them into tubes and stitching them using fishing line and a flattened fish hook for a needle. The towel for each sleeve ran from my wrist to my chest, where I sewed them together, leaving a collar-like hole for my head. I slid my chest waders back on, attaching the suspenders over top of the towels to hold the sleeves in place. Then I marched around the room, stretching and testing my sartorial achievement, pleased with my creativity. Part one of my coat was complete.

Around mid-morning I cooked half of the spaghetti noodles, eating them with an odd compliment of curry, paprika, and salt, washing them down with warm water. I could not remember eating a better meal. After lunch, I started making the rest of my coat. A thick gingham curtain covered the hut's only window, its bright red checkerboard pattern reminding me of a restaurant tablecloth. I cut a hole in the middle of the curtain, turning it into a poncho. Then I pulled foam padding from the arm of the couch to use for a hat. When the time came I would fill my chest waders with pieces of cushion for insulation and tie on my hat and poncho with cords from the curtain. By the end of the day, I had a winter coat that would have been the envy of the Donner Party.

As the sun began to set, I again checked the weather. Although snow still fell, it was not falling as heavily or as horizontally as before. I stepped out into snow up to my knees and realized that I would need snow shoes. I thought about that while I made supper, using the fillet knife to open the can of beef stew, cooking it on the stove until it bubbled.

After supper, I sat in the light of the fire fashioning snow shoes out of one-by-eight pine baseboards that I'd pried off the wall. I used nylon cords from the guts of the couch to bind the boards to the chest waders' boots. When I finished, I smiled with satisfaction and curled up on what remained of the couch for my second night in the hut.

In the morning, I cooked and ate the last of the noodles, cut the cushions into strips, stuffing my chest waders with the insulation, and put on my gingham poncho and my hat. I doused the fire with snow, and then, before leaving the hut, I used a piece of charred wood from the stove to write a message to the owner on the card table.

Sorry for mess. Hut saved my life. I'll pay for damage. Joe Talbert.

My final act was to strap the fillet knife to my hip. I could not imagine Lockwood still stalking me through the woods, but I didn't see the whiskey bottle coming either. He wanted me dead. He needed me dead. I had the ability to send him to prison for trying to kill me—if not for murdering Crystal Hagen. If he thought like me, he'd be in those woods, holed up like a hunter—rifle in hand—waiting for me to walk in front of the crosshairs.

CHAPTER 37

Although I grew up in Minnesota, where you walk on snow almost as much as you walk on grass or concrete, I had never walked in snowshoes before. And I had certainly never walked on snowshoes made out of pine boards. It took a bit of practice before I hit my stride, each step sinking in snow up to my shin, which was a pleasant improvement over the knee-deep drudgery that would have bogged me down without the snowshoes. I broke two sticks off a dead tree to use like ski poles for balance. Each step required focus to keep the timing of my step coordinated with the transfer of weight. After twenty minutes I had only covered about a quarter mile, but my arduous pace did not concern me. I was warm, the weather was calm, and the woods appeared to be devoid of Doug Lockwood. And despite the threat of dying dampening my mood, the scenery of the snow-covered forest was breathtaking.

Just as a trickle of a brook would lead to a river, I knew that the little cart path would lead to a road and to civilization. After an hour of walking, covering far less ground than I'd hoped, I came to a road. It was little more than a break in the trees—narrow, curvy, and not yet plowed—perhaps a gravel access road. A jaundiced sun bleeding through the clouds over my left shoulder told me that the road ran east and west. Because the northwest wind had been at my back when I'd escaped from Lockwood, I figured that heading west would take me back to the blacktop.

The trail rose on an easy line, heading to the highest point of a hill. I marched toward that point, keeping cadence to a song in my head—the chant sung by the Wicked Witch's guards in *The Wizard of Oz* as they marched into her castle: "O–ee–yah, ee–oh–ah." I would pause now and again to rest, to breathe, to look for human tracks, and to take in the beauty of the day: a day that Douglas Lockwood had tried to steal from me. Behind me, the land fell in grades toward a river in the distance, a good-sized river, but I had no idea which one. It could have been the Mississippi, the St. Croix, the Minnesota, or the Red River, depending upon how long I had lain in that trunk and which direction we had traveled.

As I crested the hill, I saw my first proof of civilization in two days: a blacktop road, plowed clean, rolling out to the horizon. Three or four miles up that road, I could see a farmstead, with the silver roof of its barn shining through the trees next to a grain silo: a view that could not have been more splendid if it had been the Emerald City itself. The farm was still a long way off, and I knew I still had probably an hour before I would reach it. I also knew that I hadn't eaten enough and that running would wipe me out. But despite what I knew, I ran.

I once watched a slow-motion video of an albatross trying to take flight from a sand dune, his webbed feet slapping flat on the ground, his body lumbering from side to side, struggling to stay erect, his clumsy wings stretched out to counter the lurching and pitching of his torso. I imagined that my run down that hill in knee-deep snow fairly resembled that bird—my feet strapped to pine boards, stomping a path more zigzagged than straight. I lunged from one step to the next, my arms extended to absurd lengths by the walking sticks in my hands, flailing in the air to keep balance. When I reached the blacktop, I fell backward into the snow, exhausted, laughing, enjoying the feel of sweat on my face, made cold by the winter breeze.

I removed the boards from my feet and headed up the blacktop to the farmhouse, jogging most of the way, walking when I needed to rest. I reckoned by the location of the sun in the sky that I got to the farmhouse well after noon.

As I approached the house, a dog stuck his head out of a doggie door and started barking to beat hell. He made no effort to advance, which surprised me given my appearance: green chest waders, cushion foam splaying out like scarecrow straw, arms wrapped in towels, and a red-checkered curtain draped over my shoulders and tied around my waist. I would have barked at me, too.

As I approached the porch and the dog, the door swung open and an old man with a shotgun stepped outside.

"Seriously?" I said, the exasperation dripping in my words. "You've got to be kidding me."

"Who are you?" the old man asked. He spoke in a soft voice, more inquisitive than angry. He pointed the gun barrel at the ground between us.

"My name is Joe Talbert," I said. "I was kidnapped, and I escaped. Can you call the sheriff? I can wait out here if you like."

The dog retreated into the house as an old woman stepped into the doorway behind the man, the girth of her hips taking up much of the opening. She put a hand on the old man's shoulder, communicating to him that he should step to the side, which he did.

"You were kidnapped?" she said.

"Yes, ma'am," I said. "Jumped out of a car a couple nights ago, just before the storm hit. Been hiding out in a little cabin in the woods there." I pointed over my shoulder with my thumb. "Can you tell me where I am?"

"You're about seven miles from North Branch, Minnesota," she said.

"And that river back there—what river is that?" I asked.

"The St. Croix," she said.

If I was right about why I had cinder blocks chained to my legs, then Lockwood was planning to dump my body into the St. Croix River. A shudder ran through my chest at the thought of how close he had come to completing his mission. I would have floated under the ice, my flesh washing away from my bones, eaten by scavenging fish, until the current cut me free of the log chain, separating my bones at the ankle. I would have bounced with the current, breaking into pieces as my body hit rocks and logs, the river spreading my remains between here and New Orleans.

"Are you hungry?" the woman asked.

"Very."

The woman nudged the old man, who stepped aside—although he never put the gun away. She took me inside and fed me cornbread and milk and waited with me until the sheriff arrived.

CHAPTER 38

The sheriff was a big man with a bald head and a thick black goatee. He asked me politely to have a seat in the back of the squad car, but I knew that his request was one that gave me no choice in the matter. I told him my story from beginning to end. When I had finished, he called my name into dispatch to see if I had any warrants for my arrest. I didn't. But I didn't come back as a missing person either. I hadn't told Lila where I was going. She probably assumed I had to go to Austin to deal with Jeremy and my mother.

"Where are we going?" I asked when he started the car and pulled out of the turnabout.

"I'm taking you to the law-enforcement center in Center City," he said.

"You're taking me to jail?"

"I'm not sure what to do with you. I suppose I could arrest you for breaking into that hunting cabin. That's a third-degree burglary."

"Burglary?" I said, my voice rising with anger. "Lockwood was trying to kill me. I had to break in."

"That's what you say," he said. "But I don't know you from Adam. I never heard of this Lockwood guy. There is no missing-persons report on you, and until I get to the bottom of this, I'm going to put you someplace where I can keep an eye on you."

"Oh, for God's sakes!" I crossed my arms in disgust.

"If your story checks out, I'm not gonna hold you, but I can't let you go until I get this straightened out."

At least he didn't handcuff me, I thought. In the confinement of that back seat I could smell the pungent odor of the towels, the couch cushions, and the chest waders: an odor I hadn't noticed before. As

I contemplated my scent, a thought popped into my head. I knew someone who could convince the sheriff that I was telling the truth.

"Call Max Rupert," I said.

"Who?"

"Detective Max Rupert. He's with the Homicide Division in Minneapolis. He knows all about Lockwood and me. He'll vouch for me."

The sheriff got on his radio and asked dispatch to contact Max Rupert in Minneapolis. We drove for a while without talking, the sheriff whistling in the front seat while I desperately waited for dispatch to confirm that I was not a nut job or a burglar. As the sheriff pulled into the sally port of the jail in Center City, the female dispatcher crackled through the radio telling the sheriff that Max Rupert was off duty, but they were trying to locate him. I dropped my head in resignation.

"Sorry," the sheriff said, "but I have to lock you down for a while." He parked the car, opened my door, and cuffed my hands behind my back. He led me to a booking room where a jailer had me change into the orange uniform of a convict. When he closed the door to the holding cell, I felt strangely content. I was warm; I was safe; and I was very much alive.

A nurse came in about an hour later to clean up my cuts, putting bandages on the deeper ones and antibacterial cream on the rest. The tips of my toes and fingers still lacked feeling from having been frozen, but she said that might not be permanent. After she left, I lay on my bunk to rest. I don't remember falling asleep.

Later, I woke to the sound of whispering voices. "He looks so peaceful. I almost hate to disturb him," said a voice that I vaguely recognized.

"We'd be more than happy to keep him here for a couple days," said another voice, which I knew to be that of the sheriff. I sat up on my bunk, rubbed the sleep from my eyes, and saw Max Rupert standing at the doorway to my cell.

"Hey there, sleeping beauty," he said. "They told me you might need these." He tossed me a sweatshirt, a coat, and a pair of winter boots three sizes too big.

"What are you doing here?" I asked.

"Giving you a ride home," he said. "We have some catching up to do." He turned, walking with the sheriff back toward the dispatch room while I changed clothes. Ten minutes later I was in Rupert's unmarked squad car—the front passenger seat this time instead of the back—leaving Center City and heading to Minneapolis. The sun had gone down, but its dying glow still marked the western horizon. I told Rupert what had happened, and he listened patiently even though I was sure that the sheriff had already filled him in.

"I think he was going to dump me in the river," I said.

"That's a pretty good bet," Rupert said. "When I heard that you wandered out of the woods like some deranged mountain man claiming that Lockwood kidnapped you, I checked out a few things. Ran your vehicle information. Your car got ticketed and towed yesterday. It was parked on a snow-emergency route in Minneapolis. I stopped by the impoundment lot before heading up here." He reached into the back seat and grabbed my car keys and backpack with my cell phone in it. "These were in your car."

"You didn't happen to find a wallet or digital recorder?"

Rupert shook his head. "But we did find a hand-held ice auger and sledgehammer in the back seat. I'm betting those aren't yours."

"No," I said.

"He was probably planning on slipping you through the ice on the St. Croix. We'd have never found you."

"I think he thought I was dead."

"Must have," Rupert said. "When you strangle someone, they tend to pass out because the blood stops going to their head, but they're not dead yet. With the cold weather dropping your body temperature, I'm sure he thought you were just a corpse."

"I almost was," I said. "You said they found my car on a snow-emergency route?"

"Yeah, parked about a block from the bus depot," Rupert said. "Lockwood could be on a bus heading anywhere."

"He's on the run?"

"He could be. Or maybe he wants us to think he's running. We checked for credit-card purchases under his name but didn't find one. He may have bought a ticket with cash though. I also have a couple officers going through the surveillance footage from the depot. So far they haven't found Lockwood on the tapes. We put a BOLO out on him."

"BOLO?

"Be on the lookout."

"So you believe me?" I asked. "That he's the guy who killed Crystal Hagen?"

"It's looking that way," he said. "I've got enough to arrest him for kidnapping you, that'll give us his DNA . . . when we find him."

"We can go to his house," I said. "He was drinking from a whiskey bottle. It'll have his DNA, or we can grab his toothbrush."

Rupert pursed his lips and sighed. "I sent a squad out to Lockwood's house already," he said. "When they got there, the fire department was just wrapping up. The place was burned to the ground. The fire marshal is pretty sure it was arson."

"He burned down his own house?"

"He's trying to cover his tracks—tie up any loose ends that might point at him. We couldn't even find a cigarette butt or beer bottle—nothing that might have his DNA on it."

"So what are we gonna do next"? I asked.

"There is no 'we' in this anymore," Rupert scolded. "You're out of this. I don't want you poking around looking for Douglas Lockwood. Am I clear? We have an investigation going. It's just a matter of time."

"But time is the problem—"

"This guy almost killed you," Rupert said. "I know you want to wrap this all up before Iverson dies. I'd like that, too. But it's time for you to fall back under the radar. "

"He won't come after me now—now that you guys are involved," I said.

"You're assuming that Lockwood is rational, that he isn't the kind of guy to kill you just to make things even," Rupert said. "You've met him. Would you say he's rational?"

"Well, let's see," I said with an edge of sarcasm. "In the short time that I was with Douglas Lockwood, he cried, spouted crazy Bible verses, hit me with a whiskey bottle, strangled me, shoved me in a trunk, and tried to shoot me. I think we can rule out rational."

"That's my point," Rupert said. "You need to watch your back. If he's still around, there's a chance he'll try to come after you. He'll see you as being the cornerstone of all his problems. I assume he has your name and address. It was in your wallet, right?"

"Damn."

"Do you have someplace you can stay for a while, someplace he won't look—your parents' maybe?"

"I can stay with Lila," I said quickly. "You met her." I didn't mention that Lila only lived a few feet down the hall from me. I wasn't about to go back to Austin.

Rupert reached into the console between us and pulled out another of his business cards. "Just in case he shows up. I wrote my personal cell number on it—if you need to reach me, twenty-four/seven."

Rupert telling me to stand down put a foul taste in my mouth. This was my project. I dug it out of the dirt. I brought it to him when he didn't want it. Now that we were so close, now that Lockwood was at the tips of our fingers, he wanted to dismiss me. He said: "We have an investigation going." But what I heard was: "We'll add this case to the stack of ongoing cases, and if Lockwood shows up, we'll arrest him." I closed my eyes, and a vision invaded my thoughts. I saw Carl thrashing in a river, slipping under the water, my grandfather's lifejacket twisted around his arms. In my vision I was holding on to that anchor rope— not letting go, not saving his life. Not again, I told myself. I was not finished with this project. I would figure out a way to keep my shoulder to the wheel. I would do what I needed to do to keep the investigation moving at a pace that would put Lockwood in jail before Carl died.

CHAPTER 39

I called Lila and asked her to pick me up at City Hall. The police were holding on to my car as evidence to be dusted for fingerprints and the like. On the phone, I told Lila some of what had happened. I finished telling her the story as she drove me back to our apartments. She touched the side of my head where the Jack Daniels bottle cut me open, letting her hand slide down to the abrasion on my neck where his belt roughed up the skin on my throat. She asked me to repeat the words that Lockwood said after reading the diary. I struggled to remember.

"I think he called Crystal the whore of Babylon," I said. "He was rambling on about how I didn't understand his love for her . . . that it was biblical and she was . . . what was it . . . something about children being man's reward from God. Then he said that he does the thing he hates, and he hit me with the bottle."

"He sounds insane," she said.

"No argument."

I kept a lookout on the drive home, scrutinizing the face of every man we passed. When we parked at the apartment, I looked around the area, examining car windshields for signs of a body in the driver's seat or a face peeking over the dash. A streetlight flickering at the end of the block made the shadows move. I thought for a second that I saw the slumped shoulders of Douglas Lockwood hiding behind a dumpster, but it turned out to be a used tire. I didn't tell Lila the reason for my new-found paranoia, but I think she understood.

I hadn't fully appreciated the toll that my ordeal had taken on my body until I walked up the narrow stairs to my apartment. So many parts of my body burned with pain: my calves, shoulders, and back felt like one giant charley horse from having been knotted up during my convulsive shivering. Cuts and scrapes crisscrossed my chest and arms and thighs as though I'd been wrestling a razorback. I stopped at the turn in the steps to make a mental note of everything that hurt before I continued to the top.

I didn't have to ask Lila to let me stay in her apartment that night—she offered. She also offered to make me some chicken noodle soup. I took her up on both. Then she led me to her bathroom and started the shower for me and left. The water felt wonderful against my skin, loosening the knots in my muscles, washing the dried blood from my hair, and cleaning the dirt from my cuts. I stayed in the shower longer than normal and would've stayed even longer than that had I not known that Lila was making soup for me. I patted myself dry, being careful not to reopen my cuts and abrasions. When I stepped out of the shower, I found some of my own clean clothes folded neatly on the toilet seat. Lila had fished my apartment key out of my pants pocket and gone next door, returning with clean boxer shorts, a t-shirt, and my bathrobe. She also brought my razor and toothbrush so that I could shave and brush my teeth for the first time in three days.

When I walked out of the bathroom, Lila was pouring soup from the saucepan into a bowl. She had changed into her favorite oversized Twins jersey and her pink pajama bottoms with matching slippers. I liked her Twins jersey.

"You look like you're in pain," Lila said.

"Yeah, I'm a bit sore," I said.

"Go lay down," she said, pointing toward her bedroom. "I'll bring your soup in."

"I'd feel better if you let me sleep on the couch," I said.

"Don't argue," she said, pointing at the door to her bedroom. "You've had a rough time. You're gonna sleep in that bed. End of story."

I didn't argue further. I'd been looking forward to sleeping in a bed, with a pillow, sheets, and a warm comforter. I propped a pillow against the headboard and climbed into bed, closing my eyes for a few seconds to savor the softness of her bed against my sore body. Lila brought the soup with a complement of crackers and a glass of milk. She sat on the edge of the bed, and we talked about my ordeal some more. I told her about starting the fire in the cabin and the designer outfits I wore to my rescue, gingham coat and all. When I finished my soup, Lila took my bowl, plate, and glass, and I listened to the clinking as she put the dishes into the sink. Things got quiet for a moment before Lila came back to the bedroom.

When she walked in—when I saw her—I stopped breathing. Lila had unbuttoned her jersey almost to her navel, the curves of her breasts peeking out from behind the fabric, the tails of the shirt sliding across the smooth silk of her bare legs.

My heart thumped so hard in my chest, I was certain she could see it. I wanted to speak but could find no words. I simply looked at her, taking in her beauty.

Slowly, gracefully, she raised a hand across her chest and slid the shirt off of her right shoulder, the cloth falling to her elbow, her right breast revealed. Then she slid the shirt from her left shoulder, letting the jersey fall to the floor, her only clothing being a pair of lacy black panties.

Pulling the covers down, she slipped in next to me, kissing the scrape on my chest, a cut on my arm, then my neck. She moved gently down my body, kissing my wounds, caressing my strained muscles, and touching me with a tenderness I had never known. She brought her lips to mine and we kissed, gently, my fingers lacing through her short hair, her body pressed against mine. I ran my other hand down the curve of her back, her hip, reading the magnificence of her form with my fingers.

We made love that night—not the sweaty, clumsy, bounce-off-the-walls type of love born of alcohol and hormones, but the slow-melting, Sunday-morning type of love. She moved over me like a breeze, her lithe, sinewy body weightless in my arms. We cuddled and nuzzled and danced until she sat astride me, slowly writhing and churning. A slice of moonlight slipped through a gap in the curtains and fell across her body, her back arched, her hands braced on my thighs, her head tossed back, eyes closed. I stared in awe, taking her in, locking that vision into a place in my mind where the memory would keep forever.

CHAPTER 40

I woke before the sun came up. Lila was still in my arms, her back pressed against my chest, her hips and thighs curving with mine. I kissed the back of her neck, causing her to stir a little, but she didn't wake. I gently breathed in the scent of her body, closed my eyes to replay last night in my head, and let the memory lull me like a fine intoxication until I fell back to sleep. I didn't wake again until my cell phone went off at around 8:30. It took me a little while to locate my pants in Lila's bathroom and fish the phone out of the pocket.

"Hello?" I said, walking back to bed.

"Joe Talbert?"

"Yeah, this is Joe," I said, rubbing my eyes.

"This is Boady Sanden from the Innocence Project. I didn't wake you, did I?" he said.

"No," I lied. "What's up?"

"You won't believe the stroke of luck we've had."

"What?"

"Have you been following the news story about the Ramsey County Crime Lab?"

"It doesn't ring a bell," I said.

"St. Paul has its own crime lab separate from the BCA—the Ramsey County Crime Lab. A couple months ago three of their scientists testified at a trial that they did not have a written protocol for many of their procedures. The defense attorneys in the area went nuts and raised a huge stink about it. So the county stopped running tests until the protocol problem is fixed.

"How is that a stroke of luck for us?" I said.

"Well, it occurred to me that they won't be doing any DNA testing

241

because without proper written protocols in place, any mediocre defense attorney will get the evidence thrown out. But in your case, it's the defense that is asking for the test. The prosecutors will never challenge the reliability of the test because to do so would force them to argue that the evidence they've been using for years is bad."

"I'm sorry, I'm not following."

"We have a lab full of scientists who are not testing anything right now because of administrative issues. I have a friend down there, and I asked her to rush our fingernail through. She said no at first, but when I explained the situation about Mr. Iverson being on his death bed, she agreed."

"You got the DNA test done?"

"I got the DNA test done. I have the results right here."

I couldn't breathe. I think Sanden held off telling me the results for a moment just to let the anticipation build. Finally I said, "And?"

"And they found both skin cells and blood on the fingernail—both male and female DNA. We can assume the female DNA was Crystal's.

"What about the male DNA?" I asked.

"The male DNA does not belong to Carl Iverson. It wasn't his skin, and it wasn't his blood."

"I knew it," I said. "I knew it wouldn't be Carl's." I pumped my fist in the air in a triumphant burst of energy.

"All we need now is a swab of Lockwood's DNA," Sanden said.

And just like that, the balloon of my elation burst. "You haven't talked to Max Rupert yet, have you?"

"Rupert? No. Why?"

"Lockwood's on the run," I said. "He burned his house to the ground and took off. Rupert said he destroyed any trace of his DNA." I didn't tell Professor Sanden why Lockwood was on the run. I didn't tell him about my visit to his house, about the kidnapping. I knew that my actions, however well-intentioned, had caused Lockwood to flee. I felt sick.

Lila sat up in bed, interested in my conversation. I hit the speakerphone so that she could listen in.

"Well," Sanden said. "We have the diary, the pictures, Lockwood's flight from justice and burning his house down—that might be enough to get us back into court."

"Is there enough to exonerate Carl?" I asked.

"I don't know." Professor Sanden spoke as if he were talking to himself, letting the pros and cons tumble from inside his head. "Let's assume that the DNA came back to Lockwood. He would simply say that he argued with Crystal that morning, that she scratched him. They lived in the same house after all. It's possible the DNA got there without him killing her."

Lila spoke up. "He said he didn't go back to the house until after she was killed. Wait a second." Lila scrambled out of bed, throwing on her Twins jersey as she ran out of the room.

"Who was that?" Sanden asked.

"That was my girlfriend, Lila," I said. It felt good to say it. I could hear her bare feet padding to my apartment. A few seconds later she came back with one of the transcripts open in her hand, her eyes skimming its pages. "I remember Danielle... Crystal's mom testifying..." She flipped another page and ran her finger down the lines. "Here it is. Crystal's mom testified that Crystal had been acting depressed, so she let Crystal sleep in that morning. After Doug and Danny left, she woke Crystal up..." She read to herself for a few seconds before she read the passage aloud. "'I woke Crystal up and told her to get in the shower because it always takes her so long to get ready for school.'"

"She showered after Doug left the house," I said.

"Exactly." Lila closed the transcript. "The only way for Doug Lockwood's DNA to get on that that fingernail is if he saw her after school."

"If that is Lockwood's DNA," Sanden said.

"If you were a betting man?" I asked.

Sanden thought for a second and said, "I would bet that it's Doug Lockwood's DNA on that fingernail," he said.

"So I go back to my original question," I said. "Is there enough evidence without the DNA to exonerate Carl Iverson?"

Boady sighed into the phone. "Maybe," he said. "I have enough to get a hearing. If we could nail down whose DNA it is . . . I mean she could have scratched her boyfriend or another boy at school. Without a match, there's too much wiggle room."

"So we need Doug's DNA or we're sunk," I said.

"Maybe we'll find him by the hearing date," Sanden said.

I hung my head again. "Yeah," I said, "maybe."

CHAPTER 41

ila and I visited Carl that day. I needed to tell him about the DNA and about Lockwood being a fugitive. I left out the part where Lockwood kidnapped me and tried to kill me. I also left out that Lockwood may still want to kill me and that every shadow I passed made me want to jump out of my skin. We walked into Hillview, nodded to Janet and Mrs. Lorngren as we passed, and turned down the hall toward Carl's room.

"Wait, Joe," Mrs. Lorngren called out. "He's not there anymore."

My heart dropped into my gut. "What? What happened?"

"Nothing happened," she said. "We moved him to a different room."

I slapped my hand to my chest. "You 'bout gave me a heart attack."

"I'm sorry," Mrs. Lorngren said. "I didn't mean to scare you." She led us down a corridor to a corner room, a nice room, where Carl lay in a bed facing a large window that framed a pine tree bent under the weight of the snow. They had decorated the room for Christmas with pine garlands looping high on the wall and Christmas ornaments hanging from the blinds and taped to the walls. Four Christmas cards stood upright, half opened, decoratively arranged on the table next to his bed. I glanced at the cards and saw that one was from Janet and another was from Mrs. Lorngren. Even though Christmas was over two weeks away, I called out, "Merry Christmas, Carl," as I entered the room.

"Joe," Carl smiled, whispering his words in short puffs. He had a tube in his nose feeding him oxygen. His chest rose and fell with labored breaths, his lungs barely strong enough to gather air. "Is this Lila? How nice." He held his trembling hand over the edge of the bed, and Lila grasped his hand lovingly between her own two hands.

"It's nice to finally meet you," Lila said.

Carl looked at me and nodded toward my face. "What happened there?" he asked.

"Oh, that," I said, touching the cut left behind by the whiskey bottle. "I had to bounce a tough guy out of Molly's the other night."

Carl narrowed his gaze at me as if he could see through my lie. I changed the subject. "We got the tests back," I said. "It wasn't your DNA on Crystal's fingernail."

"I knew that . . . already," he said, with a wink of his eye. "Didn't you?"

"Professor Sanden, who runs the Innocence Project, says it's enough to reopen your case."

Carl thought about that for a few seconds, as though he needed time to let the words break through the wall he had built up over the last thirty years. Then he smiled, closed his eyes, and allowed his head to sink into his pillow. "They'll undo . . . my conviction."

And with those words, I knew that despite his stoic protestations to the contrary, he did care about being exonerated. Clearing his name mattered more to him than he had allowed anyone to see, maybe even more than he himself understood. I began to feel a weight pressing down on me, forcing my shoulders into a slump. "They're gonna try," I said, glancing at Lila. "They're gonna set a hearing. It's just a matter of time now." The words slipped from my lips before I realized what I had said. Carl chuckled weakly and looked at me. "That's . . . the one thing . . . I don't have." Then he turned his attention back to the window. "Did you see . . . the snow?"

"Yeah, I saw it," I smiled. The snow was a thing of such peace and beauty to Carl, but it had nearly killed me. "Quite the storm," I said.

"Glorious," he said.

We visited for almost an hour, talking about the snow, the birds, the bent pine tree. We listened as Carl told stories about his grandfather's cabin at Lake Ada. We talked about everything under the sun—except his case. It was like talking about the solar system without mentioning the sun. Everyone in that room knew that Carl's exoneration would not come until long after he was dead. I suddenly felt like that eleven-year-old kid again, watching my grandfather thrash in the river.

As Carl's energy waned, we said our goodbyes, not knowing if we would see him again before he died. I did my best to hide my sadness from Carl as I shook his hand. He smiled back with a genuineness I couldn't understand. I found myself wishing that I could be as accepting and certain of my life as he seemed to be of his at that moment.

We stopped off at Mrs. Lorngren's office to thank her for moving Carl to a nicer room. She handed each of us a peppermint candy cane from a box that she kept on her desk and motioned for us to sit down. "I couldn't help but overhear you say something about DNA," she said.

"One of the dead girl's fake fingernails broke off in the struggle," I said. "It still has the killer's DNA on it. They tested the DNA, and it wasn't Carl's."

"That's just wonderful," she said. "Do they know whose it is?"

"It belongs to . . . I mean, it should belong to the girl's stepfather, but we don't know for sure. Right now, all we know is that it could be any man in the world except Carl Iverson."

"Is he dead?" she asked.

"Who?"

"The stepfather."

I shrugged my shoulders. "He may as well be dead," I said. "He's missing, so we can't get a sample of his DNA."

"Does he have a son?" she asked.

"Yeah. Why?"

"Don't you know about the Y chromosome?" Mrs. Lorngren said.

"I know there's such a thing, but I'm not sure I follow."

She leaned forward on her desk, placing her fingers together like a principal about to impart a lecture to some hapless student. "Only men have a Y chromosome," she said. "A father will pass his genetic code to a son through the Y chromosome. Those genes are almost identical. There is very little change between the father's DNA and the son's. If you get a sample of the son's DNA, that'll exclude any man who is not a direct male relative of the son."

I stared at her, my jaw slackened with amazement. "Are you like some kind of DNA expert?"

"I do have a nursing degree," she said. "And you don't get one of those without understanding biology. But..." she gave us a sheepish smile, "I learned about the Y chromosome from watching *Forensic Files* on TV. It's amazing what you can learn from those shows."

I said, "So all we have to do is get the DNA of a male relative?"

"It's not that easy," Mrs. Lorngren said. "You would have to get the DNA of every male relative that was alive thirty years ago: sons, brothers, uncles, grandpa. And even then, all you would be doing is increasing the likelihood that the stepfather is the culprit."

"What a great idea," I said. "We could show that it's Doug's DNA by using a process of elimination."

Lila said, "I thought that Max Rupert said to stay out of this case."

"Technically he said to stay away from Douglas Lockwood," I smiled at Lila. "I'm not going after Douglas Lockwood. I'm going after everyone except him."

By the time we left Lorngren's office, I felt like a kid with a brand-new pair of sneakers, anxious to try them out. I could barely control the flurry of ideas that whipped around in my head as Lila and I drove back to her apartment. When we got there, we pulled out our computers. She researched Mrs. Lorngren's information on the Y chromosome, and I scanned the web for any information about the Lockwood family tree. Lila found some terrific websites on DNA, proving that Mrs. Lorngren was right. She also found that Walmart sold paternity DNA kits that had swabs and sterile packaging—kits we could use to gather skin cells from the inside of a cheek.

I, on the other hand, found very little in the way of Lockwood relatives. I found a man named Dan Lockwood, with the correct date of birth, living in Mason City, Iowa, and working as a security guard in a mall. It had to be Crystal's stepbrother Danny. I stalked his Facebook page and any other social media I could think of and found nothing to suggest he had a male relative—not even a father. That didn't surprise me. If I were Danny, I would have done my best to deny the existence of that Bible-thumping psychopath, too. I came away hopeful that we would not need to track down too many Lockwood men in order to point a finger at Douglas.

"So how should I go about getting Danny to give me his DNA?" I asked Lila.

"You could try asking him for it," she said.

"Just ask him for it?" I said. "Excuse me, Mr. Lockwood, can I scrape a few skin cells off your cheek to use to convict your father of killing your stepsister."

"If he says no, then you're no worse off than you are right now," she said. "And if that fails . . ." She let her words trail off, as if contemplating a plan.

"What?" I asked.

"All we need is some of his spit," she said, "like on a coffee cup or a cigarette butt. I found a story from California about a guy named Gallego. The cops followed him around until he threw away a cigarette butt. They picked it up and had his DNA. He went to prison. If all else fails, we follow Danny around until he drops a cigarette butt or throws a coffee cup into the trash."

"We? Who's this 'we' you keep talking about?" I said.

"You have no car," Lila said. "Yours is still in evidence, remember?" She leaned over the table and kissed me. "Besides, I'm not letting you finish this without me. Someone has to make sure that you don't get clobbered with another whiskey bottle."

CHAPTER 42

Dan Lockwood lived in the older, blue-collar section of Mason City, Iowa, a block north of the railroad tracks in a house that blended in with every other house on the street. We drove past it twice, double-checking the house number with what we found on the Internet. After the second pass, we drove through the alley behind his house, bouncing over potholes, dodging snow drifts, and looking for signs of life. We saw a garbage can overflowing with white trash bags standing guard next to the back door of the house. We also saw that someone had shoveled a path through the knee-deep snow connecting the house to the alley. We made a mental note and continued on for a few blocks to park and go over our plan one last time.

We had stopped at Walmart on the drive down and picked up a paternity test kit, which had three cotton swabs, a specimen envelope, and instructions on how to scrape skin cells from the inside of the cheek. Lila had the kit in her purse. We decided to be straightforward. We would go to Dan's house, ask him about any male relatives alive back in 1980, and then ask him to let us swab his cheek. If that failed, we would go to plan B—follow him around until he spit out his gum or something like that.

"You ready?" I asked.

"Let's go meet Dan Lockwood," she said, putting the car in drive.

We parked in front of the house, walked up the front sidewalk together, and rang the doorbell. A middle-aged woman answered the door. Her face was prematurely aged from smoking cigarettes, the smell of which hit us like the slap of a glove. She wore a turquoise tracksuit and blue slippers, and her hair looked like a wad of burned copper wire.

"Could we please speak with Dan Lockwood?" I asked.

"He's out of town," she said, her voice thick and low as if she needed to clear her throat. "I'm his wife. Can I help you?"

"No," I said. "We really need to speak with Mr. Lockwood. We can come back—"

"Is this about his ol' man?" she said. We had already started to turn from the door, but stopped in our tracks.

"You're referring to Douglas Lockwood?" I said, trying to sound official.

"Yeah, his ol' man, the one that's missing," she said.

"As a matter of fact," Lila said, "that is why we're here. We were hoping to speak with Mr. Lockwood about that. When do you expect him back?"

"He should be home pretty soon," she said. "He's on his way back from Minnesota as we speak. You can come in and wait if you want." She turned, walking back into her house, pointing to a brown vinyl couch. "Have a seat."

An ashtray on the coffee table teemed with cigarette butts, a few were Marlboro, but most of them were Virginia Slims. "I see you're a Marlboro fan," I said.

"Those are Dan's," she said. "I smoke Slims." Lila and I exchanged a glance. If Mrs. Lockwood left the room for even a second, we could simply pick up our DNA sample.

"You said Mr. Lockwood was in Minnesota?" I said.

"You guys look awfully young to be cops," she said.

"Um . . . we're not cops," Lila said, "we're from a different agency."

"You mean like social service or something like that?" Mrs. Lockwood said.

"Did Dan go to Minnesota to look for his father?" I asked.

"Yeah," she said. "Headed up there when he heard that his dad was missing. He left the day of that big storm."

I looked at Lila, confused by what Mrs. Lockwood said. "Did Dan go up to Minnesota before or after the storm?" I asked.

"Friday, just before the storm hit. He got snowed in up there. Called me a few hours ago saying he was on his way back."

I went over the math in my head. Doug Lockwood kidnapped me on Friday. The storm strengthened that night while I hid in the hunting cabin. I weathered the storm through Saturday and walked to the farmer's house on Sunday. As far as the police in Minnesota knew, Doug Lockwood wasn't missing until Sunday.

"Just so we're clear," I said. "He told you his dad was missing before he went up?"

"No," she said. "He got a phone call on Friday about . . . oh, what time was it? Late afternoon—I can't remember exactly. Was all freaked out and said he has to go up to the ol' man's place. That's all he said, and out the door he went."

"How'd you know that Doug Lockwood is missing then?" Lila asked.

"On Sunday I received this call from some cop. Wanted to talk to Dan. I told him Dan wasn't home. So he asks who I was and have I seen Dan's ol' man lately. I told him no."

"Was the cop a guy named Rupert?" I asked.

"I'm not sure," she said. "Could be. But then that bitch of a stepmom of his calls here," she said, pursing her lips.

"Stepmom? Danielle Hagen?" I asked.

"Yeah. She ain't talked to Dan in years. Probably wouldn't spit on him if he was dying of thirst. She called him Sunday to give Dan shit."

"What all did she say?" I said.

"I didn't actually talk to her," she said. "I thought it might be that cop again, so I let it go to the answering machine."

"What was her message?" Lila asked.

"Oh, let's see . . . she says something like . . . DJ, this is Danielle Hagen. I just wanted to tell you that the cops were here today looking for that piece-of-shit father of yours. I told them I hope he's dead. I hope—"

"Wait a second," I said, interrupting her. "I think you got that backwards. You mean that she called to tell you that DJ was missing."

"DJ's not missing. His ol' man's missing. Doug's missing."

"But . . . but," I stammered.

Lila picked up where I stumbled. "But, Doug is DJ," she said. "Douglas Joseph. His initials are DJ."

"No, Dan is DJ." Mrs. Lockwood looked at us as if we were trying to convince her that day was night.

"Dan's middle name is William," I said.

"Yeah, but his dad married that bitch Danielle when Dan was a little kid. She liked to be called Dani, thought it made her sound like a tomboy. And since there couldn't be two Dannys in the family, she made everyone call her Dani and call him Danny Junior. After a while they just called him DJ."

My head began to swirl. I'd been wrong about everything. Lila looked at me, her cheeks pale, her eyes telling me what I already knew— we were in the living room of Crystal Hagen's murderer.

"Well, here's Dan now," Mrs. Lockwood said, pointing at a pickup truck pulling into the driveway.

CHAPTER 43

I tried to think, to come up with a plan, but all I could hear was the cursing of my own thoughts. The truck passed by the window and rolled to a stop in the driveway beside the house. The driver's door opened, the setting sun casting enough light for me to see a man dressed and built like a lumberjack and with a military haircut step from the truck. I looked at Lila, beseeching her with my eyes, hoping that she could think of an escape.

Lila stood up as if a current of electricity had coursed through the cushion under her butt. "The forms," she said. "We forgot to bring the forms in."

"The forms," I repeated.

"We left the forms in the car," she said, tipping her head toward the front door.

I stood up beside Lila. "Of course," I said, as both Lila and I started backing toward the door. "Will you excuse us? We . . . um . . . have to get the forms from the car."

The man rounded the corner of the house, heading up the sidewalk toward the front porch. Lila walked out the door and down the three porch steps, almost running into Dan Lockwood. Lockwood paused at the bottom of the steps, his face frozen in surprise, waiting for someone to explain why we were walking out of his house. Lila said nothing, no greeting, no explanation; she walked past him, not even making eye contact. I followed, attempting to do the same, but I couldn't help but look at him. He had his father's face—long, pale, rough. His thin eyes watched me, narrowing to look at the bandage on the side of my head and then at the abrasion on my neck.

We picked up our pace as we headed down the sidewalk toward Lila's car.

"Hey!" he called after us.

We kept walking.

"Hey you!" he called again.

Lila climbed into the driver's seat and I jumped into the passenger seat. Only then did I turn to look at Lockwood, standing at the bottom of his porch, not sure of what he'd seen. Had Doug told him about the whiskey bottle? About the belt? Is that why he looked at me so carefully? Lila drove away while I watched behind us to make sure Lockwood didn't follow.

"Danny killed his sister," Lila said. "When Doug and Danny both lied about being at Doug's car dealership, I thought that Danny was lying to protect his father, but it was Doug who lied to protect his son. And the diary—"

"Danny was eighteen that fall," I said. "That's what Andrew Fisher told us. Danny was an adult in the eyes of the law."

"He was eighteen and Crystal was fourteen. That's the rape Crystal wrote about."

"Christ, that's what Doug was talking about," I said, rapping my hand across my forehead. "That night when he tried to kill me, when he was talking all crazy and spouting Bible passages—I thought he was just being a sick bastard, confessing to molesting Crystal. But he was talking about protecting his son. He knew that Danny killed Crystal. He told the cops that Danny was with him when Crystal was murdered. He wouldn't have lied about the alibi unless he knew. He's been protecting Danny all these years. When I showed up at Doug's house with the decoded diary, he tried to kill me to protect Danny."

"The call," Lila said. "The one Danny got on Friday—"

"That had to be Doug calling Danny, to let him know about me," I said. "Doug must have called him after he thought he'd killed me—to figure out what to do with me, with my body."

"It's been Danny behind everything all along," Lila said with a shudder. "I've never been so close to a murderer before." Her eyes lit up with an epiphany. "Jesus, I bet he's the one who burned Doug's house down—to destroy any trace of Doug's DNA."

"What? But—"

"Think about it," she said. "You go to Doug's house believing Doug's the murderer, that it's Doug's DNA under Crystal's fingernail. When you escape, Danny knows that you'll bring the cops looking for Doug. They'll get his DNA from the whiskey bottle or something in the house. But Doug's DNA won't be a match. It'll be close; it'll be a male relative of Doug."

"Son of a bitch," I said. "Danny destroys all traces of Doug's DNA by burning his house so that we'd go on believing Doug's the killer." I let the pieces of the puzzle fall into place for a moment before I was struck by the next horrifying step. "But he can't get rid of all of Doug's DNA unless—"

"Unless he gets rid of Doug," Lila finished my thought.

"He kills his own father? That's insane," I said.

"Or desperate," Lila said. "What would you do to avoid dying in prison?"

"Damn." I tapped my fingers against my thigh. "I should have grabbed a cigarette butt before we left. We were so close. I could have reached out and picked one up."

"I panicked, too," Lila said. "When I saw that truck pull in, I freaked."

"You freaked?" I said. "What are you talking about? You got us out of there. You were amazing." I pulled out my cell phone and started digging through my pockets.

"What're you doing?" Lila asked.

"Max Rupert gave me his private cell number." I shoved my hands deep into each of my pockets as if his card might have somehow shrunk to the size of a postage stamp. "Crap!"

"What's the matter?"

"It's on the coffee table at the apartment."

Lila hit the brakes, pulling onto a side road. "We gotta go back," she said.

"Are you out of your mind?"

Lila put the car in park and turned to me. "If we're right, then

Danny burned down his dad's house and maybe even killed his own father just to stay out of prison. His next move will be to burn down his own house and disappear. He'll hightail it to Mexico or Venezuela or someplace and it'll take years to find him—if ever. If we can get a sample of his DNA, it'll match what they found on the fingernail. There'll be no question about it. The cops might eventually hunt Lockwood down, but in the meantime we can get Carl's conviction overturned. But we have to act now. We have to get his DNA."

"I'm not going in there, and I'm sure as hell not letting you go in there."

"Who said anything about going inside," she smiled, putting the car back into drive. "All we're gonna do is pick up some garbage."

CHAPTER 44

The sun had dropped low in the west, leaving the avenues and alleys of Mason City lit with a mixture of street lamps and Christmas lights. Our plan was simple: we would drive down the alley behind Lockwood's house one time with our lights off, our eyes scanning the windows and doors. If we saw the least hint of movement in the house, we would keep driving, head back to Minnesota, and report what we'd found to Max Rupert. If, however, the night stayed silent, and we saw no sign of Lockwood, Lila would park the car behind the neighbor's garage. I would slip out, sneak up the path using my best ninja stealth, and steal the top garbage bag.

I unlocked my door as we entered the mouth of the alley, Lila's little car struggling against the dips and traps of the snow and ice. We passed behind his neighbor's garage to view the back yard of the Lockwood house, the darkness broken only by a thin light falling from the kitchen window. I strained to see any movement behind the shadows cast by the ambient glow of the neighbor's Christmas lights.

We passed the property, and seeing nothing to stop our folly, Lila stopped her car behind the next garage and covered the dome light with her palm. I clicked open my door, slid out, and crept back up the alley to the path Mrs. Lockwood had shoveled between the house and the alley. I paused one last time at the beginning of the path and listened. I heard nothing beyond the slight whistle of wind.

I stepped onto Lockwood's property, a thin layer of fresh snow crunching under my feet. My pace remained slow and cautious, as if I were walking a tightrope. Thirty feet . . . twenty feet . . . ten feet. I could almost touch it. Suddenly, the blast of a car horn cut through the cold December air about a block away and stopped my heart for a beat or two. I didn't move—I couldn't move. I stood perfectly still, expecting a face to appear at the window. I prepared myself to run back to the car, envisioning a footrace with a murderer. But nobody came; nobody peeked out.

I gathered my wits and took that last step. The lid of the can sat off kilter on top of the top trash bag. I lifted the lid carefully and laid it in the snow. Enough light filtered from the window above me to see the neck of a garbage bag. I raised it slowly, like a jewel thief avoiding motion sensors, my reflexes sharp, my balance steady, and my eye sight . . . well, a bit lacking.

I didn't see the beer bottle leaning against the top of the bag until it glinted in the thin light as it tumbled from the top of the trash can. It spun end over end, hit the bottom wooden porch step, bounced, spun some more, and fell to the sidewalk. It smashed into a thousand tiny bits, announcing my presence with authority.

I turned and ran down the walkway, clutching the bag of rubbish with a death grip in my right hand, glass and tin clanking inside the bag like a junkyard wind chime. I reached the junction of the path and alleyway just as the back porch light burst to life. I hit the ice in full stride, my feet shooting out from under me, sending me sprawling across the alley, my hip and elbow exploding in pain from the fall. I stood up and ran the short sprint to the car, the garbage bag held tight in my hand.

Lila hit the gas as soon as my ass hit the seat, not even waiting for the door to close. Her tires spun on the ice and the back end of the car slid back and forth, nearly hitting the nearby garage. A shadowy figure, silhouetted against the floodlight above Lockwood's back door, ran down the walkway toward us. Lila's tires caught a thin strip of gravel, breaking the spin and moving us down the alley and onto the street, leaving the shadow of Dan Lockwood behind us.

Neither of us spoke until we passed beyond the city limits. I kept watch behind us, expecting to see the headlights of Lockwood's truck closing in. They never appeared. By the time we reached the interstate and headed north, I had relaxed enough to peek into the garbage bag. There, on the very top, next to an old ketchup bottle and a greasy pizza box, were at least twenty Marlboro cigarette butts.

"We got him," I said.

CHAPTER 45

We had Lockwood's cigarette butts, his DNA, the last piece of an ever-changing puzzle. The DNA from one of those butts would match the DNA on Crystal Hagen's fingernail. Everything was coming together to prove that Daniel Lockwood—Danny Junior, DJ—was the man who killed Crystal Hagen all those years ago. It all fit.

As we drove north on Interstate 35, making for the Iowa-Minnesota border, we remained vigilant, exiting the interstate twice just to make sure no one was following us. We would wait and watch as the headlights passed us. Only then would we merge back onto the interstate. Soon we crossed into Minnesota, pulling over in Albert Lea to get some gas and food. We switched seats to give Lila a break from driving. As we pulled back onto the interstate, my cell phone rang with the theme from *Pirates of the Caribbean*, the ringtone I had assigned to Jeremy's number. This was the first time that Jeremy had ever called me, other than when we were practicing. A shiver ran up my back.

"Hey, Buddy, what's up?" I answered.

There was no response. I could hear him breathing on the other end, so I spoke again.

"Jeremy, you okay?"

"Maybe do you remember what you told me to do?" Jeremy spoke with more than his normal hesitation.

"I remember," I said, my voice dropping into a deep valley. "I told you to call me if anyone tries to hurt you." I felt my hand grow tight around my phone. "Jeremy, what happened?"

He did not respond.

"Did someone hit you?" I asked.

Still no response.

"Was it Mom?"

Silence.

"Did Larry hit you?" I asked.

"Maybe . . . maybe Larry hit me."

"God dammit!" I held the phone away from my mouth as I cursed through clenched teeth. "I'll kill that son of a bitch." I took a deep breath and placed the phone back against my ear. "Now listen to me, Jeremy. I want you to go to your room and lock the door. Can you do that for me?"

"Maybe I can," he said.

"Tell me when you've locked the door."

"Maybe the door is locked now," he said.

"Okay, now take the pillowcases off your pillows and fill them with your clothes. Can you do that for me?"

"Maybe I can," he said.

"I'm on my way there now. You wait in your room until I get there. Okay?"

"Maybe you're coming from the college?" he asked.

"No," I said. "I'm almost there already. I'll be there in no time."

"Okay," he said.

"Pack your clothes."

"Okay."

"I'll see you in a bit."

I hung up my phone just in time to catch the interchange from Interstate 35 to Interstate 90. I would be in Austin in twenty minutes.

CHAPTER 46

I skidded to a stop in front of my mother's apartment, throwing Lila's car into park and leaping out the door in a single motion. I covered the twenty feet between the street and the porch in a sprint of five steps, bursting through the front door and catching Larry and my mother off guard as they sat on the couch, beers in hand, watching television.

"What'd you do to him?" I yelled.

Larry jumped to his feet, throwing his beer can at my face. I swatted it away without breaking stride. He drew his fist up as I shoved my palms into his chest, lifting him off his feet and sending him sprawling over the back of the couch. Mom started screaming at me, but I walked past her and went to Jeremy's room, gently knocking on the door as if I were simply stopping by to wish him goodnight.

"Jeremy, it's me, Joe," I said. The lock clicked open. Jeremy stood next to his bed, his left eye a spectrum of red, blue, and black, nearly swollen shut. He had his pillowcases stuffed with his clothes on the bed beside him. Larry was a lucky man to be beyond my reach at that moment.

"Hey, Jeremy," I said, picking up the pillowcases, feeling their heft. "You done good," I said, handing them back to him. "You remember Lila, don't you?"

Jeremy nodded.

"She's by her car in front of the house." I put my hand on his back, leading him from his bedroom. "Take these to her. You're coming to live with me."

"The hell he is," Mom screeched.

"Go on, Jeremy," I said. "It's okay."

Jeremy walked past my mother without looking at her, moving quickly across the living room and out the door.

"What d'ya think you're doing?" Mom said in her best scolding tongue.

"What happened to his eye, Mother?" I said.

"That was . . . that was nothing," she said.

"Your piece-of-shit boyfriend beat him up. That's not nothing; that's assault."

"Larry just gets frustrated. He—"

"Then you should kick Larry out, shouldn't you?" I said.

"Jeremy pushes Larry's buttons."

"Jeremy's autistic," I yelled. "He doesn't push buttons. He doesn't know how to push buttons."

"Well, what am I supposed to do?" she said.

"You're supposed to protect him. You're supposed to be his mother."

"So I can't have a life. Is that what you're saying?"

"You made your choice," I said. "You chose Larry, so Jeremy's coming to live with me."

"You're not getting his social-security money," she hissed.

I shook with rage, clenching my fists, waiting to calm down a little before I spoke again. "I don't want the money. He's not a meal ticket. He's your son."

"What about your precious college?" Her voice pitched with sarcasm as she spoke.

For a brief second, I saw my future plans withering on a vine. I drew in a deep breath and sighed. "Well," I said, "I guess I made my choice, too."

I started for the front door only to find Larry standing in my way, his hands balled up into fists in front of him. "Let's see how tough you are when you're not blindsiding me," he said.

Larry stood sideways in an awkward boxer's stance with his feet growing roots parallel to one another, his left fist poking out in front of him, his right tucked up against his chest. He couldn't have made himself a better target if he'd tried. With his left foot planted sideways, he exposed the side of his left knee to attack. The thing about knees is that they're made to bend front to back. If you kick the back of a knee it will buckle; if you kick the front of a knee it will remain strong. But the side of the knee is a whole different story. Knees are as fragile as dried twigs from the side.

"Okay, Larry," I said, smiling. "Let's have a go."

I walked at him as though I were going to charge face first into the right hook he had planned for me. But I stopped short, turned, cocked my leg back, and drove the heel of my foot into the side of his knee as hard as I could. I heard the bone crack, and Larry screamed as he fell into a heap on the floor.

I turned, looked at my mother one last time, and then walked out the door.

CHAPTER 47

I leaned my forehead against the passenger window of Lila's car, staring off beyond the lights of the gas stations and towns we drove by. I could see my future dissolving, melting away, my vision blurred by the speed of the car, by the drops of water on the window, and by the tears that were starting to well up in my eyes. I would never go back to Austin, Minnesota. I would be responsible for Jeremy from now on. What had I done? I whispered the words out loud that had been banging on the doors of my brain since I'd left my mom's apartment. "I can't go to school next semester. I can't take care of Jeremy and also go to school." I wiped my eyes before turning back toward Lila. "I'll have to get a serious job."

Lila reached across to my seat, rubbing the back of my still-clenched fist until I let it fall open so she could hold my hand. "It may not be that bad," she said. "I can help take care of Jeremy."

"Jeremy's not your responsibility. It was my decision."

"He's not my responsibility," she said, "but he is my friend." She turned and looked at Jeremy, who'd curled up and fallen asleep in the back seat, his cell phone still grasped in his hands. "Look at him." Lila nodded toward Jeremy. "He's sleeping so soundly. It's like he's been awake for days. He knows he's safe now. You should feel good about that. You're a good brother."

I smiled at Lila, kissed the back of her hand, and turned toward the window to watch the miles go by and think. It was then that I remembered something my grandfather once told me, something he'd said the day he died while we were eating sandwiches on the river, something I had blocked out of my memory for all these years. "You're Jeremy's big brother," he'd said. "It's your job to take care of him. There's going to come a day when I won't be here to help out, and Jeremy's going to need you. Promise me that you'll take care of him." I was eleven. I didn't know what my grandfather was talking about. But he knew. Somehow he knew that this day would come. And with that thought, a caress of serenity untied the knots in my shoulders.

As we neared the apartment, the shift from interstate highway to city streets changed the musical tone of the tires, causing Jeremy to stir. He sat up, unsure at first of where he was, looking around at the unfamiliar buildings, his brow furrowed, his eyes blinking hard.

"We're almost home, Buddy," I said. He cast his eyes down to think. "We're going to my apartment. Remember?"

"Oh, yeah," he said, a slight smile building on his face.

"We'll get you tucked into bed in a couple minutes, and you can go back to sleep."

His eyes furrowed again. "Um . . . maybe I need a toothbrush."

"You didn't bring your toothbrush?" I said.

"To be fair," Lila said, "you didn't tell him he was moving. You just said to pack his clothes." I rubbed my temples where a slight headache was starting to build. Lila pulled the car over to the curb in front of the apartment.

"Can you go one night without brushing your teeth?" I asked.

Jeremy started rubbing his thumb across his knuckles and gritting his teeth, causing the muscles beside his jaw to pop like a frog's gullet. "Maybe I need a toothbrush," he said again.

"Calm down, Buddy," I said. "We'll figure something out."

Lila spoke again in her soft, calming voice. "Jeremy, how about if I take you up to Joe's apartment and get you situated, and Joe can go get you a new toothbrush. Will that be okay?"

Jeremy stopped rubbing his hands, the emergency abated. "Okay," he said.

"Is that okay, Joe?" Lila smiled at me. I smiled back.

There was a small corner store about eight blocks away, just one more detour in a long day of detours. I liked how Lila talked to Jeremy, her soothing demeanor, her genuine affection for him. And I liked how Jeremy returned those feelings, or at least his version of those feelings, almost as though he had a crush on Lila, an emotion I knew to be beyond Jeremy's palate. It made me feel a little better about all that had happened. I was no longer Joe Talbert the college student or Joe the bouncer, or even Joe the runaway. I would, from that day forward be Joe Talbert, Jeremy's big brother. My life would be defined by the chain of small emergencies in my brother's world like this forgotten toothbrush.

Lila took Jeremy upstairs to help him prepare for bed and I hopped behind the wheel to go buy a toothbrush. I found one at the first convenience store I went to. The toothbrush was green, the same color as Jeremy's old toothbrush, which was the same color as every toothbrush Jeremy had ever owned. If I hadn't found a green toothbrush at that store, I would have had to find another store. I bought some additional supplies, paid for everything, and headed back to the apartment.

My apartment was quiet and dark when I got back, the only light being a small bulb over the kitchen sink. I could hear Jeremy sleeping in the bedroom, his muffled snore signaling that his anxiety over the lost toothbrush had given way to his exhaustion. I placed the toothbrush on the bedside table and backed out of the room, letting him sleep. I decided that I would sneak next door to give Lila a kiss goodnight. I knocked lightly on her door, a single knuckle tap, and waited. No answer. I raised my hand to knock again, paused, and then let my hand fall. It had been a long day; she'd earned a good night's sleep.

I returned to my apartment and sat down on my couch. On the coffee table in front of me I spied Max Rupert's card, the one with his personal cell number on it. I picked it up and contemplated calling him. The clock was about to strike midnight. Surely the evidence Lila and I had gathered—the bombshell information about the real DJ— was important enough to warrant the late-night call. I put my thumb on the first button to call Rupert then backed off, deciding instead to get Lila's opinion. Besides, that would give me the perfect excuse to go to her apartment and wake her up.

I took Rupert's card and my phone and headed next door. As I was about to knock, my phone rang, causing me to jump. I looked at the number, a 515 area code—Iowa. I lifted the phone to my ear. "Hello?"

"You have something of mine," a low, raspy voice whispered.

Jesus. It couldn't be. "Who is this?" I said.

"Don't play games with me, Joe," the voice barked the words. He was pissed. "You know who this is."

"DJ," I said. I tapped on Lila's door, holding the phone to my cheek so that he couldn't hear my tapping.

"I prefer to be called Dan," he said.

Then it hit me. "How do you know my name?" I asked.

"I know your name because your little girlfriend here told me."

Waves of hot and cold panic convulsed in my chest. I turned the door knob; Lila's door was unlocked. I pushed it open to find her kitchen table tipped on its side, her books scattered, her homework papers strewn across the linoleum floor. I struggled to make sense of what I saw.

"Like I said, Joe, you have something of mine . . ." Dan paused as if to lick his lips. "And I have something of yours."

CHAPTER 48

"Here's what's going to happen, Joe," Dan said. "You're going to get into your car and drive north on I-35, and make sure you bring that bag of trash you stole from me."

I turned and ran down the steps as fast as my feet could carry me, my cell phone still pressed tight against my ear. "If you hurt Lila, I'll—"

"You'll what, Joe?" he said. "Tell me. I really want to know. What are you going to do to me, Joe? But before you tell me, I want you to hear something."

I heard a muffled voice, a woman. I couldn't make out her words; it was more of a grunting sound. Then the grunting sounds gave way to a voice. "Joe! Joe, I'm sorry—" She tried to say more, but the words dropped behind a wall as if he'd put a gag into her mouth.

"So tell me now, Joe, what—"

"If you hurt her, I swear to God I'll kill you," I said as I jumped behind the wheel of Lila's car.

"Oh, Joe." There was a pause, then a muffled scream. "Did you hear that, Joe?" he said. "I just punched your pretty little girlfriend in the face, very hard. You interrupted me. You made me punch her. If you interrupt me again, if you do not follow my instructions to the smallest detail, if you do anything to try and attract the attention of a cop, your little Lila here will suffer the consequences. Have I made myself clear?"

"You've made yourself clear," I said. A sickness welled up in my throat as I started Lila's car.

"That's good," he said. "I don't want to hurt her anymore. You see, Joe, she didn't want to give me your name or your phone number. I had to persuade her that it was in her best interest. She's a tough little bitch."

My knees felt weak and my stomach queasy at the thought of what he was doing to Lila. I felt utterly helpless. "How'd you find us?" I don't know why I asked him that question. It didn't matter how he'd found us. Maybe I just wanted to keep his attention on me, talking to me. If he was busy with me, he wouldn't be hurting her.

"You found me, Joe. Remember?" he said. "So you probably know I run security at a mall. I know the cops. I got the license plate number off her car when you went through my alley. That brought me to little Miss Lila here, and she brought me to you. Or should I say, she's bringing you to me."

"I'm on my way," I said, again trying to turn his attention back to me. "I'm turning onto I-35, like you said."

"To make sure you don't do something stupid like call the police, you and I are going to talk as you drive. And I can't stress this enough, Joe: if you hang up, if you go through a dead zone, if your battery dies, if anything happens to disconnect us . . . well, let's just say you'll need to find a new girlfriend."

I sped down the on ramp, one hand on the wheel, the other holding the phone to my ear, the car screaming as it ran through its gears. A tractor-trailer hogged the lane, so I floored the accelerator. The truck seemed to speed up, as if the driver were trying to assert some misplaced testosterone-fed dominance. I gripped the wheel so tightly my fingers ached. My merge lane grew thinner as I raced toward an oncoming viaduct rail, the truck's tires whining next to me, inches from my window. My lane turned into a shoulder as my car inched past the front bumper of the truck. I jerked onto the interstate, my back bumper narrowly missing his front bumper, his horn blaring his displeasure.

"I hope you're driving carefully, Joe," Dan said. "You don't want to get pulled over. That would be tragic."

He was right. I couldn't allow myself to get pulled over. What was I thinking? I slowed down to match the speed of the other drivers, blending in as just another set of headlights.

"Where am I going?" I said, once my pulse returned to a manageable pace.

"You remember where my old man's house is, don't you?"
I shuddered with the thought. "I remember."

"Go there," he said.

"I thought it burned down," I said.

"So you heard about that. Terrible thing," he said, his voice flat, uninterested, as if I was an annoying child interrupting his morning read.

I began looking around the car for a weapon, a tool, a scrap of anything that I could use to wound him . . . or kill him. Nothing lay within reach except a plastic windshield scraper. I flicked on the dome light and looked again—fast-food trash, some spare winter gloves, papers from one of Lila's classes, Dan's bag of garbage, but no weapon. I heard bottles clinking in the garbage bag when I was running from Lockwood's house. If nothing else, I could grab one of those. Then I saw a glint of reflection in the back seat, something silver, half tucked in the crack where the seatback and cushion met.

"You seem quiet, Joe," Dan said. "I'm not boring you, am I?"

"No, I'm not bored, just thinking," I said.

"You're a thinking man, are you Joe?"

I hit the speakerphone button and laid the cell on the console between the two front seats, turning up the volume. "I don't make it a habit, but it happens every now and again," I said. I quietly pulled the lever allowing my seat to recline as far as it would go.

"Tell me, Joe, what's on your mind?"

"I was just remembering my visit with your dad. He seemed a little out of sorts when we parted." I slid back in my seat, holding the steering wheel with the tips of my fingers, waiting for a straight section of highway. "How's he doing?" I asked the question partly to hear his reaction and partly to get him talking as my straight section of highway appeared.

"I guess you could say he's seen better days," Dan said, his tone shifting cold.

I let go of the steering wheel, flopped back on my seat, and grabbed for the shiny metallic object on the back seat. I got one finger around one side and a knuckle on the other side and pulled. My fingers slipped off. I reset my grip and pulled again. Jeremy's cell phone slid out from between the cushions, spinning forward, stopping on the front edge of the seat.

"Of course," Dan went on, "it's like they say: you shouldn't send an old drunk to do a man's job."

I sat up to find the car drifting off the road, heading toward the shoulder. I grabbed the wheel, correcting with a slight squeal of the tires. Had there been a cop anywhere in the area, I would have been pulled over. I watched the rearview mirror for cherries. I watched, waited—nothing. I breathed.

"But he meant well," Dan finished.

"He meant well . . . by trying to kill me?" I said, trying to keep him talking. I pulled the seat lever, allowing the seatback to shoot into the upright position.

"Oh, Joe," Dan said. "You're not getting naive on me, are you?"

I reached back, picked up Jeremy's cell phone, and turned it on. "Was it his idea to kill me?" I said. "Or was that yours?" I arched my back, reaching into my pocket to pull out Max Rupert's card.

"The bottle to your head, that was his idea," Dan said.

I put my finger on the first digit of Rupert's personal cell number, held the phone against my leg to silence the tone, and pressed the button.

"Imagine my surprise," he continued, "when he called me to tell me what you found in Crystal's diary?"

I continued pressing numbers.

"After all this time, you figured it out," he said. "You really are a thinker, aren't you, Joe?"

I checked the number one last time and hit send, holding the phone to my ear, praying that Rupert would answer.

"Hello?" Rupert's voice came through. I clapped my thumb over the phone's speaker so that Dan Lockwood wouldn't hear Rupert, but Rupert would hear my conversation with Dan.

"I'm not as smart as you think," I said, holding Jeremy's phone near my phone. "All this time I thought DJ stood for Douglas Joseph Lockwood. You can imagine my surprise today when your wife told me that you were DJ. I was shocked. I mean, your name is Daniel William Lockwood. Who would think that anyone would call you DJ?"

I tried to be obvious enough with my words to clue Rupert in on my plight without clueing Dan in on my plan. I had to trust that Rupert was listening and understanding what was going on, that this call in the middle of the night was more than a misdialed number. I needed to engage Dan Lockwood and force him to tell his secret.

CHAPTER 49

In the minutes that I spent driving north to face Dan Lockwood, an errant thought had been lurking in the shadows of my mind—mercurial, unformed, hiding behind my fear. I sensed its presence but paid it no heed while I scrambled to come up with a plan to save Lila. Now that I had Rupert on the phone, and hopefully listening to my conversation with Dan Lockwood, I calmed down and gave voice to that errant thought, allowing it to grow in clarity and volume until it screamed—Dan Lockwood had no choice but to kill us.

Why had I been panicking? I knew what lay ahead. He would bring me to him and then he would kill us both. He couldn't let us live, not with what we knew. I felt a strange solace wash over me. I knew his plan, and he needed to know that I knew.

"Dan, you ever play Texas hold 'em?" I asked.

"I'll bite," he said. "Sure, I've been in a tournament or two."

"There's that moment when you have your two cards, and I have my two cards, and the dealer throws down the flop."

"Yeah . . . and?"

"And I go all in. I lay down my cards, and you lay down yours. I know what you have and you know what I have, and now we just wait for the dealer to play it out, to see who wins. No secrets."

"Go on."

"Well, I'm going all in," I said.

"I'm not sure I follow," Dan said.

"What's going to happen when I get out to your dad's place?" I said. "Surely you've thought this through."

"I have an idea or two," he said. "The better question is: have you thought it through?"

"You're bringing me out there to kill me. You're using Lila to make sure I come, and after you kill me, you'll kill Lila." I took a breath. "How am I doing?"

"And yet you're still on your way. Why?"

"The way I see it," I said, "I have two options. I can run to the police, give them the DNA, tell 'em you killed your sister—"

"Stepsister!"

"Stepsister," I repeated.

"In which case," he said, "poor little Lila here dies tonight." His voice grew cold again. "And what is your second option?"

I took another deep breath. "I can come out there and kill you," I said.

There was silence on the other end of the phone.

"You see," I said, "I'm still on my way because you have Lila. If she's not alive when I get there, I have no reason to stop, do I? You'll have another murder on your hands, but I'll have you. The cops will hunt you to the ends of the Earth. Lila will be avenged. You'll die in prison, and I'll piss on your grave."

"So you're going to kill me, are you?" he said.

"Isn't that what you're planning to do to Lila and me?"

He paused.

"And then what?" I said. "Dump us in a river or burn us in a shed?"

"A barn," he said.

"Ah, that's right, you're the firebug. You torched your dad's place, too, didn't you?"

He went silent again.

"I'm betting you also killed the old man to save your ass."

"I'm gonna enjoy killing you," Dan said. "I'm gonna do it so damned slow."

"Your old man cleaned up your mess by going after me, but in the process he made himself the perfect scapegoat. He tells you about the DNA, about the diary, about the evidence that led me to him instead of you. It's perfect. So you kill him, hide his body where no one will ever find him, and burn his house down to keep the police from testing his

DNA. I gotta hand it to you, Dan, that was clever—fucking twisted, but clever."

"Oh, it gets better," Dan said. "When they find your body in this barn near his house . . ." He waited for me to connect the dots.

"They'll blame him," I finished. "That is, unless I kill you first."

"I guess we'll see in about ten minutes," he said.

"Ten minutes?"

"I know how long it takes to get here. If you're not here in ten minutes, I'll assume you made a colossal mistake and tried to bring a cop to our little party."

"Don't worry," I said, "I'm coming. And if I don't see Lila standing on her feet and alive when I drive up, I'll assume that you made a colossal mistake. I'll drive on by, and I'll bring the world down on you."

"Then we understand each other," he said.

CHAPTER 50

With a ten-minute limit to drive a five-minute distance I was ahead of schedule. I tried to think of what else I could do to prepare.

I had been driving with my thumb over the speaker of Jeremy's cell phone, keeping Rupert's voice away from Lockwood's ear. As the county road twisted through some frozen wetlands, I eased back on the throttle, giving Rupert every possible second to catch up. Had I given him enough clues? Dan and I talked about his father's house, the one he burned down, and a barn nearby. Rupert knew where the house was; he's the one who told me about the fire. He was a cop, a detective. He would figure it out.

I carefully lifted Jeremy's phone, removed my thumb, pressed the speaker tightly to my ear, and listened. No voice. No breath. No white noise of a car engine in the background. Nothing. I looked at the face of the phone, at Rupert's number backlit on the screen. I listened again. Silence. I cupped my hand around the mouthpiece, whispering "Rupert" into my hand in a soft breath, enunciating the consonants, spitting them out so that Max might understand me and answer.

He didn't answer.

I stopped breathing. My hand trembled. Had I been leaving a voice message this whole time? "Rupert," I whispered again. Still no answer. I dropped Jeremy's phone onto the floor behind the passenger seat, my mouth suddenly dry. I had no plan now—no way of saving Lila.

I could smell Lockwood's garbage, his DNA, the evidence of his crime, decaying behind my seat. If I had been recording on Rupert's voice mail, then Rupert would get the message and know that Dan Lockwood killed us. I decided to drop the trash in the ditch. If things went bad, Rupert might find it and use it to nail Lockwood. As a backup plan it sucked, but it was all I had.

I reached behind my seat, easing the bag up and onto my lap, the cans and bottles rustling slightly as it settled. I felt the neck of a beer bottle pushing against the side of the bag. Using my fingernail to tear a hole in the side of the bag, I eased the bottle out and set it next to me on the seat.

"Five minutes, Joe," Dan called over the speaker on my cell phone. "Let me hear Lila's voice."

"You don't trust me?"

"What's it matter to you?" I said, with more than an edge of frustration, or maybe resignation, in my voice. "Consider it a final wish."

I heard Lila mumbling as Dan removed the gag. The phone would be away from his ear, giving me an opportunity to pitch the bag. I slowed the car to a crawl to limit the wind noise, lowered the window, and, steering with my knees, slid the garbage bag out, giving it a toss so that it landed in the snow-covered ditch.

"Joe?" Lila murmured.

"Lila, are you okay?"

"That's enough chitchat," Dan said. "You have two minutes. I don't think you're going to make it."

I closed my window, picked up my speed again, and crested the last rise before my turn onto the gravel road where Doug Lockwood once lived. "If you're at your old man's place, then you can see my headlights," I flicked the brights on and off a few times.

"Ah, at last, the hero approaches," Dan said. "There's a tractor path just past my dad's place; it leads to a barn. That's where I'll be waiting."

"With Lila standing where I can see her," I said.

"But of course," he said smugly. "I'm looking forward to meeting you."

I turned onto the gravel road, my eyes searching the darkness for movement. The chimney of Doug Lockwood's house was a lone spire rising from a pile of ashes. Spurs of ice left behind by the fire hoses dangled from its edges like frozen plumage.

I drove past the house and paused before turning into the tractor path. I followed the tire tracks laid down in the snow by Dan Lockwood's four-wheel-drive pickup. The trail wound back eighty feet to a dilapidated gray barn, the planks of its walls rotting and separating like old horse teeth. I knew that I would get stuck in the snow before I got anywhere near the barn.

I clicked the high beams on and gunned the engine, ramming Lila's little car into the snow. A wall of white exploded high into the air, the crystalline flakes shimmering in the glow of the headlights. I plowed along for ten feet before I ground to a halt, the tires spinning impotently, the engine revving in futility. I took my foot off the accelerator and watched as the final mist of powdery snow drifted away in the breeze. A single, heavy, insistent thought filled my mind—now what?

CHAPTER 51

My headlights fell across the snow-covered pasture, illuminating the barn in the distance. Lila stood in front of the tattered door, her arms stretched above her head, her hands tied together by a rope that reached up to a hoist outside of the hayloft. She appeared weak, but she stood under her own power. Dan Lockwood stood next to her, a gun in one hand pointed at her head, a cell phone in his other hand.

Seventy feet of snow-covered field separated me from the barn. The field between us was bordered by a tree line about fifty feet to my left and a creek off to my right. Both the tree line and the creek extended from the road back beyond the barn. Both could provide cover. But the creek might get me within thirty feet of Lockwood.

I lowered the car window, grabbed my phone and the beer bottle, and slid out the window—no creaking door hinge to announce my intention. Putting the phone against my cheek to hide the light of the display, I moved around the back of the car, heading for the creek.

"I think you should bring my garbage to me," Dan said.

I needed to stall. "I'm afraid I can't," I said, as I sidestepped my way into the creek. The headlights shining in Dan's eyes covered my movement in the shadows. "The snow's too deep."

"I'm getting tired of fucking around here," he yelled.

The ice crackled under my feet as I moved closer to the barn. I paused for a moment to peek over the creek bank to see Dan still focused on the car. A thin surface of ice had crusted over the snow, making a light popping noise with every step, barking my arrival into the quiet night. I moved faster when Dan spoke, hoping that the noise of his own voice in his head would cover my approach.

"Get out of your fucking car, and walk your ass down here," he yelled into the phone.

"I think you should come here and get it," I said.

"Do you think that you have any say here, you little cock weasel?" He put the gun to Lila's head. "I hold the cards. I'm in control." I turned my walk into a scamper as he yelled—my head lowered, the phone still tight to my ear. "You get your ass here or I'll kill her right now."

I was close enough now that he might hear my voice coming from the creek instead of the phone. I lowered my volume to a whisper, the change in tone giving my words a menacing edge that I had not expected. "You kill her, and I'm gone. The cavalry will be on your ass before the echo dies."

"Fine," he said. "I won't kill her." He lowered the muzzle of his gun to her knee. "If you're not in my sight in three seconds, I'll take out her pretty knees, one at a time. You have any idea how painful a bullet in the kneecap can be?"

I had gone as far as I could in the creek.

"After that," he said, "I'll start on other body parts."

If I charged, I'd be dead as soon as I came into the glare of the headlights. If I stayed in the creek, he would dissect Lila with his gun. From this distance, I would hear her screams of pain through the gag in her mouth.

"One!"

I looked around for a better weapon than the beer bottle: a rock or stick, anything.

"Two!"

A fallen tree jutted out from the opposite shore, its dead branches within reach. I dropped the bottle and grabbed a branch as big around as a stair rail and jerked it with all my weight and strength. It snapped off with a deafening crack. I stumbled back.

Two shots rang out from Dan's gun, one hitting a cottonwood tree above me, the other bullet disappearing into the darkness.

I grunted as if I had been shot and threw my cell phone like a Frisbee onto the frozen surface of the snow on the far bank of the creek, its display casting a beam of light that could be seen from the barn.

I crept up the near bank, hiding behind the cottonwood with my stick. I waited for Dan's approach, hoping that his attention would be focused on the light from my cell phone on the opposite bank.

"You're a persistent fuck," Dan called out. "I'll give you that."

I raised my stick, gauging his distance by his voice, listening to his footsteps draw closer.

He stopped walking just out of reach of my stick, probably letting his eyes adjust to the darkness away from the headlights. Two more steps, I thought to myself, just two more steps.

"It's not gonna work, Joe," he said, taking another step toward the creek, his gun still pointed toward my phone, his voice lowered, almost whispering in my ear. "I hold the cards, remember?"

He stepped again.

I lunged from my hiding place behind the tree, swinging my stick at his head. He pulled his gun around, raising it at me as he ducked away from my swing.

My aim failed. The stick crushed into his right shoulder instead of his skull. But his aim failed as well, the gun firing a bullet into my thigh instead of my chest, the hot lead tearing through the skin and muscle, punching into the bone, turning my leg into useless weight.

I fell face first into the knee-deep snow.

CHAPTER 52

If I stopped my attack, I would die—Lila would die.

I pushed my body up with my arms, only to crash back into the snow, the full weight of Dan Lockwood driving down on my back. Before I could react, he pulled my right arm behind my back, a cold metal handcuff ratcheting around my wrist. Why hadn't he shot me in the head? Why keep me alive? I fought to keep the other arm away from him, but his weight on my shoulder blade and neck brought my struggle to an end.

He stood up, grabbed my collar, and dragged me through the snow, leaning me up against a fence post at the edge of the barn. His belt made a zipping sound as he pulled it from his pants. He wrapped it around my throat, buckling me to the fencepost. Then he stood back, admired his handiwork, and kicked me in the face with his snow-covered boot.

"Because of you my dad is dead," he said. "You hear me? This was none of your damn business."

"Fuck you." I spit blood from my mouth. "You killed your dad cuz you're fucking insane. You raped and killed your sister cuz you're fucking insane. See a theme?"

He kicked me in the face with his other foot.

"Bet you're wondering why I didn't just shoot you," he said.

"It crossed my mind," I mumbled. I could feel a tooth rolling around in my mouth. I spit again.

"You're gonna watch me," he smiled. "I'm gonna rape the shit outta your little girlfriend here, and you're gonna watch. You're gonna hear her scream and beg, just like they all do."

I lifted my head, my eyes blurry, my ears still ringing from his kicks. "Oh yes, Joe," he said, "there have been others." He walked over to Lila and lifted her chin in his hands. I could see a patchwork of red and purple bruises crossing both her cheeks. She looked weak. He slid his hand down her neck, grasping the zipper of her sweatshirt between his fingers and pulling it down.

I fought against the belt around my neck, pulling at the thick leather, trying to stretch it or break it or pull the post out of the ground. Nothing budged.

"You can't get away, Joe. Don't hurt yourself." He put his hand on her breast, and she came to life as if waking from a trance. She tried to wiggle away from his touch, her tether making resistance impossible. She tried to kick him with her knee, but she was too weak to have any effect. He punched her hard in the gut for her effort, emptying her lungs of air. Lila gulped and wheezed, trying to breathe.

"In a few minutes it'll all be over, and you'll be burned up in a blaze of glory." He wet his lips, drawing in close to Lila, reaching one of his hands down to undo the buckle of Lila's pants while moving his gun up her body, brushing the muzzle over the contour of her torso, pausing at her breast for a second. He slid it up her throat, then her cheek, before raising it to her temple.

He started to lean in as though he might lick her face or bite her, but he stopped, interrupted by the difficulty he was having undoing her belt with a single hand. He took a step back to get a better look at the buckle. When he did, the nose of the gun tipped skyward for just a second, away from Lila's head.

Suddenly, three quick gunshots erupted from the tree line. The first bullet entered Dan Lockwood's left ear, exiting the right side of his head in a spray of blood, bone, and brains. The second bullet ripped through his throat with similar results. Lockwood was dead before the third bullet cracked through the plate in the side of his skull. He fell to the ground, a lump of meat and tissue.

Max Rupert stepped from the shadows of the tree line, his gun still pointed at the pile of waste that used to be Dan Lockwood. He walked over and kicked the body onto its back, Lockwood's eyes staring blankly up at the sky. Two more figures stepped from the shadows, sheriff's deputies, each wearing brown winter coats with badges on the left lapel.

One spoke into a radio microphone pinned to his shoulder, and the horizon lit up red and blue, as if the officer had called in his own personal Aurora Borealis. Soon the lights of the squad cars crested the rise, their sirens piercing the night.

CHAPTER 53

The shootout at the barn made the news and started the snow-ball rolling. The press wanted to know why a man from Iowa took three bullets in the head, and why two local college kids were at the scene. In order to justify the shooting and clear Max Rupert of any wrongdoing, the city scrambled to put flesh on the bones of what Lila and I had discovered. Within twenty-four hours, not only had they reopened Crystal Hagen's murder case, but they'd moved it to the head of the line. By the time they issued their first press release the following morning, they had confirmed Lila's deciphering of the code and that Dan Lockwood had been called DJ by Crystal and other family members back in 1980.

On the second day after the shooting, the Minnesota BCA verified that the DNA found under Crystal Hagen's fingernail belonged to Dan Lockwood. Not only that, but when the BCA ran Lockwood's DNA profile through CODIS, the national DNA database, they got a hit. Lockwood's DNA matched the profile in a case from Davenport, Iowa, where a young girl had been raped and killed, her body found in the rubble of a burned out barn. The city held a press conference to declare that Dan Lockwood had likely killed Crystal Hagen in 1980 and that he had been on the verge of killing one or both of the college students when Detective Rupert had fatally shot him. The city and the press united in their praise of Max Rupert, holding him up as a hero for killing Lockwood and saving the lives of the unidentified University of Minnesota students—who likely would have been his next victims.

One reporter learned my name, and that I'd been at the scene when Rupert shot Lockwood. She called my hospital room to ask me some questions, referring to me as a hero and buttering me up real good. I didn't feel like a hero though. I had nearly gotten Lila killed. I told the reporter that I didn't want to talk to her and that she should not call me again.

My professors all granted me extensions for my final exams and term papers. I took them up on their offers—all, that is, except for my biography class. Lila brought my laptop to the hospital, and I spent hour after hour propped up in my bed typing. Lila also brought Jeremy to the hospital to see me every day. She had spent a couple hours in the emergency room that night, getting checked over by the doctors before being released with bruises on her face and torso and abrasions on her wrists where the rope had cut into them. She'd slept on the couch in my apartment after that with Jeremy sleeping in the next room.

The doctors kept me in the hospital for four days, releasing me two weeks before Christmas with a bottle of pain medication and a pair of crutches. By the time they discharged me, I had written twice as many pages as were required for my biography of Carl Iverson. I had completed the project with the exception of the final chapter—Carl's official exoneration.

On the morning they discharged me, Professor Sanden met me in the hospital lobby. He seemed winded as he crossed the room to greet me, smiling like he had just won a raffle. "Merry Christmas," he said. Then he handed me a document: a court order with a raised seal on the bottom. My pulse quickened as I started reading the formal language of the heading: *State of Minnesota, Plaintiff, versus Carl Albert Iverson, Defendant.* I continued reading the document line by line until Professor Sanden interrupted me by flipping to the final page and pointing to a paragraph that read:

IT IS HEREBY ORDERED that the conviction of Carl Albert Iverson for the crime of murder in the first degree, found by Verdict dated January 15, 1981, and entered as Judgment on that same day, be hereby VACATED in its entirety, and that the civil rights of said Defendant be fully restored effective immediately upon the signing of this Order.

The order was signed by a district-court judge and dated that very morning.

"I can't believe it," I said. "How did you—"

"It's amazing what you can get done when the political will is there," Professor Sanden said. "With the story about the shooting making national news, the county attorney was more than happy to expedite things."

"So does this mean . . ."

"Carl Iverson is completely and officially innocent," Sanden said, beaming with delight.

I called Virgil Gray and invited him to join us when we went to visit Carl that day. Janet and Mrs. Lorngren also came with us to Carl's room. I thought about framing the order but decided against it, as that didn't seem the kind of thing that Carl would have wanted. Instead, I simply handed him the document, explaining what it meant, explaining that in the eyes of the world it was now official—he did not kill Crystal Hagen. Carl rubbed his fingers across the raised seal on the bottom of the first page, closed his eyes, and smiled a melancholy smile. A tear trickled down his cheek, which caused Janet and Mrs. Lorngren to start crying, which made Lila, Virgil, and me tear up, too. Only Jeremy remained dry eyed, but that's Jeremy.

Carl struggled to reach his hand out to me, and I took his in mine and held it. "Thank you," he whispered. "Thank you . . . all."

We stayed with Carl until he could no longer keep his weak eyes open. We wished him a merry Christmas and promised to come back the next day, but that didn't happen. He died that night. Mrs. Lorngren said that it was as though he simply decided that the time had come for him to stop living. His death was as peaceful as any she had ever seen.

CHAPTER 54

Not counting the minister, thirteen mourners attended Carl Iverson's funeral: Virgil Gray, Lila, Jeremy, me, Professor Sanden, Max Rupert, Janet, Mrs. Lorngren, two other staff from Hillview, and three guards from Stillwater Prison who remembered him fondly from his time there. He was buried at Fort Snelling National Cemetery, laid to rest in formation next to hundreds of other Vietnam veterans. The minister kept the graveside ceremony short, in part because he had never met Carl Iverson and had little to say about him beyond the standard text, and in part because a cold December breeze swept unfettered across the broad open expanse of the cemetery.

After the service, Max Rupert left with Boady Sanden, but not before insisting that Lila and I meet them later at a nearby restaurant for coffee. I could tell that they had something they wanted to talk about, something that apparently required a modicum of privacy.

I went to say goodbye to Virgil, who had been carrying a paper sack with him for the entirety of the service, clutching it to his chest. Once we were alone, he opened the bag and pulled out a display case—an oak box about the size of a dictionary with a glass face. Inside, pinned to red felt backing, were Carl's medals: two Purple Hearts and the Silver Star. Below the medals were arm patches signifying that Carl had been promoted to corporal before his discharge from the army.

"He wanted me to give these to you," Virgil said.

I couldn't speak. For at least a minute all I could do was stare at them, at the way their polished edges glistened, the way the silver and purple popped against the blood-red background. "Where did you find these?" I finally said.

"After Carl got arrested, I snuck into his house and took 'em." Virgil shrugged as if I might fault him for the theft. "Carl didn't have much in the way of possessions, and I figured that one day he'd want these back. They are . . ." Virgil pursed his lips to hold in his sobs, ". . . were his only possessions." Virgil held out his hand, and I shook it. Then he pulled me in and gave me a hug. "You did good," he whispered. "Thank you."

I thanked Virgil and then turned to make my way to the car, where Jeremy and Lila waited. Virgil remained at the gravesite, apparently not ready to leave his friend.

At the restaurant, Lila and I were warming our hands on our coffee mugs when Max and Boady arrived. Jeremy sipped hot chocolate from his mug, slurping to draw it out from under a layer of marshmallow. I introduced Max and Boady to Jeremy. Jeremy said a polite hello, as he had been taught, then turned his attention back to his hot chocolate. I gave a brief explanation of how Jeremy came to live with me, leaving out the part where I broke Larry's knee.

"That's going to make school a little more difficult," Boady said.

I dropped my gaze to the table. "I won't be going back to school."

It was the first time I'd spoken those words aloud, even to myself. Though I had officially dropped all my spring-semester classes, saying it out loud made it all the more real. When I looked up, I saw Boady and Max exchanging a glance and—to my surprise—a smile.

"I want to show you something," Max said, retrieving a piece of folded paper from his jacket pocket and handing it to me. I opened it to find an e-mail that had been sent to Max from the sheriff from Scott County, Iowa:

I've looked into the reward for solving Melissa Burns's murder. It was posted back in 1992 and is still available. It appears certain that Lockwood killed her. He worked as head of security for the mall here in Davenport and must have abducted Melissa as she was leaving the mall. Melissa was the granddaughter of a bank owner in this area, and he put up the $100,000 reward. If you give me a bank account for Mr. Talbert and Ms. Nash, I can have the bank wire it up once our case is officially closed.

I stopped reading, my head nearly ready to explode by that last part. "A hundred thousand dollars?" I said, louder than I'd intended. "Are you kidding?"

Boady smiled and said, "Keep reading."

I am aware that Mr. Lockwood is being looked at for two other abductions and murders, one in Coralville, Iowa, and one outside of Des Moines. It is the same modus operandi, and is likely the work of Lockwood as well. I've been informed that there are $10,000 rewards on each of those cases. You should let your people know that they will be entitled to that money if those cases clear.

I handed the e-mail to Lila. I heard her gasp when she read about the money and then read her name. When she finished she looked up and said, "Is this for real?"

"Absolutely," Max said. "It goes to you two."

I tried to speak but could do little more than swallow a lump of air. When I finally managed to speak, I said, "That's a lot of money."

"It's more than you normally see for a reward, I'll grant you that," Max said. "But it's not out of the ball park—especially for the death of a banker's granddaughter. If Lockwood was the perp in all three cases, you'll be looking at a hundred and twenty thousand."

Lila looked at me. "I want you to have the reward," she said, "all of it. You need it to take care of Jeremy."

"Absolutely not!" I said. "You almost died."

"I don't need it like you do," she said. "I want you to have it."

"We split it equally," I said, "or I'm not taking any of it. That's not open for discussion."

Lila opened her mouth to argue, paused, and said, "We split it three ways." She nodded at Jeremy. "Without him, we would never have solved the code. He gets a third."

I started to refuse, but she held up a hand, looked me in the eye with the seriousness of a woman who would not be moved, and said, "That's not open for discussion."

I looked at Jeremy, grinning at me with a marshmallow mustache. He hadn't been listening to the conversation. I smiled back at him, and then I leaned in and kissed Lila.

A heavy snow began to fall outside, and by the time we left the restaurant, Lila's car had been covered by an inch of it. She and Jeremy climbed in while I stayed outside to clean the snow off the windows. I could not stop smiling. With that money, I could go to school *and* take care of Jeremy. An incredible sense of lightness filled me as I brushed the snow off the windshield. A young couple entered the restaurant, releasing a wave of warm air fused with the scent of fresh-baked goods. The aroma sailed on a light breeze and swirled around my head. It caused me to pause and remember something Carl had told me—that heaven could be here on Earth.

I scooped snow into my bare hand and watched as it melted in my palm. I felt its coldness against my warm skin and studied the crystalline flakes as they changed into water droplets that trickled down my wrist, evaporating into another existence. I closed my eyes and listened to the music of the breeze as it hummed through the nearby pine trees, punctuated by the chirp of some chickadees hidden in the needles. I drew in a breath of crisp December air and stood perfectly still, savoring the feel, the sound, and the smell of the world around me, sensations that would have passed by me unnoticed had I never met Carl Iverson.

ACKNOWLEDGMENTS

I would like to offer my heartfelt gratitude to my agent Amy Cloughley who went above and beyond to bring this book to life. I want to thank my editor Dan Mayer and all of those at Seventh Street Books for their help and guidance.

I would also like to acknowledge the great assistance given to me by my beta readers: Nancy Rosin, Suzie Root, Bill Patten, Kelly Lundgren, Carrie Leone, Chris Cain, and my many friends at Twin Cities Sisters in Crime.

A special thanks to Erika Applebaum of the Minnesota Innocence Project for her advice.

A NOTE TO THE READER

I hope that you enjoyed reading *The Life We Bury*. There is no greater honor for a writer than to know that his or her work is enjoyed by the reader. And if you enjoyed *The Life We Bury*, please tell others and consider posting a reader review online, for there is no greater support you can give a debut author than your word-of-mouth recommendation.

Visit me online at http://www.alleneskens.com, on Facebook as Allen Eskens - author, and on Twitter @aeskens.

Turn the page for a SNEAK PREVIEW of

THE GUISE
OF ANOTHER

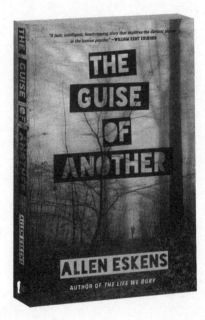

Available now, wherever books are sold

PROLOGUE

That night, there were a few things that the man knew to a religious certainty. He knew that he'd soon be having sex with the woman sitting in the passenger seat of his Lexus. He knew that neither his wife nor the woman's husband yet suspected their infidelities. And he knew that any whisper of guilt he may have felt would soon be silenced by the tumult of their act.

There were other things, however, that the man did not know. He didn't know where or how they would be having sex. He didn't know whether his feelings for this woman reached beyond the carnal pull of her body. And he didn't know that their recklessness that night would trigger a chain of events that would ripple far beyond their self-absorbed little world.

For six months now they'd been acting like mindless teenagers, pushing one another to limits neither had ever experienced, getting bolder with each passing week. Their trysts were all about variety and risk, finding the precipice and pressing everything to the point of catastrophe. If she'd wanted tried-and-true, staring at the same ceiling fan until it was over, she wouldn't have been cheating on her husband. If he'd wanted a menu of only three positions, he could've been at home with his wife. Ordinary was what they were running from.

As they prowled the near-empty streets of Minneapolis—in that part of the city where the glass and granite walls of downtown melded into the paint and mortar of the warehouse district—the woman became restless.

It was time.

She removed her seatbelt and leaned over and unbuckled his. Then, with a practiced grace, she started to undo the cinch of his pants. He must have looked disappointed, because she paused, mid-zip, and said, "You'll like this." Thinking that he knew what she had in mind, he drove in the direction of Third Street, a lightly traveled one-way that became a four-lane highway, nearly desolate at that late hour.

She leaned into his ear and whispered, "Move your seat all the way back." The tease of her perfume—the way it mingled with the scent of the new leather seats—made his breath grow shallow. The seat motor whirred, moving him back until his fingertips barely held the steering wheel. She slid her dress up and eased onto his lap, sliding a knee on either side of his thighs. He smiled as she took over.

Neither saw the rotation of the city shooting by in an ever-increasing blur of streetlights and shadows. At a place where opposing lanes were separated by a concrete median barely as high as a man's knee, the woman let herself go. She rocked on top of him, teeth gritted, hands clenched as the pleasure surged through her body.

Had she known that those sensations would be the last thing she would ever feel originating from below her L-4 vertebra, she would have paid far greater attention. Later, after she'd been fitted for her wheelchair and he for his cane, they would denounce each other with a fierce enmity reserved for blood feuds. She would say that he lost control in the heat of his passion, jerking the car sharply to the left. He would swear that her butt cheek caught the steering wheel, catapulting them over the divider. Those who heard their stories—or read the salacious details in the newspaper—would hate them both.

The crash ruptured the calm fabric of the night. And in the span of a single gasp, the northbound Lexus hurtled over the median and into the opposing lane, slamming nose-first into an oncoming Porsche Panamera.

The driver of the Porsche, a guy known to the world as James Erkel Putnam, went for his brake, barely touching the pedal before the grill of his car kissed the steel frame of the Lexus. The cacophony of screaming metal could be heard for miles as the two cars spun counterclockwise, intertwined in a grisly pas de deux, the Lexus leading the dance.

That night, James Erkel Putnam—a man who walked in daylight but lived in shadows, a man who thought he had all the time in the world to seek forgiveness for his many sins—never stood a chance.

CHAPTER 1

Detective Alexander Rupert descended the worn marble staircase into the depths of City Hall, pausing on the bottom step to let the clench of knuckles in his gut relax. He breathed in the tired air of the basement, and when he exhaled, his breath carried with it the residue of his frustration. With each new day and each new trip down that staircase, he found it harder to convince himself that he didn't own this new routine, this reassignment into the Frauds Unit. He wore this new job like a suit one size too small, a suit he swore he would never claim as his own. This was a temporary bump in his career path, nothing more. Yet, as the weeks turned into months, as hard edges began to form on the stories that triggered his departure from Narcotics, he began to doubt that he would ever find his way out of that basement.

He took another cleansing breath as he turned the corner and entered the long, stale hallway that led to the Forgery and Frauds Unit of the Minneapolis Police Department, the place where he landed after his ignominious fall from grace. The hallway, with its moss-green walls and mat of tiny white tiles underfoot, reminded him of the men's restroom at the old Metrodome. All it needed was a stainless-steel pissing trough and a few sinks, and he'd feel like he was at a Vikings game.

His transfer from Narcotics to Frauds had been termed a temporary reassignment, just a place to land until the dust settled. But Alexander knew better. He knew that the powers that be intended that he languish there until the federal investigation either exonerated him or sent him to prison. He also knew that when the grand jury came back with a finding of no bill—and he was certain that they would find no bill—that exoneration would not completely pull him out of the hole he'd fallen into.

He sat down at his desk, a gray, metal, standard-issue desk wedged into a cubicle identical to the one he sat in eight years earlier when he first became a detective. That first promotion to detective sent him to the Sex Crimes Unit, a job that had its good side and its bad side. He got a kick out of the prostitution stings, especially when he plastered the mug shots of the patrons all over the Internet. But the child-abuse cases sickened him.

One day, during an interview with a man who videotaped his abuse of a mentally disabled girl, Alexander leaned into the man and whispered, "You'd better hope that you go to prison, because if you walk away from this, I'll hunt you down and kill you myself."

That incident ended Alexander's stint in Sex Crimes. It wasn't a demotion or a punishment that moved him out of Sex Crimes; in fact, his commander never found out about that comment. As far as she was concerned, Alexander did a bang-up job of getting a sexual offender off the street. But Alexander told that story to his big brother, Max, also a detective, but in Homicide. It was Max who prodded Alexander into asking for the transfer. That's how, after three years in Sex Crimes, Alexander moved to Narcotics and from there joined the Joint Drug Enforcement Task Force.

And then came the fall of the Task Force.

Alexander sat down at his cubicle in the Frauds Unit and stared at the stacks of reports awaiting his attention. He felt as though he'd been sent back to the kiddie table, removed from the adult conversations that whispered around him. He could feel the icy stares of the other detectives in the room—men and women who, when Alexander approached, parted like a school of anchovies in the path of a shark. They fed on the rumors and knew nothing about the hell that Alexander went through in his days in Narcotics. They knew nothing about the gray areas that a man had to walk when working undercover. They had no inkling of the sacrifices that it took to get in tight with the right group of bad guys. They knew little beyond the dark whispers that swirled in his wake as he passed by.

During his days on the Task Force, Alexander stood shoulder to shoulder with men who would one day try to kill him. He had set up one of the biggest sting operations in Minnesota history, an operation that led to his first—and only—bullet wound, a shot to his pelvis that cracked his ilium. But that arrest also led to his Medal of Valor and the parade of well-wishers, everyone from patrol officers to senators congratulating him on his outstanding work as a detective.

But that was before the fall of the Task Force, before the newspaper articles, the federal investigation and the grand jury. That was before the backslide that landed him in the Frauds Unit in the basement of City Hall. Because of the stupidity of others, he'd become a pariah, a man so loathsome that none of his fellow detectives even deigned to offer him a cup of coffee.

Now, every day, Alexander Rupert walked to his cubicle in the Frauds Unit, where he would sit and gnaw on the bridle and bit of his resentment. He cursed those detectives from the Task Force whose ineptitude stained them all. He also cursed the detectives around him who had judged him without giving him a chance. After three months, he still found it hard to fight through the muddle of bad thoughts that stirred in his head.

Yet, in a way, he preferred the agitation of that resentment to the calm that lay behind it. On those rare occasions when his bitterness fell quiet, he could feel the loneliness, the stigma of being an outcast. He could feel the full force of his ostracism, powerful and cold like a winter wind. He'd never known anything so consuming.

CHAPTER 2

Alexander glanced at his clock. His first appointment of the day, a personal-injury attorney named Reginald Dogget, was already late. Alexander sensed an edge of disrespect in Dogget's tardiness and slowly began to despise the man. When Dogget finally arrived, Alexander watched him walk to the interview room with the stride of someone who owned every inch of the ground he trod. Alexander recognized Dogget from his ads on television, the man railing against insurance companies, jabbing a finger at the camera and vowing to make them pay.

The receptionist called Alexander to let him know that his appointment was waiting in interview room number 2. Alexander grabbed a pad of paper and a pencil and started to rise, but then paused, sat back down, and sharpened the pencil, once, twice, and three times, grinding off nearly an inch of wood and graphite while Dogget waited for him. When he figured Dogget had waited long enough, Alexander walked to the interview room with a pad of paper, his newly sharpened pencil in his hand and a bead of irritation infecting his mood.

"Mr. Dogget?" he asked.

"That's me," Dogget said in a big voice as he rose and stretched out his hand. Alexander shook it and sat down.

Alexander took a moment to scratch a few unnecessary notes on the page before saying, "I'm Detective Alexander Rupert. What can I do for you today?"

Dogget cocked his head slightly as if taken off guard by something. "Alexander Rupert. Now why do I know that name?"

"I'm sure I don't know." Alexander tapped his pencil on the pad of paper.

"Are you the detective who shot down that killer . . . that guy at the barn?"

Alexander closed his eyes and shook his head before answering. "No. I'm not that guy. That guy is Max Rupert. I'm Alexander Rupert."

"You related?"

"Only by blood," Alexander said. "Now, about your—"

"No, that's not it. I've heard your name before. I've got a great memory for names." He scratched his chin. "Alexander Rupert . . ." Then he lit up and snapped his fingers. "Now I know. You were in the news a few months ago. You were one of the cops in that Task Force that they shut down."

And there it was, like a foot stepping on Alexander's fingertips, the reminder of how far he'd slipped down the ladder. Alexander gritted his teeth, stared at Dogget, and wondered how big of a handprint he would leave on the side of Dogget's head if he stretched out his fingers and smacked the man.

"I thought all you guys got suspended or fired for stealing drug money," Dogget continued.

A pretty big handprint, Alexander thought. He'd always been told that he had big paws. "Mr. Dogget, I have a lot of work to do. If you have a crime to report, I'll take that report. But if all you want to do is sit here and bullshit, well, then you're wasting my time."

Alexander started to stand up and Dogget held out his hands, palms down, over the table. "Hang on there, Detective. I have a crime to report. At least I'm pretty sure it's a crime."

Alexander sat back down. "'Pretty sure'?"

"Yeah." Dogget nodded his head as he considered. "It's like this. I have a decent law practice where I make money suing people for car accidents and the like."

"I've seen your ads."

"Well, thank you."

"That wasn't a compliment."

Dogget cleared his throat and continued. "I have sources that feed me leads on cases."

"Ambulance chasers?"

"If you want to use that term." Dogget shifted uncomfortably in his seat at the interruption. Then he continued. "So I get a call from one of my feeders about a car accident in Minneapolis—this Lexus plowed into a Porsche. That's usually a good sign. An expensive car means that they have deep pockets beyond the insurance. The Lexus is being driven by the owner of a chain of jewelry stores. Now we're talking big bucks. And to put icing on the cake, there's no question about who's at fault. The jewelry guy was getting his world rocked by a woman who wasn't his wife, and they crossed the lane. I mean the woman was actually screwing him as they jumped the median into oncoming traffic. The criminal complaint referred to that as 'gross negligence.'" Dogget cracked a smile as if he'd made a joke.

"I heard about that accident," Alexander said. "One guy died."

"Yeah, the guy in the Porsche in the oncoming lane, the guy who was minding his own business, not doing a damned thing wrong."

"Highway Patrol handled the accident," Alexander said. "They would've done the reconstruction. Not us."

"I'm not looking for accident reconstruction. I have all that." Dogget tapped his finger on a file lying on the table in front of him, a file he'd brought to the interview.

"Then what are you looking for?" Alexander said. He made no attempt to hide his growing impatience. "This is the Fraud Unit. We don't handle accidents or deaths."

"I'm getting there. When I got the lead on this case, I had my investigator try to scrounge up a relative—someone I could send a letter to."

"A relative?"

"It's a wrongful-death action. The heirs of the dead get to sue the people who caused the death."

"So you stalk the relative of the guy in the Porsche, hoping to take a cut of what his heirs should get for his death."

"Hey, I provide a valuable service," Dogget said, pointing his finger at Alexander. It was all Alexander could do not to reach out and break the finger in half. It would have been so quick, so easy. "I go after the deep pocket once the insurance company offers up their meager policy limits."

"So did you find a relative?"

"Sort of." Dogget shrugged.

"'Sort of'?"

"The guy in the Porsche lived with a woman named Ianna Markova. I sent a letter to her that same day. I normally wait and make sure that the significant other is a wife because a girlfriend does me no good. The heir has to be a blood relative or a wife. Girlfriends are shit out of luck."

"Sucks to be her," Alexander said.

"Don't it, though." Alexander's sarcasm floated right past Dogget. "So this Ianna Markova calls me up. Wants to come in and see me. I clear my calendar to get her in. You know, get 'em while they're hot. And boy was she hot. Late twenties, maybe early thirties, blond hair, knockers..." Dogget gave a sideways glance up to the camera in the corner of the ceiling, cleared his throat, and continued in a manner more professional than before. "So she's all bereaved, and I'm taking my time with her. Then I ask her if she and James were married."

"James?"

"The guy in the Porsche. His name was James Erkel Putnam. She had just come from making the funeral arrangements. She tells me that she and Putnam never tied the knot. I almost started crying myself. So I ask her if there were any brothers or sisters or parents. I tell her that we need the names of all of his living relatives. At first she says that James doesn't have a living relative."

"So no lawsuit? You must've been heartbroken."

"I don't give up that easy. I've never met a man with no blood relatives. You shake a family tree hard enough, someone always falls out. So I laid it on the line. I told her that without a blood relative, there's no lawsuit. No money."

"Why would she care? The girlfriend gets nothing, remember?"

Dogget gave a sly grin, like a man about to share a dirty joke. "I kind of told her that she still gets part of the settlement. I said that once we had the blood relative, she can stake a claim against the jewelry mogul."

"So you lied to a woman who just lost her boyfriend." Alexander leaned into the table and aimed his stare at Dogget. "Is that the crime you came here to report?"

"You're funny, Detective." Dogget tapped his knuckles against his chest as if trying to pass a burp. "I come in here to do the right thing, and you bust my chops."

"You understand this is the Fraud Unit, don't you? Lying to Ms. Markova is the first thing I've heard so far that sounds like a fraud."

"I'm getting there," Dogget said.

Alexander could see tiny beads of sweat starting to form on Dogget's temple, and he took some pleasure in it.

"So, the next day, she came back with a box of documents: birth certificate, Social Security card, and some letters."

"Letters?"

"Yeah, letters that James received years ago from a brother in prison in New York. I had my investigator check into it and, sure enough, Putnam has this older brother doing a stint in the Clinton Correctional Facility for a drug conviction—what they called a class A-1 felony."

"So why'd she tell you that James had no relatives?"

"She said that she found the stuff in a hidden box full of James's personal things. She said she wanted to respect his privacy. My thought is that she just didn't want to share with the brother in prison. But who knows?"

"What's the brother's name?"

"William Bartók Putnam. We followed up on the information, compared the birth certificates with city records. Putnam's parents are dead, died in a car crash back in '98, and the older brother's legit."

"So you have your heir. You can rape the jewelry king to your heart's content."

"You would think so, but not so fast with the happy ending." Dogget folded his fingers together in order to give his words some dramatic weight. "I sent William Bartók Putnam a contract to sign, allowing me to file a lawsuit on his behalf. I also sent him a copy of the obituary of his brother. A week later, I get the whole mess back with a simple note that read: 'That is not my brother. That is not James Erkel Putnam.'"

ABOUT THE AUTHOR

Allen Eskens grew up in Jefferson City, Missouri, before migrating north to attend the University of Minnesota. After graduating with a degree in journalism, he went on to law school and eventually settled in Mankato, Minnesota, where he started a law practice and raised his family. He honed his creative-writing skills in the MFA program at Minnesota State University and at the Loft Literary Center and the Iowa Summer Writer's Festival. He continues to live quietly in the country near Mankato, husband to Joely, father to Mikayla, and pet owner to many.